DITCH LANE DIARIES:

SANDY'S STORY

D. F. JONES

SANDY'S STORY
Ditch Lane Diaries, vol. 3
Copyright © D.F. Jones 2016

ISBN: 978-0-9861227-6-7 paperback
ISBN: 978-0-9861227-5-0 ebook

Cover Art by Jones Media
Editing by Alicia Street
Proofreading by Jody Wallace
Formatting by Author E.M.S.

With tremendous thanks to my readers,
your support, encouragement, and comments
fill me with great joy and inspires me daily
to continue my incredible writing journey.

Acknowledgments

To the best support team ever, I want to thank Kristi, Erin, Tammy, Alice, Regina, Brandy, Jessica, Mark and Pat for taking your time to beta read Sandy's Story. Your suggestions, comments, and insights are invaluable to me.

Thank you, dear husband, for encouraging me to follow my dreams and for listening to my story ideas. You inspire me daily. Thank you to my mom for listening as I read my manuscript to her. She loves romance novels and movies.

Thank you, Alicia, my editor, for your insight, comments, and suggestions. Thank you, Jody, my proofreader, for catching everything that slips through the cracks and your comments crack me up.

After working in advertising for years, I need creative individuals to give me feedback. All of you who offer constructive suggestions and comments help me to grow as a writer.

Thank you, Amy Atwell for awesome formatting and to Amanda, for designing my cover and marketing materials. You always make me look great.

And most importantly, to my readers, thank you for supporting the Ditch Lane Diaries. Your word of mouth referrals, written reviews, messages, and comments keeps me writing.

Fun Fact: Chapter Titles are songs from the 1980's. Enjoy.

Contents

Prologue

What Becomes of the Brokenhearted

Ohio 1966

NINE-YEAR-OLD SANDY WOKE from a slumber to the handsome face of her dad's boss, Mr. Ben, as he gently shook her leg. "Wake up, honey. I came to tell you the story I promised."

Sandy wiped the sleepies out of her eyes and smiled. "I thought Daddy said you couldn't."

Ben smiled back and rubbed his hands up and down his thighs. "Your dad thinks I'm outside for a smoke. Come here, sweet child. Would you still like to hear a story?"

Sandy jumped up and down on the bed. "Oh, yes, please tell me a story."

Ben bent down as Sandy reached up to wrap her arms around his neck. He sat Sandy on his lap and began to stroke her long, silky chestnut hair. "You're more beautiful than Sleeping Beauty. You're fairer than all of the princesses in all of the stories ever told, my darling."

Sandy snuggled into his arms as Ben told her the story of Sleeping Beauty. She relished every detail, and her innocent eyes were bright with excitement. Near the end of the story, Mr. Ben ran his hand under Sandy's nightgown and began to rub her bare leg. Sandy frowned and tried to push him away. She struggled with all of her might to wiggle her way out of his grasp, but Mr. Ben held her tightly.

He whispered, "It's all right, darling. Prince Charming did the same thing to Sleeping Beauty." Mr. Ben pushed her down on the bed, placed one hand over her mouth and the other hand inside her panties. Sandy tried to fight him, but she wasn't strong enough.

Baldric, her guardian angel, appeared, and Sandy rapidly blinked tears. He whispered, "Do not be afraid, little one. Your father is here."

Sandy's father, Hugh, burst into the bedroom, jerked Mr. Ben up in the air and punched him in the stomach. Sandy pushed with her feet against the wall, her teeth chomping down on the blanket as she shook uncontrollably.

Hugh yelled a steady stream of curses as he smashed Mr. Ben's face with his fists, splattering blood on her bed and toys. "You perverted son of a bitch. I'll kill you, motherfucker, for touching my daughter. I'll kill you." Hugh wrapped his hands around Ben's neck and began to choke him.

Sandy's mom, Sally, ran into the room screaming, "Stop it, Hugh! You're killing him. Stop it." Sally smacked Hugh several times across the face before he released Mr. Ben, who lay unmoving on the floor.

Hugh rubbed his face with his hands. With a crazed look, he said, "Call Dad. Tell him to get over here now." He walked over toward Sandy, and she burst into tears. Frightened and confused about what had just happened, Sandy recoiled from her father.

"Is he dead?" Sally scooped Sandy into her arms and said, "You call your dad. She's in shock, and I'm going to put her in the tub." Then Sandy fainted.

Sandy didn't know how much time had passed between the chaos in her room and the time her mom placed her in the bathtub. The warm water soothed her aching privates. "I'm sorry, Mommy. I'm sorry. I wanted the story."

Sally reached over in the tub and hugged her daughter. Her voice quivered. "Honey, there's nothing for you to be sorry about. Let's get you dried off. You can sleep with us tonight."

Wide awake, Sandy lay in her parents' bed when she heard Papa come inside the front door. Hugh and Papa were shouting at each other downstairs. Suddenly, heavy footfalls rushed up the stairs and into her bedroom. Sandy slid out of her parents' bed, went to the door, and cracked it open.

Papa said, "Thank God, he's alive. Jesus, son, you have to get out of here. The Salingers own this town. Sam will see you behind bars for beating his son."

"Are you kidding? Me, arrested? The son of a bitch ruined my baby girl. Dad, I caught him with my baby. I want to kill the bastard."

Sandy squeezed the doorknob. She didn't understand what her daddy meant by ruined.

Her mom sounded frantic. "My aunt lives in Tennessee. She's all alone in that big house of hers. I'll call her. She's been so lonely since Uncle Dale died. We'll move to Tennessee. Hugh, I can't lose you."

Papa let out a deep sigh. "Rumors have circulated about Ben's preference for little girls, but I never believed it. I've been friends with Sam since we were boys. I'll take Ben to Sam and tell him what his boy did to Sandy. Just in case, you start packing. What you can't take with you, I'll bring to Tennessee later. Be on the road by daylight. I want you as far away from this mess as possible."

Sally cried, "Sandy needs a doctor. She needs to go to the emergency room."

Papa said calmly, "Look, Sally, Hugh could get arrested if Sandy goes to the hospital. Sam's on the damn board. He'd have them bury the records. I know how Sam operates. I'll take Ben to Sam, and he can decide what to do with him. Ben will live with the scars from tonight." Papa began to pace about the floor. "I'd kill him myself if I could get away with it. No, I think it's best to take Sandy and go to your aunt's house. In the long run, it'll be the best for all of you."

Sandy moved swiftly back into her parents' bed when she saw her mom walk down the hall. Sally slid into the bed and wrapped her arms around Sandy. "Honey, how are you feeling?"

Sandy sniffled, and her voice cracked. "Are we moving to Tennessee? I'm afraid, Mommy. I'm scared of Daddy."

Sally brushed the hair away from her daughter's eyes and pressed a kiss on her forehead. "Never be afraid of Daddy. He loves you and will do anything to keep you safe. I want you to try to sleep. Tomorrow we're going on a new adventure. You're going to love the country. Tennessee is beautiful, and my Aunt Ellen's farm has cows and kittens." Sally held Sandy in her arms, rocking her back and forth.

Sandy's brain wouldn't go to sleep. It was her fault they were moving away from the only home she'd ever known. Why had she agreed to the bedtime story? Why did Mr. Ben have to hurt her?

The next morning, slivers of sunlight peeked through the curtains. Sandy covered her face and rolled over in bed. She'd been unable to sleep last night from listening to her mom and dad whisper to each over about her. Finally, Sandy got out of bed and quietly went down the stairs. She peeked through the spindles and watched her parents load the car.

Sally came in the front door, looked up at Sandy and gave her a smile. "I laid some clothes out for you in the bathroom. You don't have to go into your room. I have Teddy down here on the couch waiting for you. Are you hungry?"

Shaking her head in silence, Sandy trudged slowly back upstairs into the bathroom. She changed out of her nightgown and into her play clothes, brushed her hair and teeth. Before Sandy went downstairs, she walked back into her room and hugged herself. The room looked the same, but it was different. She used to love her room. Now it made her want to puke.

Baldric appeared before her and knelt down on one knee. She stared into his eyes that were the color of spring grass. He held her hand and said, "Daireann, you're strong. You're going to be okay, I promise."

Sandy leaned over and lightly touched his face with the palm of her hand. "I'll never be okay again. I'm ruined. Daddy said so." Baldric's eyes began to water, and she tilted her head to the side. "What's wrong, Baldric? Please don't cry."

Baldric held her in his big, strong arms, and for a moment, she felt safe. He said, "I will always be here for you. Let's go get Teddy."

Baldric led Sandy out of her room for the last time. Downstairs, she glanced at Teddy still propped on the couch. Averting her eyes, Sandy walked out the door and down the sidewalk. She'd never play with stuffed animals again. Sandy opened the car door, slid into the backseat, and waited for her parents. She stared down at her clasped hands instead of looking back at her old home.

On the road to Tennessee, Baldric kept trying to play the game where they talked to each other using their minds. She turned to him. *I don't want to play. I've ruined my family. Leave me alone.*

Baldric tilted her chin up with his forefinger. *What happened to you last night wasn't your fault. Do you hear me? Moving to Tennessee was your parents' decision, not yours. They're doing what they think is best for you.*

Sandy pressed her forehead to the glass and stared out the car window. She watched as the miles pushed her further away from Mr. Ben. Sandy couldn't erase the image of his face, the stench of whiskey and his aftershave, the feel of his fingers pushing her panties down and hurting her. His severely beaten and bloody face forced its way into her memory and shut her eyes tight trying to block the image.

Everglade, Tennessee

SANDY WATCHED AS HUGH pulled into Aunt Ellen's driveway and turned off the ignition. Aunt Ellen's smiling face lit up as she waved to greet them from the front door. The big two-story yellow farmhouse had a broad front porch and down the steps along the sidewalk lined brightly colored flowerbeds. Several kittens scurried under the porch lattice.

Ignoring her aunt and parents, Sandy bolted out of the car and ran down the driveway to the bubbling brook running along the farm's property. She sat on the ground and propped her elbows on her knees. In her peripheral vision, Sandy saw a girl riding her bicycle down the road.

The red-haired girl wore pigtails, a sleeveless orange and green plaid shirt, and white shorts which hit at the knee. The girl pedaled over to Sandy, hopped off the bike, and used her foot on the kickstand to prop it. "Hey there, I'm Ruby. My mama said Ms. Ellen had family moving in today. Wanna come over and play at my house? My friend, Anna, will be over soon. It'll be fun." Ruby placed her hands on her hips while she waited for an answer.

Sandy plucked strands of grass through her fingers. She cocked her head to the side and slowly smiled. "Yeah, but I need to ask my mom first."

Ruby extended her hand to help Sandy up. When Sandy reached for it, Ruby quickly withdrew it and wiggled her fingers. "You snooze, you lose." Ruby started laughing and said, "Come on, Slick—I'll race you." Sandy and Ruby ran to Aunt Ellen's house.

LATER THAT NIGHT, AS SANDY lay in her new bedroom, Baldric appeared and sat on the edge of her bed. "Do you like Tennessee?"

"I love it, especially Ruby. She's funny and makes me laugh. Her family is loud, and they laugh a lot, too." She pulled the blanket up to her chin and yawned.

Baldric squeezed her hand. "I'm happy for you. Ruby and Anna will be your lifelong friends."

Sandy remained silent for a moment. Emotion boiled up inside of her soul and tears rolled down her cheeks. "Mr. Ben changed me on the inside." Sandy placed her right hand over her heart. "I never want to be a princess, and I never want a prince. Fairy tales aren't real. Friends are real. That's what I want. Don't look so sad, Baldric. You told me I was strong, and you're right. I am strong."

Sandy pushed the horrific memories of Mr. Ben to the furthermost corners of her mind, buried them, and locked the door. It would be nineteen years before Sandy reconciled what happened to the little nine-year-old girl.

Chapter 1

When The Going Gets Tough,
The Tough Get Going

Nashville 1986

SANDY MONITORED THE NASHVILLE POLICE Department (NPD) frequencies on her scanner to pick up leads for news stories while getting ready for work. Listening to the hunt for a shooter, she pulled a black cashmere turtleneck over her head. "All points bulletin for a white male, wearing a black or dark blue hoodie and driving a 1985 black Ford Explorer, license plate TN3490. Ambulance and squad car being dispatched to 17th and Edgehill."

The rest of the APB description fell on deaf ears. She recognized the location from other recent crimes in the area. Sandy grabbed her new camera, her car keys and ran for the door. She didn't have time to call her boss, Art, to tell him she'd be late. He'd forgive her if she came in with a story.

As an investigative reporter for Channel 3 News in Nashville, many of the stories Sandy covered were unsolvable crimes. But on occasion, she could find the truth through her visions. Clairvoyance was a gift from The Creator she'd received at the age of fifteen, unlocked by a mystical hiddenite stone during a spelunking adventure with her best friends, Ruby and Anna. Over the years, Sandy's visions blessed her with multiple Associated Press (AP) awards, but awards didn't help her sleep at night. Sometimes, trying to understand her extrasensory abilities frightened the hell out of her.

Old Man Winter was back with a vengeance as Sandy navigated the icy roads. She skidded a time or two, but she managed to stay on the road without sliding off into a ditch. She should be driving at a snail's pace, but she needed to beat the police to the scene to have a shot at seeing the victim's past and unlocking the secrets of the early morning shooting with just a touch of her hand.

Sandy turned onto Edgehill, parked in front of the sidewalk, and exited her car. As she approached the crime scene, there were a handful of bystanders huddled together outside in the cold. One woman in the group pointed and yelled, "Hey, there's Sandy Cothran from Channel 3 News." The power of television along with Sandy's face plastered across town on billboards gave her little privacy.

Sandy strapped her camera bag over her shoulder and nodded to the group. "Good morning, everyone." A gold Lincoln Continental's engine was running with the driver door open. The upper body of a man lay off kilter on the asphalt while the rest of him remained inside the car.

Placing her camera bag on the ground, Sandy gently touched the man's forearm. His life force was draining fast. Sandy yelled back at the group of bystanders, "Where's the freaking ambulance?" The victim was unresponsive. He had a gaping bullet wound in his chest. Sandy took off her winter coat and applied pressure to the wound. He was beyond her help.

Sandy traveled through her visions on cords of light. At times, she could see millions of strands of light that sometimes ran for miles and spanned decades. Mental images flashed through her mind so fast that it made her extremely nauseated. The victim had a faint pulse as his evening unfolded in her mind at blinding speed.

A map of downtown Nashville lay across an old walnut desk in a shabby little office with fluorescent lighting. His father had opened Henry's Tailor Shop nearly thirty years ago. Nick London started working in the shop as a teenager and eventually inherited the store after his dad passed away.

Nick's finger trailed the map down the route along Broadway and stopped at the corner of First Avenue. Two red X's marked the corner block properties.

Entrepreneur, Cole Steele was trying to force him out of business. Cole owned almost all the properties along First Avenue and Broadway. Last week, Mr. Watson, the owner of the tool and die shop next door, had been in a severe car accident. He was fortunate to survive, and Nick learned today that Mr. Watson sold his business to Steele Construction. Henry's Tailor Shop was the last business on the block to hold out.

Rumor had it Cole was going to tear down all of the existing businesses along the riverfront to build another high-rise hotel to accommodate the new convention center. Cole made him a nice offer on Henry's, but the threats began when Nick refused to sell the store. During his meeting with Cole, Nick lifted what he thought was Cole's journal but later realized was some kind of relic. He placed the book in a locked box at the bank as leverage against Cole's attempts to force him to sell the store.

Nick ran his fingers through his hair and looked at his Timex watch. He folded the map, placed it with his key to a safety deposit box in a folder and wrapped it with a huge rubber band. Nick searched for a place to hide the folder. He walked over to the vent return, popped it open, and put the folder in front of the air filter before securing the latch.

It was nearly two in the morning, and he needed to get home to relieve his wife's sister, Alice. His wife, Martha, had a stroke six months ago, impairing her speech and leaving her bedridden. He picked up the phone and dialed. "Alice, did I wake you? I'm sorry I'm so late. How did she do today? Oh, good. Do you need me to pick up anything? I'll be along soon. Tell my girl how much I love her." He hung up.

Nick walked to the front door and flipped the open sign to closed. After bolting the door to the shop, he jogged across First Avenue to the parking lot close to the Cumberland River. A sudden chill ran down his spine. He looked over his left shoulder and quickened his steps.

Once inside his car, Nick started the ignition, backed out of the spot, put the car in drive, and pulled onto the street. He turned left at the intersection and drove along Broadway when a car pulled in behind him with its headlights on high beam.

Fear and panic gripped Nick as he pressed his foot on the gas pedal. The car behind him was riding on his tail. He ran a red light and decided to take a detour home through Music Row. He drove swiftly through the side streets, trying to lose the car, but the car gained speed and hit his bumper.

Nick swerved his car onto 17th and Edgehill. He lost control of his vehicle and slammed into a brick mailbox. The black Ford Explorer swooped in and blocked his exit. He was trapped. Nick slammed the car into park, reached into his coat pocket and pulled out his gun.

His assailant was quick to open the door and knock the gun out of Nick's hand. "Where's the book, London?"

Nick pressed his lips together in a tight line. One of Cole's thugs, Hammer, backhanded him across the face. "Tell me where the book is or you're dead meat."

Nick narrowed his eyes and said, "I'm dead whether I tell you or not. So, I think not." An explosion of light and sound released as Hammer shot Nick in the chest. Nick watched his murderer race to the Ford Explorer and flee the scene.

Everything went silent and time seemed to move in slow motion. Nick didn't feel any pain. A bright light appeared before him, and he wasn't afraid. His last thoughts were of his wife, the love of his life. He muttered, "I'm sorry, Martha."

Sandy released Nick's arm. She turned left and right, looking for help. The NPD blues lights and an ambulance with blaring sirens flew into the driveway. She stepped away from Nick as the paramedics arrived and the officers secured the area.

Sandy began setting up her camera as Detective Bob Wade sauntered over with his signature Camel behind his ear. She encountered the detective nearly every week.

Bob wore a brown leather aviator jacket and a pair of Levi's with Timberland hiking boots. "How did I know you'd be here?"

Sandy flipped the camera on, reached into her bag for her mic. "Well, if it isn't *the* Bob Wire. It looks like our mystery killer has struck again. I'm glad you boys could join the party. If you'll excuse me, I have a story to cover."

Bob placed his hand over her mic and whispered in her ear, "You're playing with fire, girlie. These boys don't mess around."

"What boys? And is that on the record?" Sandy stared at him with a level gaze and straightened her shoulders.

"You know it's not. I can't comment during an ongoing

investigation." His dark brown eyes seemed to reflect compassion.

Sandy pinned the mic to her sweater. "You and I know who's behind the shooting. I'm going to prove it. Don't you get sick of it? Don't you get tired of all the bullshit? You file paperwork that's never followed up on, or worse, it disappears. You could help me."

Bob shook his head, and his shoulders slumped. "I'm doing my best. But I have to keep my job. I have alimony and child support." He walked away.

Sandy clicked on her camera light and began reporting. Thirty minutes later she pulled into the station.

Art was on her heels when she walked into the back door. "You're late. A murder came in about twenty minutes ago. I need you at Edgehill with Duncan."

Sandy pulled the Beta tape from her camera bag. "Got it. I have a lead on the shooter. I need to get to Nick's house before the police, and I have to get into his business. This murder could be what I've needed to nail our friend, Mr. Steele."

Art's eyes widened, and rubbed the top of his bald head. "Well, don't let the door hit you in the ass on your way out. Go! Give me the tape. Do you need Duncan?"

"Ah, no. My camera, my story, my angles. I'm not waiting for Duncan. Besides, I think Cole may have gotten to him." Sandy went silent as Duncan walked up. She'd saved money to buy her camera so she wouldn't have to fight for creative control at the station. Art approved her use of personal equipment since it passed all the codes.

"Are you deliberately trying to put me out of a job?" Duncan frowned at Sandy while he placed his hands on his hips.

Sandy took a deep breath and pushed by Duncan. "I wouldn't have this story if I waited on you. Art needs to key it up. You can handle the graphics. Can't you, Duncan?"

Duncan thinned his lips over his teeth. "You're a pain in the ass."

Sandy laughed. "Tell me something I don't know."

Sandy sat down at her desk, pulled out the phone book, and looked up Nick London's home address. She tossed a glance over her shoulder and huffed. "Jesus, Duncan, do I have to do everything around here?" Duncan stormed off to the control room.

Sandy scribbled down Nick's Green Hills address, roughly five miles from the station, then replenished her camera bag with extra

Beta tapes and battery backups. She hit the ladies' room and took care of business. Just before sprinting out the back door, Sandy grabbed a Channel 3 News winter coat.

A thin layer of ice had formed on her Corvette's windshield. She fired up the defrost and made a mental checklist of things she needed from Nick's house and business to solidify her story.

Baldric sudden and unexpected appearances didn't startle her any longer. She said, "I didn't sense you at the scene."

He said, "I'm sorry I didn't stay with you this morning, but I followed the shooter."

Sandy drove the slick backroads to Nick's house and began to slide toward an embankment. Taking her foot off the gas, Sandy steered slowly toward the middle of the road. Thankfully, there was little traffic this morning due to the inclement weather. Her car finally came to a stop. "Good grief. I hate ice." She took a few deep breaths as she slowly accelerated. Sandy loved her Corvette, but she needed a more efficient ride, especially in the winter.

"Nice driving, kid. Oh, I arrived on the scene just before you did. Hammer was all over poor Nick. Cole's team has staked out both Nick's house and Henry's." Chip Hammond, or more affectionately known in Nashville's underbelly as "The Hammer," was ruthless, and Cole's connections had kept him out of jail numerous times.

Sandy gripped the steering wheel and briefly glanced at Baldric. "Day-yum. Have I told you lately how much I love you? What else did you find out?"

Baldric said, "I spoke to Gabriel's angel, Alyen before he took Nick's soul. Nick left a folder with a key to a lockbox at City Bank, and the box holds Luc's Testament. Nick lifted it while he was meeting with Steele last week."

Baldric turned in the seat to face Sandy. "If it's Luc's Testament, you have to be careful. Luc's manifesto includes a list of his contracted souls and the names of his demons and their divisions along with magic spells. The book is said to give enormous power to any human possessing it. A bit of warning, the longer a person has the book, the darker their soul becomes. I don't think Nick knew what he was lifting. He hid the key to the lockbox in a folder in front of the air filer in the vent return in his office."

A shiver ran up Sandy's spine. "Lucifer's Testament? I saw where

Nick hid the folder when I held his arm this morning. I have to get the key before Cole gets it." Sandy pulled into Nick's driveway.

Baldric placed his hand on her knee. "Luc tortures humans, and he doesn't care if the human is man, woman, or child. The closer you get to his operation or his book, the more dangerous your quest becomes."

Sandy squeezed his hand. "I know it's dangerous. He tried to kill Anna last summer. Luc won't stop, and we can't either. Hey, to change the subject, if I die, will I see you in heaven?"

Baldric stared into her eyes and raised her hand to his lips. He pressed a feather soft kiss on the back of her hand. "I'm not ready for your demise, but if you die today, I will find you in the Everafter."

A slow grin lit Sandy's face. It was reassuring to hear she would see Baldric again if she died. Sandy jumped out of the car, pulled the hood of her coat down around her ears, and zipped it up to her neck. Her snow boots crunched footprints into the sidewalk as she walked up to the front door and pressed the bell.

An older woman, whom Sandy guessed was Martha's sister, Alice, opened the door. The woman's eyes were red and swollen with tears. "Yes, may I help you?"

Sandy said, "I'm sorry for your loss. I'm Sandy Cothran with Channel 3 News, and I have a lead on Nick's killer. I don't have a lot of time to explain, and we're probably being watched. Is there any way I could borrow the keys to Henry's Tailor Shop?"

Alice motioned Sandy into the den and stammered, "I know who you are. I-I think he has an extra set of keys in the bedroom nightstand. I'll be right back."

Sandy stepped into the little den and found Martha. She lay in a hospital bed, staring out a bay window into the backyard. Sandy placed her hand on Martha's forearm. Martha's mind was intact. Sandy took a deep breath and said, "Martha, I'm going to help you find Nick's killer. I promise."

Martha answered with her mind. *Poor Nick. Did he suffer?*

Sandy shook her head slowly. "I was with him until the paramedics arrived. His last words before he moved into the heavenly realm were, *I'm sorry, Martha.*"

Martha blinked several times as tears ran down her cheeks. She asked telepathically, *How do you understand me?*

Sandy said, "I can read a person's thoughts or visualize their past by touch or holding something belonging to them. I've been able to do it for years."

Alice walked in the den and pressed the keys into Sandy's hand. "Here's the extra set of keys. Please be careful, Ms. Cothran."

"I will. I'll get the keys back to you. Thanks for trusting me." Sandy squeezed Alice's hand and left the house.

EIGHT O'CLOCK IN THE MORNING and Sandy felt like it was midnight. Before starting her car, Sandy looked at Baldric sitting in the passenger seat. "Why do bad things happen to good people? Cole is a freaking wart on humanity. All for what? The love of money? Wealth?"

Baldric placed his hands on his knees. "I don't have the right answer for you. All I can say is Cole's free will is directly responsible for the agony of many. Luc has used him for decades. Luc has a stronghold here and will not relinquish it without a fight. You get the folder with the key, and I'll fight off any demons who try to stop you. We'll go to the bank, get the book, and drive straight to Everglade Farms. There's a meeting tonight with your team."

Before starting the car, Sandy placed her hands in prayer mode and batted her eyelashes a few times for good measure. "Shoot. I forgot about the meeting. Can you get me out of it? I need to work."

Baldric chuckled and said, "Nope, everyone must attend, including the guardians."

Sandy was a member of the Campbell Ridge wards along with Ruby, Anna, Jerry, and Lee. Before leaving heaven, selected humans received a specific genetic code altered by The Creator containing a part of His DNA, which blessed them with divine supernatural powers. The people who received the codes became wards. The wards worked with their assigned warrior angel in an angelic battle over the earth and the human species against Luc and his demon angels. Luc and his army had been cast out of heaven for trying to incite rebellion within the heavenly realm over six thousand years ago.

The Creator gave Anna the gift of healing and light of love. Ruby had prophetic dreams, and she'd given birth to a new ward, little Joe, in December. Jerry had the gift of writing binary code. During his code-writing sessions, sometimes he would receive encrypted messages.

Recently, Jerry received a message of a coming battle. That was why they were meeting at Everglade Farms. After Joe was born, Ruby's mom, Lee, revealed she was a ward, too. She possessed all the powers of a warrior angel.

Years ago, while Sandy attended college, she and the girls began to journal in their diaries about their supernatural powers and events in what she coined The Ditch Lane Diaries. With every passing year, the Campbell Ridge wards became stronger. Tonight's meeting would bring the wards and guardians under one roof for the first time to plan for the prophesied battle. Sandy sensed the battle and her drive to expose Cole were a part of a bigger picture. Her visions never allowed her to see into her own future.

As Sandy neared the tailor shop, the hair on her arms rose, and she felt a prickly sensation on the back of her neck. Something or someone was watching her, and it wasn't Baldric.

Chapter 2

Sweetest Taboo

HENRY'S TAILOR SHOP WAS CRAWLING with cops. Baldric turned to Sandy and said, "Wait here. I'll check." He dematerialized and seconds later reappeared in the passenger seat. "The folder is still in front of the air filter inside the vent return. Cole's boys are lurking outside while the police conduct their investigation. We have to wait until they leave the shop. You need to eat breakfast. You're too skinny."

Sandy glanced into her rearview mirror and ran her fingers over her face. "Thanks for the compliment, but I need to get inside Henry's."

With a raised brow, he said, "I'll stay. I'll make sure no one gets near the folder. Go to the diner down the street, drink a cup of coffee, and eat a bagel. You need your strength."

Sandy rolled her eyes and waved her hand at him. "Okay, okay, Big B. Get out. I'll be back in two shakes and a holler." He chuckled. Sandy had nicknamed him Big B after he'd made his presence known to her in December.

Baldric appeared back inside Henry's with his sword held in his right hand. Unnoticed by human men, He moved freely through the shop checking the place out for demon angels.

Caiojezeal (Kay-oh-jez-e-al), a commander in Luc's army, materialized behind the walnut desk, splayed his fingers over the top, and glared at Baldric. "Where's Luc's Testament?"

Baldric waved cheerily to Caiojezeal. "Hey, there CJ. Missing something? You should be shouting with joy from the rooftops. Cole has secured the last piece of property on his acquisition list."

Caiojezeal walked around the desk and stood toe to toe with Baldric. "Don't play coy with me, you big brute. I sense Luc's Testament. Where is it? Oh, shit. You sneaky bastard. You placed a protection veil over it, didn't you?"

Baldric crossed his left arm over his chest and held onto his right bicep. With a feeling of satisfaction, he lied through his teeth. "As a matter of fact, I did. I have the book. Your little team in Nashville is going down. You must make retribution for the innocent."

Caiojezeal's sinister laugh rose throughout the office. With sarcasm, he said, "Daireann, the lovely Daireann. She's working on her little news story about Cole. Did you think we didn't know? Her story will never see the light of day, my old friend."

Baldric growled and bared his teeth. "You're not worthy to say her name. I'm not your friend, and I'm not your average warrior angel. You wanna play, CJ? Let's play and you can tell your boss we're bringing his division down. Yeah, tell the arrogant bastard I have him by the balls." Baldric readied himself in the on-guard position, rotating his blade of light in front of Caiojezeal.

"Oh my, my, my, Baldric. Really? You're getting testy in your old age. Maybe Daireann's more than a ward to you. Huh? Is that it, Baldric? Nailing your ward?" Caiojezeal roared with laughter and slapped the blade away from his face. "What's up with your fetish for human females? Or could this be true love? Does the old man know? Does he?" Caiojezeal laughed so hard his shoulders shook.

Baldric pushed Caiojezeal against the wall and pressed his sword against Caiojezeal's throat. Caiojezeal tried to contain his laughter but couldn't and burst out laughing again. He seemed oblivious to the blade of light held at his throat. Caiojezeal said, "The old man isn't through with us yet. But you, my most worthy adversary, you risk your position, your status, all for a human female?"

Baldric's voice deepened. "Daireann is my ward. I love her as my ward, and I'll protect her unto my last breath. I'll risk everything for her."

"Blah, blah, blah. You've just made the game much more enjoyable. And here I thought this decade would be dull. You've given me a fantastic idea. I think I'll just pop into Luc's Arrington Estate and let my sire know you're in love with Sandy. Oh, he's going to have a field day. We didn't believe we could break the Campbell Ridge wards. Thanks, Baldric." Caiojezeal bowed and disappeared.

Baldric did a three-eighty and yelled, "Damn it. Seneca? I screwed up."

Seneca, Ruby's guardian angel, and Baldric's boss, appeared before him as the humans wrapped up their investigation of Henry's Tailor Shop. Humans rarely noticed angels, even when they appeared in front of them.

Seneca exhaled a deep breath and said, "You're heading for big trouble. Are you really in love with Sandy? Do you want to be an earthbound angel? Don't get me wrong. I want you to be happy, but Saints preserve us, does it have to be your ward?"

Seneca paced back and forth in the small office while he waved his hands in the air. "You're jeopardizing our entire mission. Is there anything I can say or do to get inside that thick skull of yours? You've given Luc bait. The Demons of Pain and Suffering have lived inside of Sandy since she was nine. Luc will use them to get to her. A few more carefully placed demons and Sandy's divine power could be used against us. I cannot reiterate enough what a colossal setback that would mean for us."

Baldric slammed his fist into the wall of the office. "Do you think I fell in love on purpose? No one in heaven or earth chooses the one. She's the one. I'll resign my post if you need me to, but I'll never leave her."

"Jesus, Joseph, and Mary." Seneca sat down in the reception chair close to the dressing room. "I knew you'd formed an attachment. Has it progressed to the physical element?"

"Ah, no. I do have scruples. I'm not sure Sandy realizes the depth of my feelings. She's behaved since she tried to seduce me the night Joe was born."

Seneca shouted, "Michael could take you from our team. I need you, Baldric. The Campbell Ridge wards need you, and most especially, Sandy needs you. Control your feelings and do your job. Have you got the book? If so, get Sandy, get the book, and get to Everglade Farms. I trust this conversation is over for now."

"No, I don't have the book, but I know where it is." The doorbell chimed as Sandy walked into Henry's Tailor Shop. Baldric stood erect, and the air backed up into his lungs. He glanced at Seneca in time to see the scowl. *Oh, he was in big trouble.*

Seneca turned back to Baldric and shouted again, "Get a grip, or I'll pull you myself. You're placing her in grave danger."

Baldric frowned and said, "I will protect her. See you later, boss."

Poof! Seneca disappeared.

Sandy ran her fingers lightly over the silk ties arranged on the cherry pedestal table as she looked about the room. "Baldric, are you here?"

Baldric appeared at her side. "I'm here, Daireann."

Sandy went into the little office in the back of the store. She stepped over to the air return, opened it, and pulled out the folder with the key. Her eyes held Baldric's stare, and she said, "It's a key to a lockbox at City Bank. I have a friend who works over there."

Baldric read her thoughts. Sandy's friend was a human male that she'd slept with in the past. It sucked to know the most intimate details of Sandy's love life. He took a deep breath and exhaled.

Sandy placed the folder under her arm and raised a brow. "What's wrong with you? I did what you said. I drank a cup of coffee and ate a bagel with cream cheese. Geez Louise, why are you mad?"

"Hmph. I'm not mad—I'm angry. Your friend at the bank. I read your thoughts, and he's not just a friend. You slept with him." Baldric placed his sword in its sheath.

Sandy shook her head and said, "You're acting like a jealous boyfriend. It's just sex, not love. Besides, I'm damaged goods. You need to quit looking at me all moon-eyed like a lovesick schoolboy unless you want to do something about it."

"You're not damaged goods. Have more respect for yourself." Baldric disappeared.

Sandy stepped over to the assistant manager's desk at City Bank. "May I speak to Ken, please?"

Without looking up from her typewriter, the woman said, "He's in a meeting." She glanced up and recognized Sandy. "Oh, Ms. Cothran, let me check for you."

"Thank you, Susan. How are the twins?"

Susan beamed with pride. "Growing like two little weeds. Would you like to sit down?"

"I'm good. Thanks." Sandy caught a glimpse of Baldric sulking in the corner with his arms across his chest. *Good grief.* She stared at him and exchanged telepathic comments. *You're acting like a child.*

He snarled. *Oh goody, Ken approaches.*

Sandy turned to Ken and gave him a huge grin. "Why, Ken. You get better looking every time I see you."

Ken pulled her up into his arms without care and kissed her cheek. "Ms. Cothran, to what do I owe the pleasure of such beautiful company today?"

Sandy poured it on as thick as dripping molasses. "Well, I've come across this little ole key, and I need to get into the lockbox. Think you could help me?"

"Why, I'd be delighted. This way, Ms. Cothran." Sandy followed Ken as he unlocked the door to a private viewing room for customers with lockboxes. He shut the door, swept her into his arms and kissed her as she draped her arms around his neck. He ran his hand down the curve of Sandy's spine, and Baldric zapped Ken's hand with electricity.

Ken yelped. "Yikes. Your outfit has electricity in it. How about you lose it?"

Sandy tilted the angle of her face and gave him a sly smile. "You know I would love to do just that, but I'm in a bit of a hurry and have to deliver the contents of that little box to my family. Raincheck?" Sandy kissed Ken again.

Baldric pinched the soft skin under her arm. Sandy frowned and waved Baldric away. He grinned and planted his feet hip-width apart and didn't move.

Ken said, "You can give me a raincheck anytime. I'll leave you to it. Number thirteen-oh-nine is located on the top row, the second box to the end. I'll be outside if you need me." He exited the room.

Baldric gruffly said, "Get the book and let's get out of here before I do something I regret."

Sandy whipped around to face him. "Look, buddy, you and I are going to have a big problem if you can't tell me what's bothering you. I've already told you I want you. If you want me, all you have to do is say the word."

Baldric threw his hands up in exasperation. "Not everything is about your sexual prowess. We have a job to do. And how can you kiss that mealy-mouthed man? I'll meet you in the car. My stomach can't take anymore."

Sandy giggled. Baldric was jealous, and that gave her hope. Maybe he felt about her the same way she felt about him. Sandy had never been in love, never wanted to be until the night Baldric rescued her from Carson Jones, another one of Cole's attack dogs.

Sandy left work to go home and change clothes before heading out to Anna and Jerry's farm to celebrate Ruby and Reed's baby party. She parked in front of her condo building in a tow-away zone and placed her press pass in the window. Sandy grabbed her purse, threw it over her shoulder, and sprinted through the double doors of her condo building to the elevators. When the doors opened, she pressed the button to the third floor. Right as the doors were about to shut, a man wearing black trousers and a black turtleneck slid inside.

As the elevator pulled into its ascent, the man leaned over and pressed the stop button. The large man slammed Sandy against the elevator wall and choked her, his forearm cutting off her windpipe. Sandy had been on the verge of passing out when a brilliant white light filled the elevator and ripped the man away. Sandy watched as this beautiful being beat the ever-loving shit out of her attacker.

Afterward, Sandy looked into the sea green eyes of a radiant being, and life on the planet changed for her. The key to a distant memory unlocked. She remembered Baldric from childhood. His heavenly scent, his warm touch—Sandy remembered her guardian angel. But it also opened up horrible memories. Memories of Mr. Ben. Memories she still didn't want to face.

Sandy opened the lockbox and found a wad of money, several titles to cars, and a brown, leather-bound book. Her hands trembled as she ran her fingers over the cover of the large book and wondered how Nick had ever lifted it in the first place. In the center of the book was an emblem of a serpent-entwined rod, and each corner had metal embellishments that looked new, but inside, the pages were old and made of vellum.

Thumbing through the pages of the testament conjured up images tracing back to antiquity. Just holding the book revealed some pretty startling information that Sandy would have to make notes on at a later time.

The Sunday sermons Sandy grew up listening to spoke of damned souls tortured in hellfire and brimstone or sulfur. In Luc's Testament, contracted souls lived abundant lives on earth while their mortal bodies existed. It was only at death that the contracted souls lived in servitude for the rest of eternity on the lowest rung of hell's ladder. Luc despised humans who were weak enough to sell their souls for any price for a mere lifetime. Eternity lasted forever.

The entries over the last several decades had recognizable names of some very influential people, not just from Sandy's home state and region but in the country and across the world. Listed in the book were leaders of industry, leaders in politics, and leaders in religion.

In earth's purgatory, Luc held the human souls who straddled the fence in the angelic war between heaven and hell until the person declared allegiance to one side or the other. His notes made it clear he thought the modern-day soft sell of religion was an edge in his favor. Many of the undeclared souls converted to Luc's church while others dug in deep for The Creator and fought for the light of love.

Luc had marked a favorite chapter in his Testament—the one regarding souls belonging to The Creator in the Everafter. The Campbell Ridge wards were among the souls listed. The faithful humans of The Creator were the ones Luc enjoyed tempting the most.

Luc's manifesto listed dozens of spells and magical incantations, including a chapter on exorcising evil spirits. In the Testament, all of the light and dark supernatural powers available through the universe were listed and named the being who possessed the power.

Further into the book, Sandy glimpsed Luc's demon angels, and their divisions seemed based on inherent human flaws. Baldric would have to help her with this chapter. The language was different than any Sandy had ever encountered. The pages and text kept changing before her eyes. If she thumbed back to a previous page, the text held different passages or was deleted entirely.

The dark energy within the book merged with the light energy of her powers. Malicious thoughts and nefarious deeds swirled inside her mind. Sandy slammed the book shut, dropped to her knees, and began reciting The Lord's Prayer.

Luc's Testament held the keys she needed to bring down his network in more places than Nashville. Sandy had enough ammunition to disrupt Luc's empire on earth. She held the power in her hands. Sandy wrapped the large book with a black velvet cloth and secured it with a leather strap.

Sandy felt weighed down by Luc's Testament as if she carried an enormous burden on her back while walking slowly to her Corvette. She placed the book in the back storage with her Ditch Lane Diaries master copy, then slid behind the wheel and cranked up the engine. A stern Baldric appeared in the passenger seat, arms crossed and jaw clenched.

"You can't stay mad at me anymore. You're right. Luc's Testament has enormous power and contains everything we need to bring him down. Nailing Cole Steele will be a bonus. Before we head out to Everglade Farms, I need to stop at the library and make copies of the pages mentioning Cole. I'll keep the original book with me." Sandy grabbed Baldric by the face and kissed him on the mouth.

Flames of desire shot up her spine as the kiss lengthened, and she melted into Baldric's strong arms. Sandy gazed at him through heavy lids, and a slow smile came to her lips. "You have sparkles floating in the air all around you. Golden sparkles. What is that?"

"Don't ask or we won't make it to the library or Everglade Farms, and I'm already in deep enough waters with Seneca." Baldric held her hand and kissed her fingertips.

Sandy turned up her CD player and began to rock back and forth to the music from Electric Light Orchestra. She teased him and sang out the words, "You like me, you love me, you want some more of me." She giggled and pulled out onto the highway.

"You're some kind of woman." He laughed.

"Yup, the kind that wants some." Baldric's response to her kiss made her heart flutter with excitement. It was the middle of February and her palms were sweating.

Everglade was thirty miles south of Nashville. Driving down I-65, Sandy's thoughts raced back to Luc's Testament. She'd followed leads on Cole for months. Not a single solitary soul would even speak to her off the record. Everyone was scared to death of him. But with the book in her trunk, Sandy had all the answers she needed to nail Cole to the wall and couldn't wait until her segment hit the airwaves.

THE EVERGLADE LIBRARY PARKING LOT was empty. The librarian, Miss Manning, sat behind the checkout counter as Sandy walked inside the door. "Hi, Miss Manny. How the heck are ya?"

Miss Manning removed her glasses and allowed them to dangle on the gold chain next to her chest. She walked from behind the counter and gave Sandy a quick kiss on the cheek. "Aw, it's so good to see you, child. You're making big waves in Nashville. I watch you every night on the news. So what brings you to the library?"

Sandy hugged Miss Manny and then took a step back. She giggled and said, "Perceptive as ever. No beating around the bush with you, is there? May I use your copy machine, please?"

Miss Manning pressed her fingers together and leaned in closer to Sandy. With a whisper, she asked, "Is it news related? Some big scoop?"

Sandy's eyebrows popped as she held the book to her chest and nodded. "Yes, ma'am. Top-secret stuff. I promise I'll call you and give you a heads up the night the story airs. You can tell the ladies during bridge that you helped. But not until it airs. Promise?"

Miss Manny pretended to lock her lips and throw away an invisible key. "Follow me. Let's see if the machine has paper and ink."

The copy machine was located in a cramped little room in the back of the library against the wall. On the opposite side of the room, shelving held office supplies for the library. Sandy placed the book on a side table.

Luc's Testament bound in brown leather measured around nine inches wide by seventeen inches long. As Sandy thumbed the pages, wild, colorful images flashed through her mind, making her reel with nausea. The moving mental images carried her on the cords of light back to the days of Caesar.

A Roman soldier or official knelt before someone Sandy couldn't see. The Roman kissed the mysterious person's hand and then took a small knife and sliced the palm of his hand, allowing blood to fill the inkwell. The Roman dipped his pen into the blood and signed his name into the book. Sandy could only assume the unseen person was Luc.

Sandy released the book and jumped away from the machine. She was on the verge of hyperventilating. Dark moving images filled her brain with disgusting, vile profiles of possessed and deranged humans throughout civilization. The images zipped along the cords of light as Sandy braced herself against the wall and gripped the lip of the book shelves.

Baldric appeared next to the copy machine loudly enough to make the door vibrate against the jambs. "Ah, what's wrong? You're pale as a ghost."

Sandy shook her head and said, "That book is disgusting. Vile images fill my mind every time I turn a page."

Baldric placed his hands on top of her head and closed his eyes. His positive energy seeped into her bones like hot butter and drained the negative energy right out of her body. She sighed and said, "Thanks. I thought I was going to get sick."

Baldric leaned against the wall and crossed his arms over his chest, watching her as she made the last copy from the book. "Once you get the info you need to do your story, burn those pages and give me the book. I'll see it gets to the right hands. Oh, and one more thing. I told one of Luc's demon angels I had the book. I placed a veil of protection over Luc's Testament to prevent them from finding it. At least until your story airs."

Sandy stomped her foot and stopped the machine. "Can't I get a freaking break? Dad gum it." She turned to Baldric and said, "If Luc's demon knows, then I've not only placed myself in danger but my best friends along with Martha, Alice, and Miss Manny. Would you set up a protection veil over them, too?"

Baldric grabbed her by the shoulders. "Listen to me. Luc's Testament causes great pain. The only reason I'm allowing you to use the book is that you might save lives which could otherwise be ruined. Even if you only expose Cole and his cronies. I won't lie to you. Luc will come for the book. Your story may never see the light of day, but it won't be for the lack of you trying."

As if to gather his thoughts, Baldric closed his eyes for a brief second and then stared into her eyes. He continued, "Ruby, Anna, Jerry, and Lee know the risks. Guardian angels protect the innocent, but Luc and his demon angels can make hell on earth for them. Revealing the truth opens more light into the world."

Sandy tilted her head. Her eyes widened as the revelation hit her, and she shouted, "Hell's on earth, isn't it? That's why Luc wants to destroy humans."

Baldric retold the story of how Luc was one of the three mightiest angels in the universe. He told her about Luc's obsession to overrule The Creator, which got him cast out of heaven to earth while it was still null and void. "Luc's lived here ever since."

With determination, Sandy tucked the copies in her briefcase. She wrapped up Luc's Testament with the velvet cloth and tied it with a leather strap. "Let's boogie, my Big B."

Sandy walked over to Miss Manning as she placed returned books back on the library shelf. Sandy tapped her on the shoulder. "Thanks for letting me make copies."

Miss Manny turned as she held Jane Austen's *Mansfield Park* in her hand. "I'm delighted to help, and I can't wait to see your story on the news. Won't Daisy Allen be jealous?" She snickered as Sandy left the building.

Sandy said a quick prayer for Miss Manny. The book she held in her arms had killed a man today. She didn't think he would be the last.

Chapter 3

That's What Friends Are For

SNOW BEGAN TO FALL AS Sandy pulled into Everglade Farms. The place looked like a postcard with its old two-story brick house and wraparound porch. Two rockers sat on the front porch next to empty flower containers. Smoke filtered slowly from the chimney on the snow-covered rooftop. Sandy parked down the tractor lane next to the big red barn. She gathered Luc's Testament and the copies into her arms and exited the car.

Sandy's teeth chattered from the cold walking up the cleared sidewalk that made passage around the house and up the front stairs less treacherous. Sandy opened the front door without knocking and yelled out, "Honey, I'm home."

Lee walked from the kitchen wiping her hands with a dishtowel. "Darling, you must be freezing. I have a big pot of vegetable soup on, and cornbread is baking in the oven." Lee looked at the book, and her right hand flew to her chest. "You found Luc's Testament. Where?"

Sandy followed Lee into the kitchen while she told her the events of the last fourteen hours. She noticed concern lines etched Lee's face. Sandy placed Luc's Testament and her briefcase on Lee's baker rack. Sandy glanced at a collage of photos of little Joe with Ruby and Reed, a few of George and Lizzie, and one snapshot of Granddaddy Campbell with Harry and Lee.

Sandy went over to the stove and took off the lid and sniffed. "God, that smells good." She grabbed a bowl of soup and sat down at

27

the table. Lee brought her a glass of buttermilk because she knew it was Sandy's favorite. Sandy asked, "How are George and Lizzie? I haven't seen them since Joe was born."

Lee joined Sandy at the table with a cup of coffee in her hands. "They've separated. George hasn't told me what's going on, but Lizzie did before she left for her mother's house in Florida. She can't have kids and doesn't want George to miss out. Her depression escalated after Ruby gave birth to Joe. Lizzie thinks she's doing the right thing. I tried to talk her out of it. Now my boy's fun-loving personality has turned dark and grumpy. I've spoken to Ruby, and she said I needed to stay out of it. What do you think?"

"Ah, lawd, don't ask me. I'm the world's worst person for love life advice." Sandy blew on the hot soup before she sipped it and still burned her tongue. "George and Lizzie have been together for a long time. It doesn't seem right they should be separated. You know, back in the day, I had a huge crush on George. He kissed me once. Did you know that?"

Lee took another sip of coffee and sighed. "Yeah, I knew you were kinda in love with him before he met Lizzie and they started dating."

Lee pushed her chair away from the table and walked over to the sink. Looking out the window at the sheets of snow, she said, "I'm having battle dreams. I think it's the same one Jerry's message revealed. I believe it's about Luc coming for his book." Lee turned and looked at Sandy. "You're messing with real fire, this time, Sandy D. This isn't your run of the mill news story."

Sandy remained silent.

Lee leaned against the counter. "Luc's book is proof of a supernatural world most humans choose to ignore. It's not just the fact that Luc will come for you, but the longer you possess the book, the darker your soul will become. It has enormous power and yields destruction. The book will destroy you if you don't rid yourself of it soon."

Sandy said, "Mama Bear, Baldric's already given me a lecture, but I need to do the story on Cole. I know I only have the book for a short time. But Baldric and I agree the story may save lives. It won't stop Luc or even slow him down. But it's one more victory for the home team."

Sandy washed down the rest of her soup with a big glass of

buttermilk and wiped her mouth with a red linen napkin. "Um, Mama Bear, I had no idea what the book was until I held it and made copies. The news story should be ready to go live tomorrow evening. I haven't called Art because I'm afraid Cole has placed people inside the station. I don't have time to train. I need to work tonight."

Lee walked over and squeezed Sandy's hand. "But that's precisely why you need to train. You need the additional skills if Luc knows you have the book, and I can assure you he does by now. Training will give you the edge on whether you live or die. Put your piece off. Stay here tonight. You can leave in the morning."

Sandy placed her forearms on the table. "Do you have any idea how hard it is for me to sit on this story? Nick London is dead. We have a councilman missing, and countless small business owners have gone out of business because of Cole. I have to write the story, shoot the scenes, and edit them for air. I can't do it here." *And that's if Luc or Cole doesn't get to me first.*

Sandy pushed away from the table and brought her dishes to the sink. She turned and said, "I have to expose Cole's illegal activity and include those people who have helped him circumvent the system to make millions, and do it in such a way the powers that be will have to investigate my allegations."

Footfalls thumped outside the kitchen door, and a smile lit Lee's face. "Aw, I hear my baby boy." She walked to the back door and opened it. Ruby and little Joe came inside. A clump of snow fell out of Ruby's hair onto the chubby baby's forehead making him scream bloody murder in his mother's arms.

Sandy clapped her hands and went over to Ruby. She grabbed the little boy out of Ruby's arms and twirled Joe in a circle. "What are you doing to your mama? You precious boy. Man, you have a huge set of lungs." Sandy glanced at Ruby and added, "You may have given birth to this child, but he's going to look like his daddy." The abrupt departure of his mother stunned Joe into silence as he stared at Sandy. Joe's face began to turn shades of red as he held his breath and then screamed some more. Sandy quickly passed off the explosive package to his grandmother.

Lee placed the baby on her shoulder and began to pat and rub his back. Joe let out a belch of a much larger person. "See there? He just had air in his belly."

Ruby shook off her coat and hung it on the hook next to the back door. She gave Sandy a hug and kissed her cheek. "Sweetie, how are you? I've missed the heck out of you, stranger."

Sandy whistled and waved her hand back and forth. "Wowzer, you're back to your pre-baby weight. Dang, motherhood looks good on you."

"Oh, girl, flattery will get you everything. I didn't know if you'd make it tonight. Jerry's battle prediction has Mom nervous. Big training session in the barn. Did you bring workout clothes?" Ruby stepped over to the stove and raised the top of the pot. "Yum, I'm starving." She reached into the cabinet next to the fridge and pulled out a bowl, then ladled vegetable soup to the brim.

"If I'm staying over tonight, I'll have to borrow clothes from Lee. Ruby, brace yourself." Sandy paused for effect, and Ruby stopped and stared. "I have Luc's Testament. With it, I have the tools to bring down Cole Steele."

Ruby's face paled, and she dropped her spoon in the bowl of soup. "Holy moly. That's why Jerry received the encrypted message. Holy cow. Luc has to be pissed. I'm surprised the house is still standing."

Anna and Jerry came through the back kitchen door, taking off their coats, grab-assing and snickering like two teenagers. Anna turned from Sandy to Ruby. "What? Can't I give my husband some sugar?" She went to Sandy and hugged her. "Hey, we've missed you around here, Miss Reporter of the Year."

Sandy kissed Anna's cheek, and Jerry came over to get into the action. Sandy wrapped her arms around their necks and said, "I miss you guys, too. It looks like the honeymoon is still going strong."

Ruby began to eat and pointed to the pot of soup. Jerry quickly grabbed bowls for him and Anna and joined Ruby at the table. Ruby said, "Jero, your message is on point. Sandy has Luc's Testament." She glanced up at Sandy and said, "Spill it. Short and sweet please."

Sandy walked over to the baker's rack, grabbed the book, and placed it in the middle of the walnut kitchen table. "I have horrible visions from the book. The book seems to be alive. Revelations filled my brain regarding human souls. Luc breaks human souls into categories. The book lists magic spells and Luc's military strategies for his demon angels. The pages are in a constant state of flux, adding some pages while deleting others. It's like one of your software programs, Jerry. The book incriminates Mr. Steele, and that'll be the focal point of my story."

Sandy quickly told them about Nick and Henry's Tailor shop. "Nick lifted the book while meeting with Cole. I'm not sure how he did it. Look at that thing—it's huge. I don't think Nick had any idea what he was stealing or why in the world Cole left the Testament out in the open in the first place. Nick taking the book signed his death warrant. I have to develop a story and get it on air before they silence me."

Lee came back into the kitchen with Joe in her arms. He was trying to stick his fingers into Lee's mouth. She kissed his fingertips and gave him a plastic teething ring to occupy his time. "The guardians are waiting for us in the barn. Harry's going to babysit. Where's Reed?"

Ruby stepped over to her mom and kissed Joe on the forehead. "Reed's mad. He's feeling a little insecure at the moment. He thinks he can't protect us. Reed wants to become a member of our team. It's not my call, but he's sure as shit acting like it's my call."

Harry walked into the kitchen, and little Joe's eyes lit up for his granddaddy. Harry grinned from ear to ear as he opened his hands and extended them to Joe, who squealed and reached for him. "I remember when I found out about you and your mother. I wasn't very happy either. I made the decision to accept her position and respect her for it. The responsibility each of you shares is enormous. The least I can do is support you and care for this little guy. Listen to Lee, listen to the guardians. It'll save lives and souls." He left the room with Joe in his arms.

Lee stepped over to the stove and turned the burner off. She turned around to face her daughter and the others whom she regarded as her own children, or so Sandy thought. "I'm changing into my training gear. Sandy, I'll leave you some clothes in Ruby's room." Lee paused before walking out of the kitchen. "My prayer has been to keep all of you safe. The guardians called tonight's training session. It's serious, so I need you all to be serious, and that goes for you, too, Jerry."

Ruby, Sandy, Anna, and Jerry exchanged questioning looks, then

Ruby said, "Mom, we're not teenagers anymore. We get it. It's serious."

Lee placed her hand on Ruby's shoulder and kissed the top of her head. "My darling, you don't get it, but you will when you walk into the barn." She looked at her watch and said, "We have fifteen minutes. Don't be late. Erinelle is the senior commander of Campbell Ridge and she is by-the-book tough." She left the room.

"Ew-whee, someone's in trouble." Jerry snickered and slurped his soup.

"I think Mom is scared we'll embarrass her or something in front of her guardian." Ruby started cleaning up the dirty dishes.

Sandy pulled out a drawer and reached in for a clean towel to dry. "This will be the first time we've seen all of our guardians together. It's exciting. I mean, didn't you feel Lee's electric vibe?"

Anna stood, finished drinking her water, and handed the empty glass to Ruby. "I've seen them together. I've watched the guardians fight, and I'm glad that they're finally going to include us. I have a feeling this is why we went to the cave in the first place. How long ago was that? Things happen for a reason, or at least I think so."

Jerry turned his bowl up and quickly finished his soup. He handed the empty bowl to Ruby. "Look, it wasn't that long ago I lost Anna and by His Grace got her back. Demon angels are real, and they're real nasty. If they're coming for us, then we have to know what to do. Some of the messages I receive I don't think I'm supposed to understand. It torments my sleep. But the battle message, it specifically said we would fight Luc's demons."

Sandy folded the dishtowel and laid it on the counter. "Give me five minutes to change clothes and we'll go to the barn together."

THANKFULLY, SANDY AND LEE WORE the same size clothes. She pulled on a pair of black sweatpants and a gray sweatshirt. Running shoes were a tad big, but an extra pair of socks did the trick. Sandy bounded down the stairs, and everyone stood at the door waiting for her. "We have two minutes to get to the barn."

Ruby said, "Let's fly." They grabbed their coats and left out the back door from the kitchen and ran across the backyard, down the hill, and into the barn.

The big red barn had three separate double doors at the entrance, two at the back, and several side doors. Ruby opened the side door of the barn closest to the main house, and they walked inside.

Along every wall and up to the rafters, angels filled the barn. It took Sandy's breath away. The warm glow of love inside the barn made her want to weep with joy. Unconditional love filled every nook and cranny of her soul. She had a complete sense of peace, and then she locked eyes with Baldric. He gave her a big smile. *Baldric, do you feel this kind of peace every day?* He nodded and winked.

Sandy noticed that her best friends seemed to be experiencing the same kind of awesome feeling. Sandy wondered what the angels thought of them. Lee stood next to an incredibly tall and beautiful female angel with long, dark red hair, and she was armed to the teeth with weapons.

The female warrior angel said, "Good evening, wards, please join us. As you see, this is a training session for us as well as it is for you. Sandy's in possession of Luc's Testament and Jerry's prophecy states we'll be joining forces in a battle. It's time to prepare." The female warrior angel motioned toward the Campbell Ridge guardians who fell into rank beside her. "To my right, we have Seneca, guardian of Ruby Jane, Baldric the Warrior, guardian of Sandra Daireann, Luwenia, guardian of Jerry Douglas, Raphael, guardian of Anna Faye, and I'm Erinelle, guardian of Georgiana Lee."

The side door opened again, and all eyes turned to Reed as he strolled inside the barn. He nodded to his friends as he crossed the room to stand next to Ruby. Reed stood tall and proud as he held Ruby's hand. "I apologize for my tardiness. I just received the phone call from Harry that I was to attend tonight's session. Is this correct?" Lee smiled at Reed and tilted her head toward Erinelle.

Erinelle stepped up to Reed and at eye level, she said, "You want to fight, human?"

Without wavering and with steady eyes, Reed replied, "I'll lay my life down for anyone in this room. I'm willing to do what's necessary to protect my family."

Erinelle turned and whistled. A boy who seemed to be around the age of ten approached the female angel. She said, "Are you willing to train the human?" The boy nodded and approached Reed.

With reverence, Reed said, "I mean no disrespect, but surely you don't mean to send this kid into battle?" The boy grabbed Reed's arm and flipped him to the ground, placing his foot on Reed's throat. Laughter rumbled throughout the barn.

The boy chuckled and said, "Be careful who you call a kid. I'm three thousand years old, and I've seen more battles than most of the angels in this barn. Who do you think taught them?" The boy raised his foot and extended a hand to Reed.

Reed grabbed his throat and choked out, "My apologies, sir."

After the laughter had died down, the boy said, "Meh, no apologies needed. My name is Simon. You listen and do what I say, and I'll make you a warrior fit for the AAF." A roar of whistles and clapping erupted throughout the crowd of angels. The Angel Armed Forces were under Michael's command and protected all of the known universes, including earth.

Erinelle placed her hand on Simon's left shoulder, and he fell in rank with the guardians of Campbell Ridge. She extended her arms outward and said, "Tonight's training session is a crash course for fighting Luc's demon angels. It's a prelude to the coming battle. There are no rules, no wrong or right way to send a demon angel to the Eternal Darkness, which is the abyss where one is separated from The Creator forever."

Erinelle commanded the room as she walked about the straw- and dirt-covered floor. She looked at the wards and the angels in the rafters. "Single combat battles are rare. Most demon angels will try to tag team to destroy the soul of possession. The light of love or The Creator's light draws the demon angels into the open. The light triggers a memory of heaven. The demons still long to be in The Creator's presence. The light of love gives our legion the opportunity to descend from heaven and send the demon angels straight to the Eternal Darkness."

Erinelle approached Ruby and Reed and searched their eyes. "Demon angels are cast into divisions based on personal flaws, human weaknesses. Any act perpetrated on oneself or others that destroys the soul—you can safely assume Luc's demon angels have compromised their spirit of light. The little voice within you telling you the difference between right and wrong began at creation when humans made the decision to choose for themselves. It's been a constant struggle between good and evil ever since."

Erinelle stepped in front of Sandy and placed her hands on her hips. "Demon angels are highly territorial by nature, and it isn't uncommon for an internal battle between groups to occur. We use their territorial nature to divide and conquer."

Last, Erinelle faced Jerry and Anna. "Keep in mind as we break up into groups you'll be fighting a contest of wills and sometimes it's your free will that may hinder you from victory. Commence to your guardians." Erinelle waved her hand and walked over to Lee.

The barn had been set up into quadrants. Luwenia took Jerry to the back right of the barn to practice archery. Anna went with Raphael to the back left where he rolled several daggers out on a table and pointed to Harry's old scarecrow nailed to the wall of the barn. He and Anna would be in charge of the triage but needed to train in case they needed to defend themselves. Ruby and Seneca went to the front right of the barn to practice throwing what looked like blue golf balls into peg holes along the wall.

Lee and Reed along with Erinelle and Simon set up sparring partners.

Sandy tilted her head to Baldric and said, "What are you going to teach me?"

A smile crept into the corners of his mouth as he pulled out his sword. "She's a beauty, isn't she? I selected one just for you." He sheathed his sword and brought her to their training area. Baldric revealed an extraordinary, almost feminine sword and fitted her hand around the hilt. He whispered in her ear, and a shiver ran up her spine. "Feels good in your hand, doesn't it? Now watch me." Baldric took out his sword and made slow circle eights with his wrist. "Just try to get a feel for the blade. Slow and easy."

Sandy mimicked Baldric's movements, and she felt better about herself with the sword in her hand.

With a rich, velvety smooth voice, Baldric said, "Fully extend your arm before taking any movements." He demonstrated the proper form. "Now look at my feet. The on-guard and the retreat on-guard." Baldric moved fluidly back and forth along a forty-foot-long pathway. "I want you to practice these simple exercises here and in your condo."

Sandy imitated his movements. "This feels a little like dancing."

Baldric chuckled and said, "Yeah, it does. There's a rhythm, a tempo, and timing when you enter a bout."

Sandy stopped and pointed her blade to the ground. "I pray I don't have to fight anytime soon."

Baldric placed his hands on her shoulders and gazed into her eyes. "The Creator will bestow and enhance your new skill within days, not weeks. You'll practice after work and in your dreams. The movements, exercises, and techniques will become second nature."

Sandy lifted her chin and said, "I believe you. The angels in this room and my best friends fill and recharge my soul. I'll work hard, I promise, but I have to be honest: Erinelle scares me a little."

Baldric threw his head back and laughed. "She scares all of us. Erinelle is fearsome, loyal, and will fight unto her last breath for the wards of Campbell Ridge."

Two hours later, Sandy labored to breathe as she held onto her knees. Sweat streamed down her face and back, and her legs and arms were weak as a kitten.

Erinelle whistled and roared, "Time. Desist practice and come to me."

Everyone in the room, angels, and wards alike, gathered in a circle from the floor to the ceiling of the barn. Erinelle's beautiful shimmering wings jutted upward to the heavens. Erinelle spread her arms wide and sang the sweetest song. "Come to me, my little sparrows. Come to me unto this day. Fill my heart and soul with your song. Fill my heart and soul with your joy. We sing together in our flight to serve He who created us—He who fills my heart and soul with His love." She bowed her head, and everyone bowed their heads. The barn glowed with an incandescent light.

The love of light filled each being—mortal and immortal—in the room with a vibration of energy that shook Sandy to her core. Erinelle's words seared her soul and revealed an understanding she wasn't alone. The angels and the wards of Campbell Ridge stood together for the good of humanity.

After the session had ended, most of the visiting and some of the guardian angels vanished into the air. Sandy glanced over at Baldric as they strolled to the side door of the barn and went out into the chilly wind of winter. "If Luc knows we have the book, why hasn't he come for it?"

Baldric draped his right arm around her shoulders. The heat of his massive body warmed her in the frigid air. He leaned next to her ear and said, "Open your eyes, Daireann. Open your mind. Allow the veil of the supernatural to reveal itself to you. Look around, and tell me what you see."

At first glance, Sandy saw the weather vane on the roof of the barn. Then a mysterious cloud lifted and revealed warrior angels standing guard. She turned and found warrior angels stationed around the house, the barn, and along the property lines of Everglade Farms. Sandy angled her face toward Baldric and said, "Angels are everywhere?" She paused and looked around the property again, and she understood. "Angels *are* everywhere."

Baldric exhaled a deep breath, kissed the top of her head, and hugged her tightly. "Exactly."

Chapter 4

I Didn't Mean To Turn You On

WORD REACHED LUC WHILE HE was in the midst of creating conflict among rival tribes that would result in thousands of deaths in Asia. He became furious when Caiojezeal appeared before him with the news. Someone stole his Testament, and someone was going to pay.

Luc strolled through a picturesque village with children running through the streets and women covered from head to toe with only their eyes exposed to the world. In a few years, the village would be a war zone with tall walls of barbed wire, and every few feet a soldier would be toting a machine gun. "Damn it. How in the hell did my book get stolen? Oh, wait, of course. Cole checked out the book several weeks ago. I should've known the human was too inept to protect it. Who stole the book from him and where is it now?"

Caiojezeal walked into a nearby tea house. "Nick London of Henry's Tailor Shop in Nashville lifted the book. I went there to search myself and ran into Baldric. He has the book."

Luc kicked a chair away from the table and sat down to talk with Caiojezeal. The waiter took one look at Luc and returned swiftly with two teas and snacks. Luc placed his hand on the man's forearm. The man began praying incessantly. Luc growled, "Leave us in peace." The old man exited into the kitchen, walking backward while he continued to pray loudly.

Luc shook his head in disbelief. "Humans and their prayers. The funny part about prayer and religion is all the humans on the planet think their religion is right, and everyone else's is wrong. Unless The Creator has changed philosophy, there's only one faith and it's all directed to Him." Luc took a bite of his cake and drank his tea while he contemplated what to do about Baldric.

Luc's Testament held incredible power, and he controlled his followers with its accounts. "Baldric has my book, huh? Well, it looks like I'll be paying his ward a little visit, but not before I meet with Cole. Stay close to Baldric. I want to know his every move. I need his ward alone. We get his ward, and we get Baldric and my book. It's a win-win for me."

"You may count on me, sire." Caiojezeal bowed his head toward Luc before taking a sip of his tea.

Luc reached over to place his hand on Caiojezeal's left shoulder. "I have to stop by Egypt before returning to the States. Place a couple of your warriors with Cole and his guards. He has a short fuse, and I won't allow another one of his mistakes to jeopardize my work." Luc manipulated both time and space within earth's realm. He often used astral travel, and today he ported to Egypt before returning to his estate in Middle Tennessee where his servant, Cole, resided.

Luc had designed Arrington Estate as a reflection of a home he once owned in the French countryside. Luc's stately manor offered a kind of rustic charm with curved arches, stonework, and a steep hip roof. He loved the symmetry of the estate as well as the underground tunnels leading to his domain. The interior reflected more of a mountain lodge retreat. The living area housed a large stone fireplace surrounded by rich, dark wood paneling, thick Aubusson carpets, and luxurious leather couches.

Cole sat on the sofa drinking a cocktail while he had an argument with Hammer, his senior assassin. "You weren't supposed to shoot him, idiot. Now how will we find the book? Carson and Walt worked with their police informant with the police. They didn't find it."

Luc materialized behind Cole. He placed his hands on Cole's shoulders and the room became intensely quiet. Hatred and anger exuded from Luc as his fingers dug into Cole's flesh while he spoke in a gentle manner. "Do you want to know who has my book?"

Luc released Cole and walked to the fireplace. He spanned his fingers out over the flames and engulfed the tips. After a minute, Luc blew the flames out and stepped back over to Cole. Luc wrapped his steaming fingers around Cole's neck, burning Cole's skin, while tears formed in the corners of Cole's eyes. Cole opened his mouth to speak, but Luc shook his head back and forth.

The interior walls shook as Luc shouted, "Baldric, the warrior angel from the AAF, has my book, and I want it back. You'll see I get my book back, or you'll be taking a trip down memory lane. To, ah, let's see, 1929, as you sat in your bedroom after killing your wife. Yes, that's where we'll travel if I don't get my book back soon."

Luc stepped away from Cole and glared at Hammer, Carson Jones, and Walt Reese. "All of you face a fate worse than death if I don't get my book soon. Do I make myself clear?"

The men stammered their apologies and reassurances. Luc waved his hand in the air to silence them. "Why are you standing around with your thumbs up your ass? Leave now, and find my book!" The four men rushed from the room. Luc watched from the wall of windows as they flew down the snow-covered sidewalk, slipping and sliding along the way. They jumped into the black Ford Explorer and sped away into the night.

Luc glanced up to the shimmering stars dotted across the black velvet sky. As soon as Caiojezeal gave Luc word Baldric had left earth's realm, Luc would take Sandra Daireann. Capturing her would be the best way to recover his book of souls and incantations. It took Luc centuries to create his version of the Bible, and he would be damned if Baldric kept it. He thought of Baldric. Baldric and Luc had been friends once before he'd been cast out of heaven.

After the worship cycle, Luc made plans with Baldric and Michael to spar in the courtyard. Luc, a warrior angel, had been relegated to leading one-third of heaven's angels in daily praise of The Creator. He didn't want to lose his edge, so he frequently met with the two best warriors in all the known universe to train.

The Creator made the courtyard for a variety of reasons, such as sparring, theater, and festivals. At the end of every work rotation, angels gathered to socialize along the walls and immaculate lawn with its ancient trees.

Baldric entered the arena with a scowl on his face. Luc had watched him grow into an elite warrior angel. Angels never aged past the date of maturity. Luc teased him on occasion but had never seen Baldric angry.

Baldric withdrew his sword and held it in his right hand. He went into a battle stance. "You'll pay for what you did to Barbellina. Her parents promised a pairing between us, and you took her innocence." The young angel glared at Luc.

"A female is why you're so worked up? Come on. Baldric, son, there are many untouched angels to choose from for a mate, and Barbellina came to me, not the other way around. Back down or I'll have to teach you a lesson." Luc withdrew his sword and presented himself in the on-guard position, extending his right arm toward Baldric.

Michael stood between the angels and threw up his hands. "Drop the swords. If you're to fight, do it with fists. I'll not allow injuries to either of you that'll require treatment." Michael turned to Baldric and said, "Did you talk to Barbellina? Did she tell you Lucifer took her innocence or are you assuming that's what happened?"

Baldric glanced at Michael as blood rushed to his cheeks with anger. "I didn't have to ask her. Every angel in heaven including the outbound angels knows Lucifer snares the females in a trance and leads them like lambs to the slaughter. Lucifer has no honor."

Lucifer threw down his sword and charged Baldric. He lifted the young warrior off the ground and body-slammed him against the stone wall. Baldric ducked and weaved out of Lucifer's grasp. He punched Luc hard in the left kidney, making Lucifer's knees hit the ground. Baldric hit Lucifer with quick jabs, each finding a spot on Luc's body. Baldric pinned Luc to the field. The crowd of male angels let out a roar of applause and whistles.

A smile curved the corners of Baldric's lips. "The next time you take a maid be sure to ask if she's promised first. It may save your ass getting whipped in front of the legion." He released Luc and dusted off his hands.

Luc jumped off the ground, grabbed Baldric by the arm, and flipped him around to face him. "I will lay with any female I choose, especially if she's promised to you. If you can't keep your woman, don't blame me. She's evidently looking for something you don't have." The male angels watched the scene unfold. The crowd began *to laugh at Baldric, and several angels made snide remarks. Baldric stormed away, and Lucifer raised his arms to the crowd. "Females love me, what can I say?"*

LUC BEGAN TO CHUCKLE. "OH, Baldric, it's finally time for a little payback. Hmmm, if memory serves, Sandra is quite beautiful and promiscuous, too. Oh, I'm going to have some fun."

Luc opened the door to the caverns under the estate. The mysterious underworld belonged to Luc, and he would enjoy introducing Sandra to its unique properties.

SANDY TOOK LEE UP ON her offer to spend the night. After Baldric's intensive fencing workout, her legs and arms felt like jelly. Unfortunately, sleep didn't last long, and a few hours later, Sandy delved into Luc's Testament along with her master copy of the Ditch Lane Diaries. Her journal documented dates and times of crimes related to business takeovers and suspected corruptions in local government leading to the disappearance of Councilman Stevens. Sandy also discovered Cole's partners were listed within Luc's Testament.

A dated entry into Luc's Testament on November 10, 1929, was about Cole. Notes in the side column stated Mr. Steele had shot his spouse and placed the gun to his head when Luc arrived on the scene. Sandy put her hand on the page and closed her eyes to see what transpired between the two.

Luc appeared before Cole. At first, Cole thought the angel was a hallucination brought on by a state of shock, but then Luc said, "You have no need to put a bullet in your brain. You were rich, and no doubt your wife has seen better days. What if I said you could be truly wealthy beyond your wildest dreams? Would you shoot yourself or would you come and work for me?"

Cole laid the gun on the nightstand next to his bed where his wife's body oozed the last of her life force onto the mattress. Without giving it a second thought, Cole said, "How rich are we talking?"

Luc laughed and slapped Cole on the back. "Filthy, stinking rich. It comes with a price. Are you interested?"

Over the last twelve days, Cole had watched billions of dollars disappear in the stock market crash. Cole made the decision to kill Maggie first and then himself because his creditors weren't friendly people. Death seemed the preferable answer to torture. He couldn't bear what the sharks would do to Maggie. Rape and prostitution were on the top of their list. So he shot her in the head without warning as she slept.

Cole glanced over his shoulder at his dead blond bombshell with great gams. Maggie had come on to him nearly five years ago because he lived in a Manhattan penthouse suite overlooking the Hudson and had money to burn. Maggie hadn't loved him, but when she made love to him, she'd been worth every penny. Cole asked, "What's the price, Big Cheese?"

Luc walked over and peered out the window. His wings spanned the width of the room as he turned back around. He held a thick brown leather book in his hands. Luc said, "I require your soul. You'll remain immortal and serve me personally while I train you. In a few decades, after I deem you can handle the dough, I'll set you up. I'm looking for a human soldier to run my Southeast Division in Nashville. You will agree to do anything and everything I ask with no arguments. Agreed?"

Cole placed his hands on his thighs. He looked up into Luc's eyes and raised a brow. "Who are you again?"

"Atta boy, ask those questions now while you still have the chance. I'm Lucifer. Earth is my domain. The way I see it, I have your soul either way. You've committed a mortal sin, and you were at the point of eating a bullet. I can use your body, and you will enjoy the fruits of my labor. Do we have a deal?"

Cole nodded and said, "Well, when you put it that way, cash or check?"

Luc laid the mysterious book with a quill and inkwell on Cole's nightstand. He punctured Cole's forefinger and squeezed Cole's blood into the inkwell. "Sign and date, please. I'll fill in the particulars."

Sandy released the book and shook her head.

There was a soft knock, and the door opened. Lee stuck her head inside. "I saw the light when I got up to pee. Okay for me to come in?"

Sandy leaned against the headboard and waved Lee inside. "I'm getting into some deep shit." She quickly relayed her vision to Lee. "Cole's associates have signed the book. The downtown area is a coverup for a larger conspiracy. Luc's using the area as one of his home bases, and Cole's using it to line his pockets. Several judges, a couple of legislators, and the chief are working with Cole to keep Luc's cover. That's just the tip of the iceberg."

Sandy crossed her legs and said, "I have enough information from my journal to tie Nick's murder and the disappearance of Councilman Stevens to Cole. I'm going to drop off what I have to the D.A. to investigate further. I'll use Luc's Testament as one of my sources using my reporter's privilege to keep it confidential. The story should air tonight."

"I understand your need to air the story. I even agree with it, but you'll be placing a price on your head. You know what I'm saying?" Lee squeezed Sandy's hand.

"Airing the story is my best protection."

SANDY WALKED INTO STEELE ENTERPRISES to request an official comment before her story aired tonight. Hammer met her at the elevator door. Her ankle turned, and she reached out and grabbed Chip's forearm to prevent her falling headfirst into the door. Another astounding revelation swept through her mind with detailed moving images.

Hammer slung the body of Councilman Stevens onto the back of the boat. He wrapped Stevens in burlap purchased from a local feed mill store and secured Stevens with a rope. Cement blocks dropped off the sides of the Bayliner bumper rails just below the surface of the water. Walt had obtained the bags earlier in the day.

The engine silently purred as Hammer backed out of the slip and drove past the dock restaurant before slamming the boat full throttle past the no wake zone. The crescent moon and cloudy skies gave him the perfect cover. He drove down the channel until he reached the deepest part of the lake.

Hammer placed the boat in neutral and threw out the anchor. He lifted the body and tossed it over into the water. The body bobbed back and forth in the waves until he secured the cement blocks to the body and then he released the blocks into the lake. In a matter of minutes, the councilman disappeared into the murky black water.

Hammer turned his ball cap around backward and jumped behind the wheel. He drove the boat to a different dock several miles downriver. Hammer pulled into a vacant slip, turned off the ignition, and secured the boat. He hopped out onto the boardwalk and strolled to the waiting black BMW at the top of the hill.

Hammer's eyes widened as he pried Sandy's fingers off his forearm. "Let go of me, you crazy bitch."

Sandy released his arm and stepped away from him. She'd add her latest vision of Councilman Stevens' demise to a growing crime list from Cole Steele's goons.

Minutes later, Sandy stood in front of Steele Enterprises while Eddie, her camera operator, videotaped her story. "Federal and state investigators issued search warrants today for Steele Enterprises and Cole Steele's home in Arrington on the disappearance of Councilman Stevens and the murder of Nick London.

"Both Stevens and London had documentation listing times and dates of meetings with Mr. Steele, and shortly after, Mr. London was found shot in the chest on Music Row while an ongoing investigation continues into the disappearance of Councilman Stevens.

"District Attorney Matthew Dillard has requested additional help from the TBI to investigate General Court Sessions Judge Rogers, Chief Dyer, and business associates Chip Hammond, Carson Jones, and Walt Reese. Records indicate the named individuals are listed as partners in the newly formed Steele Construction. The company's recent acquisitions of the downtown properties are the site for the proposed Steele Hotel.

"Please keep in mind, the federal investigators become involved only when public corruption is suspected. Everyone noted in this story is presumed innocent until proven guilty. I'm Sandra Cothran, Channel 3 News." Sandy dropped the mic and asked Eddie, "How was that?"

Eddie turned off the light and smiled. "Looks like another AP for

Ms. Cothran. Let's book it back to the station and get this baby live for the evening news."

"I like the way you think, Ace."

ON ANY GIVEN DAY, THE chaos of a newsroom would drive a sane person mad. There was a constant battle against time to shoot, edit, and get approval for a story to go on air. Sandy and Eddie worked feverishly to edit her piece in the control room before handing it over to the news director, Art Hayes.

Sandy watched the ten o'clock news from inside the control room with Eddie as News 3 weather girl Dawn Frost wrapped today's forecast. Camera A switched to the anchor, Adam Wesley. "Bringing you a breaking investigation, here's Sandy Cothran."

Sandy held her breath as her story aired, and when it was over, she didn't feel relief. Baldric materialized beside her as she walked downstairs to her cubicle. "The story was excellent. Why the sad face?"

She tilted her head and answered, "I have a target on my back. They'll come after me."

"And we'll kick their asses. Let's celebrate. You've worked months on this story. Whatever happens with Cole and his thugs, it's with the authorities. You did your best, and that's all anyone can do." Baldric was like the sun in the middle of a rain storm.

Sandy lifted the corners of her lips. "I'm glad you think so. I have a few loose ends to tie up, and we'll stop by the store for champagne. I know how you love the bubbles."

Baldric's face lit up like a Christmas tree. "Aw, you remembered." His smile widened, and he got little crinkles around his dreamy eyes. Sandy could get lost in Baldric's eyes forever.

The truth hit her square in the chest. She was falling in love with Baldric, and she didn't want to fall in love with anyone. It wasn't just the physical attraction, which was freaking hot. She enjoyed his company. Baldric made her laugh. He made her feel loved, and he made her feel safe.

Before Sandy searched her feelings any further, Art rounded the corner. "You did it, kid. You knocked 'em dead tonight. The guys upstairs say our ratings are shooting through the roof. Can you work late? I need you to help me man the calls. Good." Before she could reply, Art strode rapidly in the other direction. What was another couple of hours?

Baldric made himself comfortable on the top of her credenza. "I'm starving. You think the station will call out for sandwiches?"

"I believe they have food in the break room. Just pop in and get one. It's not like anyone is going to see you." She chuckled.

"Yeah, that's what I thought, too. I'll be right back" Poof, Baldric vanished. Her guardian could eat more than anyone she knew.

Sandy glanced at her Rolex watch. Man, time flew by as she talked with callers over the last couple of hours. She was the last to leave the station again, except for the night watchman, Buddy. Sandy pushed the chair away from her desk in her gray and maroon cubicle. Sandy was ready for a bottle of Dom and a hot bath. Art had rewarded her with a few days off, and she didn't have to report back to work until the middle of next week.

The telephone rang. *Don't answer, don't freaking answer, oh, for crying out loud.* Sandy grabbed the receiver and said, "Channel 3 News, this is Sandy Cothran."

Breathing, heavy breathing. *Good lord, not another one of those calls.* Right as she began to hang up, the man said, "You're dead, bitch." Dial tone.

Well, if that wasn't the icing on the frigging cake. There was something familiar in the voice that made the hair on her arms rise. *Shit, shit, shit, Cole Steele.* He meant to kill her. "Baldric, are you here?"

An invisible hand caressed her cheek, and he whispered in her ear. "Always, Daireann."

Sandy exhaled a deep breath. Baldric would keep her safe.

OVER THE LAST DECADE, SANDY'S clairvoyance had increased to the point she was afraid to shake hands with people. She stopped by the twenty-four-hour grocery for a few items before heading home from work, the internal thoughts of others crowding her mind. The man in the bread aisle: *I left the coffee pot on, I know I left the coffee pot on.*

The woman in produce: *How am I going to tell my family I have a brain tumor? Oh God, I'm going to die, I don't want to die.* The teenage boy barely brushed Sandy's arm when she saw flashes of him having sex with a much older woman: *Man, my mom's friend is really hot, wonder if she'll let me do it to her again.* As if Sandy were reaching inside their souls and what she found sometimes offered her mind-boggling revelations.

Sandy shook the thoughts from her mind as she walked into the liquor store next to the grocery. She splurged on a bottle of Dom Pérignon. Back in the car, she heard Baldric chuckle.

Baldric's eyes were bright with excitement. "Oh, I love the bubbly stuff. It makes my nose tingle." Sandy shook her head. Baldric was a bad-ass warrior, but he also had a tender side. It was just another reason why she loved him. She sighed.

Sandy pulled onto Lafayette Street and drove to her condo on Second Avenue. "I kinda like the bubbles, too. I'm going to draw a hot bath, light some candles, and get drunk." She glanced over and teased him. "Wanna join me?" Part of her wished he would.

Baldric chuckled again and said, "You're completely oversexed, woman."

Sandy laughed and turned into her parking garage. "I did grow up in the '70s. Sex, drugs, and rock 'n' roll, babe. If it makes you feel any better, there's been very few moments of real happiness during my sexual escapades. Now, with you, that could be an entirely different story."

Baldric rolled his eyes, reached over, and placed his hand on her thigh. "Little girl, whatever this thing is that's happening between us—it's just not possible."

Sandy pulled into her parking space and turned off the ignition. She leaned against the steering wheel and turned to face him. "Nothing's impossible, and that's from years of watching Lesley Anne Warren play Cinderella." She grabbed her groceries and the booze and left him sitting in the car.

Sandy swiftly walked along Second Avenue as snowflakes swirled in the air and the gusty wind chilled her to the bone. People were singing and laughing in the streets. Wednesday nights were always jumping on Second and Broadway. Music blared from several bars, and a group of college girls or wannabe Madonnas passed her.

Sandy shook her head. She missed the carefree days of college. Life seemed simple then. Sandy would be twenty-nine on March fifth. God, she hated getting old but despised the alternative.

After Sandy's attack in December, the condo's super installed a security system. She punched in her passcode. Baldric appeared as the doors opened, and he made her safer than any security system. Sandy glanced around the foyer. The place was empty except for the large angel. Scoping the place out, Baldric readied himself for battle with the enormous sword in his right hand. The blade could be either a laser of light or blade of steel with a simple flick of his wrist.

The elevator opened and the couple who lived on the second floor stepped out. Sandy never remembered their names, but they knew her name, thanks to the power of television.

The woman always acted like they were friends or something. With chirpiness, the woman said, "Oh, hi, Sandy, are you going out tonight?"

Sandy shook her bottle of Dom in front of the couple. "Nah, I'm partying at home. Y'all have fun."

The man smiled and winked. "You're more than welcome to join us. The more, the merrier."

Sandy glanced at the woman, who smiled and shook her head like one of those bobblehead dolls. The man's visions flashed across Sandy's mind, and she saw herself with his wife in a threesome. Sandy inwardly cringed and wanted to punch her neighbor's lights out, the pervert. Instead, Sandy politely said, "Thank you for the invitation, but I'm going to party with the cast of *Dynasty* tonight." She recorded her favorite TV shows on her VCR because she rarely made it home to watch them during their regular time period. Sandy pressed the third-floor button and the elevator doors shut.

Baldric burst out laughing. "The man can't help himself. I assure you he's harmless. I read his soul. He's confused about his life, and you're his unattainable dream."

"You bet your sweet ass, honey. But you're not the only one who read his mind. Gross. Here, help me with these grocery bags. My arms feel like they're going to break in two." Baldric's sword mysteriously vanished as he grabbed the bags.

Inside her condo, Sandy threw her purse on the table next to the door and unzipped her boots, pulled them off, and wiggled her toes.

She sighed in relief. Sandy loved her cosmopolitan condo. All white and black décor with a splash of red in her local art collection and a few decorative pillows. Sandy had recessed and track lighting with dimmers installed and reached over to turn on the lights. She went into the kitchen and began to put away the groceries in the fridge and pantry.

Sandy went into the den after she had stored the groceries. She fired up Whitney Houston on her state of the art sound system and hit the dimmer switch on low. She watched as Baldric opened her best friend for the night with a loud *pop!* Sandy quickly grabbed the Dom from Baldric's hand and drank the bubbles rushing from the bottle.

Baldric reached up to the top kitchen cabinet for a couple of crystal flutes. He took the bottle from Sandy and poured champagne into their glasses. He took a long drink before placing the champagne bottle in the stainless steel ice bucket.

Sandy went through her spacious warehouse condo lighting vanilla and jasmine scented candles then made her way into the bedroom. She placed her glass on top of the black armoire before taking off her clothes. Opening the double doors, Sandy glanced at her nude reflection in the mirror. She yelled, "I'm going to jump in the tub. If you get bored, you can come in. I promise to behave. Or watch TV. I won't be long."

Baldric's brows rose as he looked at her over the rim of his glass. "I think I better wait out here. I'm going to play the VCR and check out MacGyver."

"Suit yourself."

Soaking in the tub soothed Sandy's aching muscles and released the tension in her shoulders. The last couple of days had drained her physically, mentally, and emotionally. The murder, Luc's Testament, Cole's threat, and the realization she was falling in love with a being from an entirely different realm made her drain her glass. She shouted, "Baldric, hey Baldric, my glass is empty. Can you hear me?"

Baldric walked into the bathroom looking too fine. He had to be at least six foot six, and Sandy estimated his weight at two hundred and fifty pounds of pure muscle, or what she thought was muscle. He was solid nonetheless. Baldric had long wavy blond hair cascading over his shoulders like spun silk, and she stared into the depths of his iridescent eyes.

Baldric topped off her glass with champagne. His eyes seemed to smolder, and she noticed his nostrils flare. His decadent scent of cocoa and vanilla filled the air. Sandy took a sip and said, "You're doing the sparkling thingy again. What is that?"

Baldric sat on the edge of the tub and trailed his fingers along the top of the bubbles. "Angels release varying types of energies under certain circumstances. I can't control it. It's like a wolf who marks his territory."

Sandy's stomach flipped. She took another sip, stared into his eyes and her gaze dropped to his full sensual lips. He wet them with the tip of his tongue. Sandy submerged her head under the water and came up seconds later and spewed water onto his face. She laughed and said, "You're flirting with me."

Baldric splashed water toward her. "I am not." He chuckled.

"Oh, you are totally flirting with me. Unless you want to follow through with it, I suggest you move on into the den, Big B." He pushed her head under the water before leaving the room. Sandy came up coughing. "Paybacks are a bitch."

Sandy slipped into a pair of midnight black silk pajamas and went into the den. She jumped into Baldric's lap. "*Dynasty* time. I love their clothes. Who do you like better? Krystle or Alexis?"

Baldric draped his arm around her shoulders. "Total Alexis fan. She's as feisty as you are."

"Good answer."

Baldric reached to the side table, grabbed his champagne, and raised his glass. "To the most beautiful girl in the world, my Daireann." Sandy reached over and picked up her glass and touched his. As she took a sip, their eyes locked in an embrace. Damn, Baldric was pretty. She chuckled and thought, *Yeah, pretty damn hot!*

Sandy ran her fingers through his silky hair and stared at his face, his hair, and his skin. Baldric's image could've been painted on the Sistine Chapel ceiling. She hugged him tightly and buried her face in his neck. "Don't give me compliments because it's not like you're going to kiss me or anything remotely in that fashion. I have a confession to make. I have to tell you on the off chance I get hit by a bus or something. At least you'll know if I can't find you on the other side."

Baldric brushed her cheek gently with his fingers. "Why are you crying? Oh, Daireann, please tell me what I've done wrong."

"You know me better than any of my friends. You know my secrets about Mr. Ben. You know me, not who I pretend to be. I'm falling in love with you. I didn't think I would ever fall in love with anyone. But I love you." Sandy had never said those words to anyone and held her breath for his response.

Baldric wrapped his big arms around her. "I've made so many mistakes, and I've broken many rules when it comes to you. I've existed for over two millennia, and I've had my share of relationships, but you're different." He placed his hand over his heart. "My feelings for you endanger both of us, especially you. I'm not objective anymore. Luc and his demon angels will use it against us if given the chance. I don't mean to cause you additional pain or confusion. I can't, I won't jeopardize your safety any further."

Sandy pushed him away from her and walked to the window. Her view of the Cumberland River was spectacular. She tried to focus on the boats, but the little girl in her cried. He didn't want her as she wanted him. She wanted to shout at him but wouldn't humiliate herself again.

Baldric walked up behind her and placed his hands on her shoulders. He leaned down close to her face, the warmth of his breath kissing her cheek, and the heat of desire rushed between her legs. Her head fell against his solid chest, and she closed her eyes. Neither of them spoke as her heart shattered.

Sandy turned and looked up into his eyes. "It's okay. Don't sweat it. I'm exhausted, and I'm going to bed. Goodnight." She left him standing next to the window. She couldn't bear to look back at him again.

BALDRIC WATCHED AS SANDY LEFT the room. He'd broken her heart. The worst part of the whole situation—he loved her like no other. They were star-crossed. She was human and he, an angel. Their union would never be sanctioned. Their pairing would set up a precedent that Michael, Gabriel or The Creator didn't want because humans and angels weren't allowed to mate.

It was times like these that Baldric wondered about destiny. Why had he been assigned to her? If The Creator was all knowing, why would He do this to them? He knelt on the floor and looked out at the moon and the stars. He spoke to The Creator. "Forgive me, Lord, I am weak. I'm not worthy to be her protector. Would you ever consider her as my mate, my pairing partner? I could place a million years between Daireann and me and never get over her. You've ruined me. I'm not able to protect her without putting us both in jeopardy. My unyielding love for her has made me weak."

Baldric waited for a bolt of lightning to strike him for the words he'd prayed to the Almighty. He waited for a sign as he looked out over the lake, and a gentle rain began to pour over the dark, inky water. The Creator heard him and the sky wept.

Chapter 5

Addicted To Love

SANDY TOSSED AND TURNED MOST of the night. She thought of all the males who had desired her and confessed their love for her. Three of those men had loved her. Rusty, her high school sweetheart, Brent her college beau, and last summer, Anna's colleague, Frank. But she didn't love them and had never cried over a man in her life.

But then again, Baldric wasn't a man, was he? Sandy rolled over onto her stomach. Her clock radio on her nightstand gleamed 6:00 a.m. *Good grief.* She had the day off and couldn't sleep. She was mad at Baldric not because he'd turned her down, but because he'd been sending her mixed signals since December. She'd never misinterpreted come-on signs before. Sandy placed the pillow over her face and screamed.

Sitting up in the bed, Sandy could smell Baldric's heavenly scent. "Stop lurking in the shadows, and stop reading my mind. It's not fair. I feel foolish enough."

Baldric appeared at the corner of her bed. "I'm sorry. It was never my intention to hurt you. I can't stand that you're still crying."

Sandy jumped out of bed and punched him in the arm. "If you tell anyone I cried over you—I swear I'll never speak to you again. The last thing I want is pity from the other guardians, and we have another training session this evening." The telephone started ringing, and she snapped into it angrily, "Hello."

Art coughed in the phone and said, "Um, sorry, did I wake you?

Hey, Cole made bail and so did everyone else. I wanted to warn you. Well, um, in case, they come for you. It's front page news."

Pissed off, she replied, "Well, ain't that just jelly to my peanut butter? Thanks for the good news." Sandy narrowed her eyes at Baldric and turned her back to him.

Art stammered, "Did you get up on the wrong side of the bed?"

"Yeah. Sorry, I snapped. Hey, I'm heading to my parents' house for a couple of days. I'll talk to you when I get back." Sandy hung up before Art said good-bye. The phone rang again. "Geez, Art, I said I was sorry."

Sandy's mom, Sally, cut her off, her voice broken up with sobs. "Sandy, your dad's been in an accident. Please come to Everglade Hospital. Please hurry."

Sandy's chin began to tremble. "What? Dad? What happened, Mom?"

"Honey, I don't know. The police came to the house and said he'd been in an accident. I'm in the waiting room now," Sally replied between sniffles.

"I'm on my way. I'll be there in forty minutes." Sandy hung up, ran to the bathroom, washed her face quickly, and brushed her teeth. She pulled her hair up, twisting and securing it with a clip. She pulled on a pair of jeans and a button-down before slipping on her boots and coat.

The phone rang again, and Sandy grabbed it, thinking it was her mom. "Mom, I'm heading out the door."

"How does it feel to lose something?" Cole asked.

Sandy froze. "What are you referring to?"

With a sharp edge to his voice, Cole said, "Oh, I think you know what I'm referring to. You take from me. I take from you." He hung up.

Sandy stood stock-still and listened to the dial tone before Baldric took the receiver from her hand.

Sandy had blinked a couple of times before she glanced up into Baldric's eyes. "Cole's responsible for Dad's accident."

Baldric held her hand and squeezed. "You need to go to the hospital. We'll deal with Cole later."

Sandy pulled out of the garage in less than five minutes. Barring any traffic on the interstate, she should make Everglade Hospital in thirty-five minutes. Sandy thought Cole would come for her, but the rotten sick bastard went for her dad. "Baldric, go to the hospital. Please be with my dad. I'll be there soon." Baldric nodded and vanished.

Driving like a bat out of hell, Sandy pulled into the parking lot of Everglade Hospital. She replayed her conversation with Cole at least a thousand times. She had tightness in her chest that was making it difficult to breathe. If her daddy died, it would be her fault. A mental image of her nine-year-old self pointed an accusing finger. Once again, Sandy's actions had threatened to unravel her family.

Sandy bit her bottom lip and drew blood. The metallic coppery taste in her mouth made her open the car door and spit before she turned off the ignition. The police needed notifying about Cole's phone call. Too bad she didn't think fast enough to press play on her answering machine to record his call. However, Cole had people on his payroll with the police.

On second thought, Sandy would let the local sheriff's department check her dad's car. She'd trust her life to Sheriff Roy Robinson of Everglade. He would know what to do if any tampering had taken place with the vehicle. People in a small town took care of each other. It was a huge perk of living in a small town.

God, she wanted to kill Cole. *You take from me. I take from you.* Sandy blew out a deep breath. At a dead run from the parking lot, she entered the ER automatic doors and looked left into the waiting room.

Sandy nearly burst into tear seeing her buds, Anna and Jerry, Ruby and Reed, along with Lee and Harry. She glanced at the back of the room and spotted George and Brent. They were all in the waiting room. Anna and Ruby ran to Sandy and wrapped their arms around her. Sandy said, "Where's Mom?"

Anna was in her scrubs. "I was on shift when he was brought in. Your mom's with the attending physician. Sandy, prepare yourself. He doesn't look good. We've brought in a neurosurgeon from Nashville to examine your dad to be on the safe side."

Sandy felt numb like this was some horrible dream. It didn't seem real. Brent caught her in his arms before she sank to the floor. He said, "I got you, sweet girl. Do you want to sit down?"

Sandy shook her head and said, "I want to see my daddy."

Brent looked at Anna, and she nodded. Anna said, "The nurse station is expecting Sandy. Y'all follow me."

Anna entered her passcode into the ER, and they walked through another set of automatic doors. The sterile hospital environment and the pungent antiseptic smell made Sandy reel with nausea.

Down the hall corridor, a few doors on the right, Anna stopped in front of a door and placed her hand on Sandy's shoulder. "Be the strong person I know you are. Your mom needs your strength. I'll be in the waiting room if you need me." Anna brushed her hand down Brent's arm. "Stay with her."

"Not leaving my girl. No way, no how," Brent replied.

Sandy heard Anna and Brent talking. She just didn't register what they were saying as she walked into her dad's room. Sandy wasn't prepared to see her father's severely swollen face, tubing running into every orifice, monitoring equipment. She overheard the hushed tones of a doctor speaking to her mom. It went over her head. Frightened and confused, Sandy stood in her dad's room, not twenty-eight but nine.

Her rock, Baldric, leaned against the concrete wall. He crossed his arms over his chest. Telepathically, he said, *I am with you, Daireann. Do not be afraid.* She rapidly blinked the tears and swiped her eyes with her forearm.

Brent stroked her back gently. "You okay, Sandy? Do you need a chair?"

She held onto Brent's arm for balance. The doctor speaking with her mom turned and said, "You must be Sandy. I'm Doctor Abnob. I was talking with your mother about your dad's condition. He's stable for the moment. He's unconscious, but no coma. He has several fractures, and we're monitoring the swelling on his brain. The good news is your father didn't suffer any internal damage. The next twenty-four hours is critical, but I'm optimistic. He's a healthy man, otherwise. I'll be back to check on him soon. Please let the nurses know if you need anything."

Yup, most of what the doctor said went right over her head, too. Her mom stepped over and wrapped her arms around Sandy. Sally seemed suddenly old and frail, fragile. With tears in her eyes, Sandy said, "Mom, what happened?"

Sally rubbed her daughter's arm and patted her hand, almost

absentmindedly. "Sheriff Robinson left a little while ago. Dad's brake lines were cut. Someone deliberately tried to hurt Daddy."

Sandy let out a wail of grief. She staggered back, and Brent held onto her. Tears ran down her cheeks, and Sandy said, "It's my fault, Mom. My story about Cole Steele did this. I have something belonging to Mr. Steele. He's going to pay for hurting Dad. I swear it."

Sally's eyes met Sandy's. "Darling, this isn't your fault. You're not responsible for the action of that man. You exposed the truth. You did the right thing. Mr. Steele is a horrible person. We need to call Sheriff Robinson, and he'll investigate Mr. Steele. Don't blame yourself for the wreck. I mean it, sweetie."

Sandy's gaze lifted to Baldric's, and he nodded. She could barely look at him after her declaration of love and his gentle rejection.

Brent held her hand and kissed her cheek. "I'm going to run and get you girls some coffee. It's going to be a long twenty-four hours."

Sandy wouldn't let go of Brent's hand. He looked down at their hands and then back at her. He said, "What is it, honey?"

"No, Brent. Stay with Mom." She turned and sent a telepathic message to Baldric. *Get the guardians here, now.*

Sandy ran out of the room, down the corridor, and out of the doors until she made it to the waiting room. Her friends sat at a white laminate table near the vending machines in the rear of the room. Sandy rushed to them and turned to Anna. "I need your powers, Anna. Please, you can heal Dad. I know you can." She turned to Ruby, Reed, and Jerry. "I need y'all to come with me to Dad's room. Our powers have to be good for something, right? Well, let's get the lead out and heal my daddy."

Anna stood, followed by Ruby, Reed, Jerry, and George. Anna said, "We need the guardians. Raphael can faze the staff and any onlookers. I haven't healed any major accidents in several months."

Jerry circled her waist with his arm and said, "Just like riding a bike, dumpling."

George frowned and said, "What the heck are y'all talking about? What guardians?"

Anna replied, "No time to explain, Georgie. You in or you out?"

George shrugged his shoulders with his palms upright. "I'm in."

Baldric called the guardians of Campbell Ridge. Raphael cast an ethereal veil called a faze over the hospital staff and visitors close to the ER area where everyone gathered. The faze made everything appear normal.

Inside Hugh's hospital room, Brent's mouth dropped open as he grabbed the back of his neck, looking at the angels in apparent disbelief. Sally blinked her eyes as she nervously wrung her hands.

Sandy draped her arm around her mother's shoulders. "Mom, we're going to heal Dad. Do you trust me?" Sally nodded with a slight head shake. Sandy squeezed her mother's shoulders with a hug. "Anna is a divine healer in addition to being Everglade's best family doctor."

Anna took control of the room. "I need the wards to grab hands and pray." Anna turned and addressed the angels, and she said, "Guardians, please concentrate your energies toward my fingertips. Ralph will assist me." The room began to hum with electricity. Anna had learned to control her healing power. She no longer knocked out the power grid or made wind tunnels during her healing sessions. However, not all injuries or illnesses could be healed by her touch.

Anna said, "Everyone pray as I lay hands on Mr. Cothran." Raphael, Anna's guardian, and master healer, started at Hugh's feet as Anna placed her hands on the top of Hugh's head. Anna and Ralph proceeded counter clockwise around Hugh's bed, tracing his body with their fingertips.

Sandy prayed. Time stood still.

OUTSIDE THE ER DOORS, THE sun burned brightly against an azure sky. Sandy closed her eyes and allowed the sun to warm her face. Anna and Raphael healed most of her father's injuries. The bruises remained, but he had opened his eyes. Her friends and guardians left Hugh's room shortly after with hugs and kisses, and Seneca, Ruby's guardian, cancelled the wards' training session until the weekend.

The hospital staff and visitors remained unaware of the medical miracle. Dr. Abnob sent Hugh for more tests, trying to determine if radiology had mixed up the reports. Hugh would stay in the hospital for another day or two in a regular room for mere observation. Sally requested a cot for Hugh's hospital room because she didn't want to leave his side.

Sandy offered a silent prayer. *Thank you. Thank you for the miracle.*

Brent walked over to Sandy from the exit door. He gently traced the curve of her face with his forefinger. "What happened in the ICU? Did I see angels?"

Sandy briefly told Brent about the cave, the mysterious stones, and how each ward possessed divine supernatural powers. Brent gazed into her eyes and said, "How in the world did I not see how amazing you are? Sandy, I miss you. I miss us."

Sandy held his hand. "Oh, Brent, I'm glad you were here for me today. I do miss you, truly I do, but my heart belongs to another."

Brent tensed and took a step away from her. He tilted his head, and with a raised voice, he said, "Where in the hell was he today? Why wasn't he here for you?"

At that moment, Baldric materialized beside Sandy. Brent's eyes went wide, and he shook his head. "Oh, you've got to be kidding. Sandy, him? Surely not him." Brent sized up Baldric.

Baldric spread his feet hip-width apart and golden sparkles like pixie dust released around Sandy. His wings released, his chest puffed out, and he let out a low growl.

Sandy gently touched Baldric's forearm. "Baldric, please be gentle. Don't hurt Brent. He didn't know. It's not his fault I'm in love with an angel."

Baldric immobilized Brent into a trance. "I'm not going to hurt you, Brent. You'll only remember good things about Sandy. You won't remember anything about the wards' powers or meeting the guardians today. You're going to fall in love and have three kids, but it's not, nor will it ever be, with Sandy. Are we cool, bro?" Brent nodded, and Baldric dematerialized, leaving Brent staring at Sandy, dumbfounded.

Brent glanced around the hospital property and scratched his cheek. He glanced up at the sky and then back at Sandy. "Um, glad your dad is okay, and it's been good to see you again. I'm going to leave now."

Sandy rushed to Brent and wrapped her arms around him. "Thank you for being such a wonderful friend. Take care of yourself." Brent turned around and walked slowly into the parking lot.

Sandy watched Brent get into the car and leave. She prayed that

Baldric's memory wipe wouldn't leave Brent with any long-term damage. Sandy noticed the angelic faze had worn off as she walked back into the hospital. People walked up and down the hospital corridors. Nothing seemed amiss. She stepped into the elevator and pushed the button for the second floor.

The time had come to talk to her father. Hugh nearly died today, and she didn't want to live in the past anymore. Sandy had blamed her dad for bringing Ben Salinger into her life. She'd blamed her parents for not protecting her as a child. The pain and suffering had clouded her mind from the real love her family shared together.

Hugh sat up in the hospital bed holding Sally's hand. Watching her parents, Sandy wondered why she had never noticed how much they loved each other before now.

With a little apprehension, he said, "Mom told me you wanted to talk?"

Sandy sat on the opposite side of the bed from her mother and gave her parents a little smile before pouring her soul out to them. For the first time, in nineteen years, Sandy expressed her grief, her pain, and her suffering from the child abuse she'd experienced.

Sandy purged the demons of pain and suffering from her soul. The light of love lit the room with a bastion of warmth. "I blamed myself. I blamed you. I was too young to understand what happened to me and too stubborn to talk about it later in life. So I acted out as a teenager. I apologize for what I must've put you through during my wild and wooly youth. I can't take back my actions, but I'll promise, from this day forward, to try to be a better person. I love you both so much. Will you forgive me?"

Tears filled Hugh's eyes as he opened his arms to Sandy. "Come here, baby girl. It was never your fault, and we love you, too." Hugh hugged her, and Sandy broke out in a sob. Wiping the tears from her eyes, he said, "I blamed myself. I should've protected you, honey. I felt like I failed you as a father. I'm sorry I was hard on you as a teenager, but fear for your safety made me crazy. You make your mother and me very proud. Not just your career accomplishments, but you're my beautiful daughter with a big, compassionate heart."

Sandy pressed her face into her daddy's neck. All the years of pain and bad memories had been washed away with love and forgiveness. She had finally let go of her past.

Chapter 6

All I Need Is a Miracle

HOURS TICKED BY BEFORE SANDY left the hospital. She had spent hours talking with her parents like she'd never done before. Sandy's spirit soared while she drove down Highway 99.

Everglade was a one-red-light town, but Sandy missed living here. She passed Anna's Clinic and the Pharmacy with its old fashioned soda shop. Turning onto Concord Road, she drove by Ruby's Everglade General Store. Several minutes later, Sandy found herself sitting in the St. Timothy's Church parking lot. She stared at the beautiful old church with its old gray stone and high steeple that still chimed the bells every hour.

Growing up, Sandy had gone with her parents to every service. Pastor Logan was getting older, but his sermons of love and forgiveness gave her peace. He would get so emotional during his sermons that he'd cry.

Sandy opened the car door and walked slowly up the sidewalk. The sun had melted nearly all the snow and ice. The afternoon was fading quickly into dusk as the sky turned dark orange and pink. The church doors had never been locked, to her knowledge. She reached for the knob and pushed the door open.

The stained glass windows of Jesus with the twelve disciples along with Mary and Joseph and other saints and angels cast a warm glow from the fading sun. The dark red velvet carpet was worn from years of foot traffic. Plush homemade cushions fit on the walnut pews, lovingly made by the women's Bible class. The light inside was dim; only a couple of track lights lit a beautifully carved cross with Jesus mounted on the wall behind the pulpit.

Sandy sat on the front pew with her hands in her lap. She hadn't been to church since Christmas. Her hands began to tremble as the events of the past few days caught up with her. In the quiet stillness of the church, Sandy found herself on her knees praying for her many blessings. She prayed for forgiveness for any wrong to others or herself. Sandy prayed for her family and her friends. She prayed for strength.

Last, she prayed for Baldric. "You know my thoughts before I think them. You know I'm in love with the angel you sent to protect me. I know it's against your rules, against the rules of heaven. It's not an ordinary love we share. I get that part. He won't go against your wishes, and it isn't right for me to ask him to. But I love him. I love Baldric. Why do I feel like he's the one you chose for me? If this is wrong, then please, please help me to overcome my feelings. I need your help."

Baldric appeared before her and knelt down on one knee. Sandy sucked in a deep breath, and she choked up with emotion. He took her right hand and said, "I have a confession to make. Last night, as you gave me your heart, I didn't offer mine in return. You're right. It's against the rules for us. It's against the rules for humans, too." He released her hand, turned, and pointed down the aisle. "You should want to walk down the aisle of this holy place with someone worthy of you. Marry in front of your family and friends. You deserve real love."

Baldric pushed his hair off his forehead and then rubbed his chin. "But I can't stay with you if you do. I can't watch you marry a man. I can't look at you while you raise a family with another when I want you for myself."

Sandy's hand flew over her mouth.

Baldric raised his eyes toward heaven and said, "Strike me down, Lord. Take me from her and give her someone worthy of protecting her because I can't deny my love for Daireann any longer." The look he gave her had the air backing up in her lungs. Her chest tightened, and her heart fluttered. "I love you, Daireann. You're my other half. You make me whole. I want to spend eternity with you as my paired partner, my best friend, my lover."

Sandy threw herself into Baldric's arms and kissed him. The union of their kiss bathed the sanctuary in light. When they broke apart, a celestial being hovered right above them. She wore all white, and the essence of her beauty made Sandy speechless.

The female spirit said, "Baldric, you've reached a decision marking you to Sandra Daireann through eternity. However, your pairing with the human female will require His sanction. You may have this night with your partner, but you must appear before Michael in the morning. He'll make arrangements for you to meet with The Creator. I pray you both find an outcome filled with love and happiness. Take Daireann's hand."

Baldric stood and bowed deeply before the spirit. "Blessed Spirit of Man, I'm forever in your debt. You heard my prayers." He reached for Sandy's hand, and she stood beside him.

The Spirit of Man opened her arms with a sweeping motion and turned to Sandy. "Before we begin this most sacred nuptiae, you must understand, Sandra Daireann Cothran, the ceremony in which you partake. Are you in agreeance?"

Sandy had never been shy or timid, but standing before the Spirit of Man she was awestruck. She nodded and whispered, "I agree."

The Spirit of Man repeated a litany of rules and regulations regarding the pairing of angels. Since Sandy was one hundred percent human, most of the jargon was foreign to her. Sandy raised her hand, and the female spirit smiled. Sandy said, "I'm afraid I don't understand the meaning of some of the words you're using. Would you mind explaining in human terms?"

The Spirit of Man said, "You and Baldric must agree to the laws and regulations outlined in a binding agreement of what humans refer to as marriage. There are no allowances for separation under any circumstances. There are no allowances for any infidelities. You and Baldric will be bonded by the laws of heaven past your death until eternity ceases to exist. Are you willing to bind yourself to Baldric?"

Sandy had some Latin classes in college when she'd entertained the idea of becoming an attorney. She turned to Baldric and grabbed both his hands and squeezed. "*Ubi tu Gaius, ego Gaia.*" Which meant, where you go, I will follow. Sandy turned and looked up at the spirit. "I bind myself to Baldric."

The Spirit of Man turned to Baldric, who at this point had a golden halo effect around his entire body. "Baldric, do you bind yourself to Sandra Daireann Cothran?"

Baldric kissed Sandy's knuckles and repeated her choice of words, "*Ubi tu Gaia, ego Gaius.*" Baldric turned to the Spirit of Man and exclaimed, "I bind myself to Sandra Daireann." Baldric whispered to Sandy, "Clasp my right hand." Sandy did as he requested, and the Spirit of Man wrapped a glowing, golden, braided cord over their wrists.

The Spirit of Man appeared in a physical form. She held Baldric's and Sandy's hands tightly. "You have my blessing, my children. Your love isn't ordinary and falls outside the boundary of conventional pairings or marriage in the traditional sense. I'm sure all three of us will be accountable for our actions today. It is my nature to fill the universe with love, and your love is evident in my eyes. Be well and prosperous." The Spirit of Man vanished in front of Sandy's eyes.

Sandy swallowed hard as she searched Baldric's smoldering eyes. "Are we married?"

Baldric's kiss was both passionate and gentle. The electric energy between them made the hair stand on her neck and arms. The tingling of his soft, full lips against hers made her weak in the knees, and he supported her with his strength. Sandy and Baldric were married. She didn't care that she wore blue jeans and not a white dress. All Sandy cared about was that the angel in her arms loved her enough to commit himself to her for eternity.

Baldric moved slightly away from her face. "Our union won't be like normal marriages. But you'll have my love and my devotion forever. Do you think we could make it official?" He chuckled.

"You betcha! And you know I've never been normal." Sandy laughed and said, "I'm staying at Mom and Dad's. Is that okay?"

"I have fond memories of you growing up in the house. Let's go to your old room." Baldric held her tight and kissed the top of her head.

Sandy reached up on tiptoe and kissed him again, then she said, "You mean, our old room."

They walked arm in arm as they exited St. Timothy's. Stars twinkled in the jet-black sky. Sandy could see her breath in the frigid air, but she was toasty warm in Baldric's arms. At her car, Baldric opened the door, and she slid behind the wheel. He said, "It's customary for the groom to light a fire for his bride before she enters the house of their consummation. I'll go ahead to your parents' house and start the fire in their hearth and search for a bottle of wine." He leaned down and kissed her softly on the lips. "You hold my heart." He disappeared.

Sandy played Baldric's words over again on the drive to her parents' home. The mention of consummation had her squirming in the car seat. She'd lost her virginity at seventeen, but tonight she felt like a maiden again. Baldric the Warrior married her before the Spirit of Man. She pushed away any negative consequences tomorrow might bring. He belonged to her, and she belonged to him.

Aunt Ellen had passed away several years ago and left the old farmhouse to Sally. The buttery lights from inside the house were inviting as Sandy pulled into the driveway. White smoke filtered slowly from the two chimney stacks on either side of the house. She loved the old place. It was home. The front porch light flipped on, and before she could open the car door, Baldric was there.

He lifted her out of the car with one swoop and Sandy giggled like a schoolgirl. They didn't need a flashlight because Baldric emitted his golden light at least three feet in front of their path. Baldric ducked his head under the doorframe as he carried Sandy over the threshold.

True to his word, Baldric had both hearths blazing with fire. He was breathing hard, and Sandy noticed his hands shook as he sat her on the couch. The silence was too loud. She said, "We don't have to be nervous with each other. Is that glass of wine for me?"

Baldric reached for the glass and nearly toppled it over before handing it to her. "I don't know why I'm so nervous. I guess because this seems like a dream and any minute Seneca or Ralph is going to hit me on top of the head with a club."

Sandy took a sip of her wine and then set it on the coffee table next to a bowl of red apples in the center and her dad's *TV Guide* tossed to the side.

In a quiet voice, he said, "My love for you could place you in harm's way."

Sandy reached over and brought his hand to her lips and pressed a kiss. "I don't want you to think about protecting me. I want you to love me. Throw caution to the wind and give yourself to me. I want you to make love to your wife."

Baldric fell to his knees and wrapped his arms around her waist. He looked up into her eyes and said, "It is as you wish, my love. I am yours."

Sandy twisted her fingers in his thick blond hair and joined him on the floor. She kissed him, tenderly at first, before she savagely consumed him with kisses.

Baldric pulled away slightly, searched her eyes, and held her hands. The room filled with his decadent scent of cocoa. Golden sparkles like tiny stars released from his body into the air and onto her skin. Sandy began to glow with the warmth of Baldric's love. He said, "I want to make love to you, my Daireann, my wife. It sounds strange to my lips to call you my wife, but I'll get used to it."

Baldric lifted her in his arms, took the stairs two at a time, and strode to her bedroom. He kicked the door open with his boot, and it ripped off the hinges. He threw Sandy on the bed and stared down at her. Throwing his head back, Baldric opened his mouth and roared while he ripped the armor from his chest until he stood before her, magnificent and naked. The hardwood floors shook under his feet.

Baldric jumped on the bed, and the slats fell out from the mattress, throwing them to the floor. They both laughed. Then he looked at her with raw hunger in his eyes, and she wet her lips. His golden skin gleamed and shimmered as he tore the buttons from her shirt and exposed her breasts. He pulled her blue jeans off as he devoured her with his eyes.

Breathlessly, Baldric said, "I've dreamt of this moment." He lightly traced the outline of her lips with his tongue before he sucked and pulled on her bottom lip. Sandy began to bloom as his kiss lengthened. He trailed kisses along her throat, down to her breasts, and continued to her firm, flat abdominals. Baldric ran his fingers in between her legs over her soft folds of skin, and he growled. She trembled with desire from his touch.

Sandy couldn't quite believe this beautiful immortal being was making love to her. Real love, not lust. Sex she knew and understood. But even great sex was nothing like the feeling she experienced combining her soul with Baldric, the only one to whom she'd given her whole heart. The titillations of combining their arousal for one another wasn't about her or him. Making love to Baldric held the promise of all her hopes and dreams for a future she'd never allowed herself to dream about before. Sandy had no desire or impulse to run away, as she frequently felt halfway through copulation. No, on the contrary, Sandy wanted the feeling of her and Baldric, in this Oneness experience, to last forever.

BALDRIC CONSUMED SANDY'S BODY WITH the essence of his soul. The smell of her arousal drove all thoughts from his mind except for the incredible need to be inside of her warm, intoxicating body. He wanted to taste every inch of her. Sandy was his for all eternity, and he would never give her up.

Baldric devoured her with kisses, and she gave him what he needed. His hands roamed gently over her legs to the back of her knees until he held her foot in his hand. He kissed the arch of her foot and trailed his tongue along her toes, and Sandy moaned in pleasure, which drove him further to ecstasy.

Baldric kissed and trailed his tongue up along her beautiful body until he whispered in her ear, "I'm going to mark you, Daireann. Upon my entry into your womanhood, the marking process of our pairing will begin, and I won't be able to stop once the process starts. I've only heard stories about pairing couples. Some of the chemicals released and shared between us create a type of euphoria." He kissed her and cradled her face in his hands. "I tremble for you, my love."

With a throaty sigh, she said, "You're so much more than I ever imagined. Take me. I'm yours."

A burst of warm air filled the room. Energy started from the top of his head to the base of his spine as he entered Sandy, and she screamed his name. Baldric had held himself in check with regards to Sandy's sexuality for years. But she belonged to him now, and every man, every angel, and every demon angel in the universe would know Sandy belonged to him from this moment forward.

Baldric's essence marked Sandy physically through the contact of their skin, sexually through intercourse, and emotionally as their souls became one. Their pairing took him soaring to the highest mountain peak, and the beauty of their union was beyond any sex he'd ever experienced. It wasn't just the sex that was otherworldly; it was the combining of their spirits, making him whole for the first time in his existence, and the transcendental discovery of finally finding out what he knew he'd been missing in his life.

There was a magical and emotional intertwining, as well as the physical, combining his DNA into hers to seal their pairing links. The continual hum of the electrical current ringing in his ears nearly made him deaf. The light of their love had been intense, temporarily blinding him before the pairing was complete. Making love to Sandy was the most incredible and intimate experience of his life.

Later, Baldric watched the steady rise and fall of Sandy's chest as she slept in his arms. He stroked her soft, peachy cheek and ran his fingers through her silky hair. He loved her more than his life and would gladly suffer the consequences in the morning. Tonight with her had been worth an eternity of consequences. He'd have to answer to The Creator for pairing with his assigned ward. Baldric prayed He would understand and sanctify their union. At least they had the support from the Spirit of Man on their side.

Sandy snuggled further into his arms, pressed her lips against his neck, and muttered, "Make love to me again, husband. Make me glow with your love again, warrior." She arose and sat on top of him, and he arched his back and released a roar loud enough to reach the heavens. Tomorrow would come too soon.

Chapter 7

Broken Wings

THE SUNLIGHT OF MORNING BROKE through the Chantilly lace curtains. Sandy rolled over and opened her eyes. She hadn't dreamed it. Baldric smiled down at her and brushed his fingers down her spine. She lay in his arms naked. She quickly looked under the covers and smiled.

"Yeah, I'm naked, too," he chuckled.

Sandy propped her hands on his chest and kissed him. "So I didn't dream it. We're married."

Baldric kissed her lovingly while stroking her long hair down her back. "We're married or, well, paired. Either way, you're stuck with me. Any regrets?"

Sandy began trailing her fingers up and down his massive chest. "I thought I'd dreamed making love to you. But making love doesn't describe this kind of dreamland. You're spectacular. You're stupendous." Sandy threw the covers off the bed so she could inspect Baldric fully in the light of day, and he didn't need much encouragement.

"Keep the compliments coming, baby girl." He growled and rolled her onto her back and dove between her legs, and the fireworks went off again.

The little golden stars were like hits of adrenaline and pheromones rolled into one powerful formula of yum. She grabbed his head and pulled him up to her. "I could spend the rest of my days in bed with you. I love you so much, Baldric, and I'm not afraid to say it out loud. Isn't it grand? I'm not afraid to love you."

Baldric entered her and slowly began to rock back and forth into a steady rhythm. "I'm so glad you're not afraid anymore. You and I are meant to be together. I love you, and you make me feel as though I could move Mount Everest with my bare hands."

Sandy and Baldric made love while they continued talking to each other. Sandy never talked during sex. Now she couldn't stop. "I want to have your babies." He froze.

She frowned and said, "Is that wrong? Or is it impossible?"

Baldric took a deep breath and sighed, then moved away from Sandy. He stood and began to put on his warrior gear. She sat up and said, "Please don't stop talking to me. What did I say wrong? I take it back. We don't need kids. I just need you." She crawled out of bed and draped her arms around his neck.

Baldric pulled her arms away and sat on the edge of the bed. "I love you, and I'm going to fight for our sanction. I have to face the Commander in Chief this morning, and then I'll have to meet with The Creator Himself. Our pairing will be brought up to the council of nine, and we'll no doubt be the main buzz in heaven. Angels and humans consummated in antiquity. A superhuman species developed out of the union and The Creator wiped them out in the great flood."

Sandy wrapped the blanket around her and tucked it into her armpit. "I'm on birth control. I don't want to make it harder on you."

Baldric turned and pulled Sandy into his lap. His forehead touched hers. "You may be with child. Your birth control doesn't work on angels. I should've been more careful. I had no idea how powerful the pairing chemicals were between us until they were released. I couldn't stop. I couldn't help marking you and making you mine."

Sandy kissed his neck, reached up, and tugged on his sweet, full lips. "Well, let's just cross that bridge when we get to it. I'm chosen. I'm not a regular human and the Spirit of Man married us. She's on our side."

Baldric brushed the hair away from her shoulders. "I love you no matter what happens today. I love you. No one can take that from us."

Sandy's voice quivered. "You're scaring me. Do you think they'll separate us?"

"We're paired for eternity. I'll find a way to you if they take my guardianship. I've served the AAF faithfully for two thousand years; surely my service and loyalty will mean something. You must have faith and be strong while I'm away. Michael or Gabriel will send messengers to watch over you until I get an answer. The warrior angels will watch over you. Don't give up on me."

Sandy wrapped her arms around him. She put on a brave face for him because he wanted her strong. "I'll never give up on us. I'll wait for you. Just keep in mind, I'm human and humans die every day. If something happens to me, you must promise to find me in the Everafter."

"You're not dying anytime soon. You have a part of me from last night. The tiny sparkles, they're a part of my DNA, and now they're a part of yours. I could find you if worlds and years separate us, Daireann. Michael has summoned me. I have to go." Baldric kissed and hugged her, and then he was gone.

CAIOJEZEAL WATCHED FROM THE BEDROOM window the tearful exchange between Sandy and Baldric. He knew the warrior was attached to the female, but to pair with her for eternity? What a dumbass. She was beautiful, no doubt. But the earth had millions of beautiful women. Why be tied to one when there were so many to sample?

It was no skin off his ass. Caiojezeal had a job to do and ported to Lucifer's estate in Arrington. Luc's property stretched miles in the underground caverns. Caiojezeal found Luc lounging with his latest ingénue near the warm pools of Idema. Lucifer never mated with humans. He only slept with purebred angels or descendants of purebreds out of heaven.

Caiojezeal bowed on one knee. "Sire, Baldric has paired with his human ward. He's been summoned by Michael."

Luc jumped up from the blue suede chaise and knocked the female demon to the ground. "You're joking. Caiojezeal, you better not be shitting me, or you can say goodbye to earth and hello darkness."

Caiojezeal stayed on bended knee. "Sire, you asked me to report to you when Baldric left the human. I watched the Spirit of Man pair the two in a human church. He mated the female last night, and the AAF summoned Baldric this morning."

Luc clapped his hands and Taste of Honey's "Boogie Oogie Oogie" bounced off the cave walls. A disco mirror ball and strobe lights materialized out of thin air. Luc danced and sang. He pulled the demon female from behind the couch and twirled her around. "This is the best news I've had since the Spanish Flu outbreak. Get Cole and the others upstairs. I have to get my groove on, and I'll join you later. You're dismissed." Luc grabbed the female and ripped off her clothes. Caiojezeal dematerialized upstairs.

LUC STROLLED UP THE STAIRS after bathing in the pools with the sweet little ass of Sazae. He wore his black leather pants and white silk shirt. Sometimes it was just good to be him. Luc burst through the double doors to the great room. Several chief demons, including Caiojezeal along with Cole and his people, were laughing about Councilman Stevens' disappearance. He was fish bait at the bottom of Percy Priest Lake.

Luc pointed to Cole and said, "Get Sandy Cothran and get my book. If you fuck this up, Cole, I swear you'll face an eternity of hell. You catch my drift, homeboy?"

Reclining in the leather chair next to the fireplace, Cole wore a black wool blazer, a tan turtleneck, and a pair of jeans with black cowboy boots. "Ms. Cothran called my office and requested a meeting today. I'd say that's fate, wouldn't you? I was just waiting to tell you before we take off downtown. Oh, and dig this, she's bringing the book. Can you believe it? Do you still want her or just the book?"

Luc paced back and forth across the room. He wondered if the AAF was setting a trap. It would be just like them to use the human female to get to him. Baldric wouldn't have contact with earth until his meeting with The Creator was over. Time was of the essence. "Caiojezeal, take a team of seasoned warrior demon angels and go with Cole to get my book. Make sure it isn't a trap. I want my book back first and foremost, and just for shits and giggles bring me the girl. Baldric's going to get a little payback."

Cole shoved his hands into his pockets. "So, if I get your book back, can I have the girl? She's cost me a ton of money, and I still may go to jail. I think she deserves a little payback, too."

Lucifer flew in front of Cole and smacked him hard across the face. "The theft took place because of your stupidity. Ms. Cothran is mine."

Cole rubbed his jaw and said, "Yeah, whatever, man. Let's go, guys. Time's a wasting."

COLE WALKED OUT OF THE living area through the kitchen and into the garage. He'd overheard Caiojezeal talking to one of the demon angel guards stationed at the front door. Sandy was still at her parents' house. It was time to pay his nemesis a visit.

Arrington Estate was centrally located between Nashville and Everglade. Cole grabbed the keys for the black Suburban with tinted windows. Hammer jumped in the front seat while Carson and Walt got in the back. Cole sat behind the wheel and cranked the engine, pressed the remote button, and the garage door opened. He backed out and drove down the driveway. Turning onto Cox Road, Cole said, "Change of plans. Ms. Cothran didn't call me. We're heading to Everglade."

Hammer leaned his forearm on the console and said, "You do have balls of steel." He laughed loudly, and the boys joined in at the play on Cole's name.

Caiojezeal materialized between Carson and Walt, nearly making Cole run off the road. Caiojezeal said, "You're heading in the wrong direction. Are you deliberately trying to provoke Luc?"

Cole glanced at Caiojezeal through the rearview mirror. "I believe your orders were to go with me to get the girl and the book, and that's what we're doing. Like you told your buddy at the door, Sandy's in Everglade at her parents' house, alone. I need you and your team to go ahead and intercept the messengers and warriors the AAF will send to watch Ms. Cothran while Baldric is away. Give me fifteen minutes. I'm taking the back roads. Then let me do my job. I'll get the book and the girl."

CAIOJEZEAL AND HIS TEAM PORTED to the outlying property lines of Sandy's parents. After calculating there were five AAF warriors present, three on the exterior and two on the interior of the house, he said, "Take the two on the roof first, then the one at the front door. Be careful, in case my projections are wrong. Let's do this as quietly and stealthily as possible. After capturing the warriors, we'll meet in the barn to secure them."

He turned to his team and said, "I want the AAF to know we're a force to be reckoned with. I'll get the warrior watching Sandy." With a motion of Caiojezeal's hand, the demon angel team descended on the AAF warriors. The AAF managed to send two of their demon angels to the Eternal Blackness, but the demon angels eventually took possession of the house and property. Caiojezeal captured Sandy's warrior angel off guard and managed to subdue him before he alerted the AAF command center. Caiojezeal's team tied the AAF warriors with gelean wire, developed by Luc to diffuse the AAF powers and block any transmittal of messages to the AAF headquarters.

SANDY CRAWLED BACK UNDER THE covers and placed the pillow Baldric slept on over her face and inhaled, then sighed. His scent lingered on the pillowcase. She closed her eyes and allowed the cords of light to take her back to her wedding at St. Timothy's. She replayed her incredibly intoxicating honeymoon. Her husband knew her so well, and he'd pushed her every button in exactly the right places. Sandy prayed for sanction of their union.

The telephone rang. Rolling over onto her stomach and grinning like the cat who ate the canary, she reached over and grabbed the pink princess phone off the nightstand. "This is Sandy Cothran."

Ruby yelled into the phone, "Sandy, thank God. Get out of your house. Don't take a shower, just leave."

Sandy flipped over and sat on the side of the bed. "What's happened?"

Frantically, Ruby replied, "It's not what's happened but what's going to happen. The Dragon Dream is real. Luc is sending his men to you. I dreamed it, and it's as real as me talking to you now. Hang up and leave!"

"I'm outta here." She slammed the phone down and rapidly searched for her clothing. "Geez, Louise." Baldric had ripped her shirt and bra last night. She picked up her jeans and ran into her parents' bedroom. She grabbed her dad's red V-neck sweater out of his closet and pulled it over her head. She went back into her bedroom and dropped to her knees, looking for her boots. Sandy went flat onto her stomach and pulled them from under the bed slats along with her socks.

Downstairs, she scoped the room for her purse and keys and hit the door running when she came face-to-face with Cole. Sandy used the elementary school fire drill—stop, drop, and roll—to try to get away from her attackers. Her adrenaline was running a mile a minute. Her arms and legs were propelling kicks and jabs before being restrained. Lightning flashes from her chords of light filled Sandy's mind with her assailant's memories that made her stomach roll and lurch. Blood ran into her eyes and mouth. Her award-winning reporter skills had finally done her in.

Cole Steele was going to kill her. That was when someone hit her head from behind with a loud crack, and it was lights out. Right before she faded to black, an image of Baldric's handsome face appeared in her mind, and Sandy screamed, "Baldric!"

Sandy had no idea how long she'd been knocked out. She woke up in the middle of her parents' den hog-tied to one of the kitchen chairs.

Cole Steele looked down at her with a satisfied smile. "Looky, looky, looky—we have a cookie. You're not getting out of those ropes, love. So quit trying."

Sandy frowned and pressed her lips together. Damn, she was in a tight spot as she tried to relax and concentrate on her best course of action. She systematically outlined everything in her mind like she was writing out a formula back in Professor Knox's class in college and with about the same results. Cole and his thugs surrounded Sandy. She was S.O.L.

Cole leaned down in front of her and placed his hands on either side of the chair. "Now, since I have your attention, you get one shot at this, sweetheart. Where's Luc's book?"

Sandy hated that she was a tomboy because her reflex reaction worked faster than her brain. She spat in Cole's face, and he backhanded her so hard she saw stars. He grabbed her hair, and it felt like he was pulling it out by the roots. Tears formed in her eyes, but her stubbornness persisted. "Luc's book is the only thing keeping me alive. Go to hell, asshole!"

Ka-pow! Cole's fist smashed Sandy's nose and blood spewed like water. The white-hot pain nearly made her faint. Cole shouted at Walt, "Get her a towel." He turned back to Sandy and wiped the blood from her nose with his sleeve. "You like it rough. Well, so do I." He punched her in the gut, and she threw up on him. Today just kept getting better and better.

Walt pressed a cold towel to Sandy's nose, and she cried out in excruciating pain. Cole must've obliterated her septum. Cole pushed Walt out of the way. "You're going to tell me where Luc's book is, or I'll send Hammer to pick up your friends, Ruby and Anna. I know your friends and your family. I'll bring them together, and I'll beat them to death with my hands while you watch, bitch. You fucking tried to ruin everything I worked decades to build. You have a choice: tell me where the book is, or I'll send Hammer. Your call. You have ten seconds. Count 'em, Carson."

Carson began counting backward from ten when a luminous light entered the room. Sandy's heart leapt and then she realized the angel in front of her wasn't Baldric. The fierce-looking angel had shoulder-length, dark brown hair and brilliant blue eyes. He threw Cole against the wall like he was a ragdoll. "You fucking idiot. What have you done to her?"

Cole yelled, "She's mine, Caiojezeal. Mine."

Caiojezeal leaned down in front of Sandy and placed his hand over her nose. The radiant light from his hand burned her skin, but a minute later the pain was gone. He said, "You must tell me where you've hidden Luc's Testament. Cole won't harm you further, but if you don't tell me, I'm afraid Luc will be more persuasive than Cole."

Tears rolled down her cheeks, and she shook her head back and forth. "Baldric didn't send you?"

Sandy thought she'd seen compassion in the angel's eyes before she mentioned Baldric's name. Caiojezeal held her chin firmly and stated, "I'm a demon angel, servant of Lucifer and commander of his army in the south." He clasped her forearm, and she sensed Caiojezeal reading her thoughts. Damn it. She was screwed.

Two demon angels appeared on his right and left flanks. Caiojezeal released Sandy and said, "Clean her up and ready her for travel. We need her presentable at City Bank and Trust. Luc's Testament is in her lockbox." He strode over to Cole and slammed him against the wall. "You touch her again, and I'll see to it Luc terminates your mission today. Luc has commanded her into his presence, and I will ensure we proceed posthaste."

The female demon angel untied the ropes and threw Sandy over her shoulders. She flew upstairs and placed Sandy in the shower. "Ready yourself, human."

Sandy said, "Turn around while I undress."

The demon angel laughed and said, "Not a chance. Do it or I will."

Sandy undressed and threw the bloodied clothes on the floor. She quickly showered and dried off with a towel. The bruises on her face were gone but not on her ribs and arms. Whatever Caiojezeal did, the pain had disappeared. The similarities between the angels and demons were astounding, except this demon had dull and soulless eyes.

Sandy straightened her shoulders and lifted her chin. "I don't have any clothes to wear. And what did you do with the warriors sent to watch over me?"

The sinister giggle from the lithe demon made her blood chill. "Let's just say they're all tied up at the moment. We've brought you clothes from your condo. They're in your old room."

Sandy walked through the house without a stitch of clothing. She refused to allow the demon or Cole to belittle her. She'd always been proud of her physical form, with or without clothes. A Jones of New York black suit with a lavender blouse lay on the bed with her undergarments and black pumps. She dressed with care until the female demon stood behind her and Sandy felt the warmth of her breath on her neck. Sandy turned and said, "Back off, bitch. I'm ready. Let's get this over with."

The demon angel laughed again and said, "Your journey is just beginning, buttercup."

Chapter 8

Evil Ways

SANDY RODE IN THE BACK seat beside Caiojezeal in Cole's Suburban. She didn't know what transpired between the demon angel, Caiojezeal, and Cole while she was getting ready. Sandy sensed they were now working on the same page. Luc's Testament was the only thing keeping her alive. She closed her eyes and traveled on the cords of light to the book. She turned page after page of incantations and memorized them quickly. Using Luc's magic spells was her only way of escape even though the spells could turn her soul dark, but Sandy had to take a chance.

Over the last couple of days, Sandy had practiced the fencing skills Baldric taught her at home and in her mind. If she could materialize her sword, then it might buy her enough time to escape with the book and her life. On the off chance calling on her sword didn't work, Sandy memorized the spell of disappearance which would give her the ability to port her physical form from one place to another on the ethereal plane.

Sandy was already Luc's prisoner, so she didn't think she had anything to lose. Ruby would summon the wards and guardians when she didn't arrive at Everglade Store. They would come for her. The guardians would tell Baldric, and he would save her.

The chitchat among her captors was minimal, to say the least. They didn't give away any information she could use at a later date and time. Sandy had a photographic memory along with her clairvoyance. Caiojezeal seemed to possess the same skill set.

Caiojezeal walked inside the bank with Sandy, the bank staff oblivious to the supernatural warfare going on around them. Sandy's heart pounded so loud she could barely hear herself think when she entered the private room for lockbox customers.

Caiojezeal grabbed her hand and spun her around. His handsome face distorted with anger. "Dear God, woman, you do have a death wish. Do not attempt to cast a spell or any other. I'm thousands of years old and have conquered many humans with much more experience than you. I do commend your effort." He grabbed her shoulders and said, "I bind you, Sandra Daireann, from using witchcraft. I bind you from astral travel on the ethereal plane."

Sandy shook forcefully out of his grasp and, just for spite, kicked him in the shin.

Caiojezeal eye's brightened again with a flickering light, which Sandy interpreted as compassion or curiosity. He chuckled and said, "So, I see why Baldric likes you. You're quite a handful, aren't you, Ms. Cothran? Now open the damn box."

Sandy placed the key inside the lock, but before she opened the drawer, she said, "You're not like the other demon who escorted me to take a shower. You seem different."

Caiojezeal threw his head back and laughed so hard he held onto his sides. "Well, then you're seeing a side of me I haven't seen since being cast out of heaven. I was once a member of the AAF until Luc recruited me. Luc is an amazing and charismatic angel but very dangerous. Make no mistake. I'm dangerous, too. Quit stalling and give me the book."

With a heavy heart, Sandy opened the lockbox and pulled out Luc's Testament. She held it in her hands for a moment before relinquishing it to Caiojezeal. She sighed and said, "What happens to me now?"

"Luc has requested your presence. I cannot read his thoughts as I have yours. Heed my warning, Ms. Cothran. I suggest you cooperate with him. Luc is cunning and ruthless."

Sandy narrowed her eyes and said, "I am a ward of The Creator. I am wife to Baldric the warrior, guardian of Campbell Ridge. I am not afraid. Baldric will come for me, and Luc will rue this day."

Caiojezeal placed his hand gently on her shoulder. "Yeah, keep thinking that. It just ain't going to happen. Everglade Farms and all of the AAF's faze doesn't prevent us from knowing who and what we fight. I hate to see you broken, but broken you'll be."

Sandy walked out of the bank the same way she walked in. If she screamed or made a scene, the people would only think her mad. She prayed while walking to the Suburban and continued as she stepped inside. Caiojezeal sat beside her and touched the side of her neck. She slept.

She awoke sometime later on a satiny black leather couch. Around the room, black and white marbled columns shot up to twenty-foot ceilings. There were golden sconces anchored to dark plum walls illuminating the room. She looked over her head at what surely must be a replica of Peter Paul Rubens' *Massacre of the Innocents*. The grandeur of the interior was museum quality.

She quickly glanced around for a way out but couldn't find any doors, windows, or openings of any kind. Food and drink were laid out on a large black buffet across the room against a stone wall. Her stomach growled, but she had no intention of eating until she could figure out where she was. Odd, she didn't have any recollection how she got to this place, and most frightening of all, she couldn't remember her name.

In the corner of the room, someone watched her. Red eyes like fire peered at her from the dark, and the room became increasingly warm. She stood up and caught her reflection in a large gilded mirror. She wore a sleeveless white evening gown accentuating every curve. An incredible being stepped out of the darkness and appeared behind her, and she couldn't move, even though she tried. She seemed frozen in some state of paralysis.

Long, shiny black hair fell over his shoulders in waves. He was beautiful, magnificent, but something behind his blinding smile sent chills straight up her arms. He wrapped one arm around her waist and used the other to push her hair away from her neck. He kissed and sucked on her neck softly, gently, and she became aroused. It seemed wrong—all wrong as she responded to his touch while he caressed her breast.

His smooth tongue ran along her neck up to her ear, and he whispered, "Welcome home, Daireann."

LUC WHISPERING HER NAME BROKE her hypnotic trance, and Sandy wheeled around with the palm of her hand to smack him across the face, but he grabbed her wrist. "Tsk, tsk, tsk, one mustn't hit The Dragon if one is to remain whole."

Breathing heavy, she glared at him and said, "You filthy snake. You low down, dirty, rotten snake."

Luc laughed and waved his hand in the air. "Witchcraft" by Frankie played around the room. Luc sang Sandy the words and pulled her up into his arms, making her look at their reflection in the full-length mirror. "Just look at the two of us. We're a stunning couple. You're a rare beauty and, well, I'm me. Ah, what were you thinking? Oh yeah, I remember. You think I'm beautiful, magnificent."

"Go to hell!"

Luc roared with laughter and kissed her on the mouth. She remained impassive. He ran his hand over her breast and squeezed her nipples hard. "Darling, I've seen you in action. I know how to please a female like you."

With all the force Sandy could muster, she shrugged out of his grasp and pushed him away. "I'm paired with Baldric. How did he taste in your mouth?" Baldric marked Sandy the night of their pairing. Every man, angel, and demon angel would know she belonged to Baldric.

Luc shrugged and threw his hands, palms up, in the air. "*Comme ci, comme ca.* Yes, Daireann. I know you've paired with what do you call him? Oh, Big B. But The Creator will never sanction your union. So, it's neither here nor there to me. And speaking of Baldric, did he tell you of Barbellina?" He moved swiftly to her ear and whispered, "I didn't think so. He and Barbellina were supposed to pair when she slept with me. It destroyed Baldric for centuries. He was very much in love with her. She had been his match in every way. Unfortunately, she desired me, and I couldn't let her down. I do have a reputation with the females."

Luc went to the buffet. He poured red wine into crystal goblets and handed one to Sandy. "Here, you look like you need it. I hate to be the bearer of bad news. Baldric should've told you."

Sandy's hunger and thirst, coupled with the news of Barbellina, made her turn the wine up, and she emptied the glass. Sandy poured another drink. Baldric loved her. Luc was just messing with her head.

Luc made his voice sound like hers. "Day-yum, girl, you know that's what I'm talking about." He chuckled and then poured another glass for himself. His normal voice returned, and he said, "I hate to add insult to injury, but no one has come for you. No one has even inquired of your disappearance. You've been here a month, and it's like no one gives a shit."

Sandy had researched convert hypnosis on a piece she'd worked on a year ago on cults. Luc was using the same technique to discredit her love, her friends, and her family. Sandy couldn't decipher if Luc was telling her the truth or just blowing smoke up her ass. She wouldn't play his game. She had a few tricks up her sleeve, thanks to the book.

Sandy walked over to the couch and sat down. "Let's cut to the chase, shall we? Why don't you tell me why I'm here? Whether anyone is looking for me is irrelevant. I want to know what you want with me." Sandy flipped her hair off her right shoulder and pinned him with a look. She wet her lips with the wine, and Luc did a double take at her mouth.

Sandy learned from the book how to relax her mind. She'd been too flustered to use the cords of light with Caiojezeal, but she was hitting on all cylinders now. The cords of light ran through her mind, sending mixed signals to Luc. He was trying very hard to read her thoughts, but the multicolored strands thickened and blocked his encroachment into her mind.

Luc sat down and stretched his arm on the back of the couch while he studied her. "Hmmm, aren't you the clever one. Don't get me wrong. Ruby, Anna, and Jerry all have amazing gifts humans don't deserve. But you're taking what The Creator gave you plus the info from my book to block your thoughts. Touche. You and I are going to have fun. Did you know every time you use one of my magic spells you get a little closer to the dark side?"

Sandy crossed one of her long legs over the other one. Luc's eyes widened, and he licked his lips. She rolled her eyes and said, "Oh, for the record, I'd rather die than sleep with you. You have human envy because we have a connection with The Creator you'll never have again."

The couch turned around in a circle and then slammed against the wall. Before Sandy could blink, she was on her back, and Luc was on top of her. He growled and held her face with one of his huge hands. "If I wanted to fuck you there wouldn't be a thing you could do to stop me. So don't flatter yourself, human whore. I never sleep with humans. You disgust me. You angel wannabe. And for the record, you want to know why you're here? You're nothing but a big piece of cheese placed in a trap to catch a gigantic rat. I want Baldric, not you, slut. But you have given me an idea."

Sandy didn't budge. She kept her eyes locked on Luc's as she worked the cords of light to make them thicker and stronger. She didn't want Luc to see or sense her fear. Sandy stretched the cords further to her home, searching for Baldric. She had to try to warn him.

Sandy blocked her thoughts as she screamed for help. She traveled on her cords of light to the Campbell Ridge Cave, looking for the source of her power, and a portal opened in her mind. Sandy stretched the cords further into the cosmos, passing into another realm. A massive white structure stood in front of her eyes, and she screamed Baldric's name. *Baldric, be careful. Luc is using me to trap you. Baldric!* A legion of angels turned toward her voice. *Thank God.*

Sandy narrowed her eyes and said, "Baldric will rip you to shreds." She hockered up a loogie and spat in his face.

Luc wiped his face then brushed his lips across hers. He said, "You will come to regret that, my Daireann. I will use you to destroy Baldric. You will fall in love with me, and you'll beg me to make love to you. You'll open for me like the petals of a rose, and I'll devour your body and your spirit. You will break your vows to Baldric. Then I'll pass you around the division as the whore you are, and I'll use you against your friends and family one by one as I bring down the wards and guardians of Campbell Ridge." He turned into a dark wind tunnel that blew debris about the room, and Sandy was forced to hold onto the back of the sofa before Luc dematerialized.

Sandy trembled with fear. She barely held it together in front of Luc. Sandy prayed for help. She prayed for Baldric.

Caiojezeal entered the room and reached out his hand to her. "Come, I'll show you to your room. You're either the bravest human in the world or the dumbest. You're lucky. Luc sees you as a challenge, and that's the only reason you aren't being tortured. You're not the only ward in the caverns. Some of the places down here are gruesome. I told you to accommodate him, not thwart him. I have instructions to wipe your memory, and your call to the In-Between has been scrambled in the control room. I'm sorry."

Tears formed in the corners of her eyes. "Please don't take my memory. Please. I won't call out again, I promise."

Caiojezeal shoulders slumped, and he shook his head. With sadness, he said, "I cannot go against a direct order. I'm sorry. When you're in his presence, Luc will return your memory, but when you aren't, you won't even know your name. I will make your stay here as pleasant as I can." Caiojezeal raised his hands, and she tried to run, but he immobilized her. Sandy looked into his blue eyes full of sadness and then she was no more.

CAIOJEZEAL RELEASED HIS HANDS FROM Sandy. She tilted her head and asked, "Where am I?" She scratched her chin and said, "And for that matter, who am I?"

Caiojezeal placed his palm on her cheek and replied, "Your name is Dee. I have a lovely room for you. Would you like to go for a walk after you've settled?"

Dee replied, "Yes, I would love to check this place out. What's your name?"

"Call me CJ." Caiojezeal led Dee through the caverns under Luc's Arrington Estate. He opened the door to a room attached to Luc's personal quarters at his request. Caiojezeal had been assigned as Dee's jailer. He'd never known Luc to place any human within such close quarters to his own. Caiojezeal liked the human female and dreaded what Luc would do to her.

Caiojezeal used magic to give the illusion her room looked out over the Smoky Mountains, a retreat away from Luc for the time she would spend here. The room held a comfortable sitting area, kitchen, and large master bedroom and bath. The interior design reflected earth tones in the rustic furniture and art, and the light from the fire cast a soft glow around the room.

Dee ran to the window like a child and turned back to him with a big grin. "It's beautiful. Thank you, CJ. Do you know if I have any other clothes than this gown?"

Dee's smile touched a part of his soul, making him melt. Why was this human making him soft? He respected Baldric even though they played on opposing teams, and Sandy was his paired partner. He'd need to stay on his toes, or Luc would sense his weakness. Another demon angel assigned to Sandy's case wouldn't offer kindness, but cruelty. He said, "Come into your bedroom." Dee followed as he opened an enormous walk-in closet filled with clothes, shoes, purses, and undergarments along with a dressing table stocked with toiletries and cosmetics.

Dee squealed with delight as she ran her hands over the clothes. "Oh my goodness. Look at all of the clothes." She turned and hugged Caiojezeal, which made his chest tighten. "Thank you, CJ. Is it okay to shower and change clothes? I'm at a loss as to what I should do. I'm a little confused."

Damn it. Caiojezeal had wiped out too many of Sandy's natural responses. She seemed to have the demeanor of a child. "Of course, I'll show you where the linens are. The shower has soap, shampoo, and conditioner. Do you remember how to take a shower?"

Dee shoved him and jokingly said, "Silly goose, of course, I know how to take a shower. Now scoot." She pushed him out of the bathroom and locked the door.

Caiojezeal walked back into the den, dropped his face into his hands, and rubbed vigorously. He shouted, "What the hell is wrong with you? Get your shit together, or you're going to get your ass in a world of hurt."

For the duration of Dee's shower, Caiojezeal stared at the illusion he created for her. Six thousand years had come and gone. He thought himself incapable of feeling until he met her. Caiojezeal knelt and, in another first, he prayed to The Creator to help Sandy. Caiojezeal had no clue if his tie was broken, but he prayed anyway.

If Luc ever found out he'd prayed to the Almighty, Caiojezeal would be exiled into the Eternal Blackness. But if he could save Sandy, maybe, just perhaps, there was redemption, and The Creator would allow him to come home or at least become an earth angel.

Chapter 9

The Way It Is

ON THE THIRTIETH FLOOR OF the Steele Building, Cole sat in his leather chair looking at downtown Nashville. He'd built an empire with blood, sweat, and tears over a couple of decades and amassed more wealth than he ever acquired back east. Sandy Cothran had his ass in hot water with the authorities and worse with Luc.

The four televisions mounted inside a custom-built cabinet were turned on to the news stations, and there was no mention of Ms. Cothran's abduction. If Cole didn't hate the bitch so much, he would've taken her at the farm. She had slender legs all the way up to her tight ass and real tits, not those fake boobs like every woman his posse dated.

Cole beat the shit out of Sandy this morning, and just thinking about the attack made him adjust his pants. Yeah, her tits were real soft and fleshy, judging from the sweater she'd worn. Cole had recorded her stories on his VCR and played them at least a hundred times during the last two years. He'd memorized every line on her face, including the little chickenpox scar on her forehead. He would've finished her off today if Caiojezeal hadn't stopped him.

Sandy could've been a real asset to his organization, but his attempts to recruit her had failed miserably. Carson had the hit to kill her last December, but he'd only roughed her up. Baldric appeared on the scene and sent Carson to the hospital with the shit kicked out of him and amnesia to boot. Sandy had gone on air the next night with the story of her attack and even had her camera operator zoom in on the bruises on her throat. She looked straight into the camera and threatened him. Damn, the woman had cojones the size of coconuts. Her most recent exposé would probably bankrupt him and send him to jail.

The buzzer from his intercom went off, and he pushed the button. "Jackie, are they here?"

His assistant, Jackie, had been a real gem to find—trustworthy, dependable, and loyal, and she made the best coffee this side of the Mississippi. Jackie shielded him from unwanted solicitors and knew all the names of those he held in his back pocket. In exchange, she had a six-figure income and a pretty nice spread in Williamson County. She replied, "Yes, sir. Do you want me to send them in?"

"Please, and Jackie, call Nelson Doune. Tell him I'm dropping by this evening around seven. Say we have a problem. Oh, one more thing. Hold all my calls."

Cole walked around to the front of his desk and crossed his arms. The double doors opened and in walked his men. Cole's men had never questioned his decisions and never turned him down for anything. Walt, Carson, and Hammer had been with Cole since New York. "Gentlemen, please sit down. What have you heard on our prisoner, and is Luc back in town?"

Carson went over to Cole's bar and poured a shot of Chivas. "Shit, who'd have thought Caiojezeal had a soft spot for Sandy?" He sauntered back over to the couch against the wall and sat down.

Walt sat in one of the reception chairs and crossed one leg over the other. "That bastard's crazy, but he did get the book back."

Cole picked up a crystal paperweight on his desk and threw it against one of the TVs, smashing the glass screen, which released fire and smoke. "That woman and Luc's book..."

LUCIFER BLEW THE DOORS OPEN and shouted, "I'm nailing your ass to the wall. The police are downstairs. They're coming for you, Cole. You're going to spend the rest of your miserable life behind bars. It seems someone singled you out in the murder of Nick and, oops, did I forget to tell you that the authorities found Councilman Stevens' body?

Yeah, you're getting hit with the Stevens charge, too. Serves your ass right for nearly screwing up everything I've worked so hard to achieve."

Cole's face flushed red, and he balled his hands into fists. "You achieved? You turned me in to save your ass. It was my hard work that propelled this enterprise."

Luc raised a brow and waved his hand in the air, sending Cole flying into the glass windows of the office. He levitated Cole into the air, cutting off Cole's windpipe. "Carson, sit behind Cole's desk. Let's see how you look." After thirty seconds, Luc dropped Cole to the floor and left him coughing and gasping for air.

Jackie's voice came over the intercom. "Mr. Steele, there are some officers out here, and they have a warrant for your arrest."

Luc pretended to swing an invisible golf club and answered in Cole's voice. "Please send them in."

Cole crawled on his hands and knees toward Luc. "Please don't send me to jail. I'll do anything you want. Just name it."

Luc pressed his black cowboy boot into Cole's face. "But I want you to go to jail. With you in jail, Steele Enterprises will have the green light to proceed with business as usual, and the board will appoint Carson as the new President. Oh, I am the board." Luc moved to the side and allowed the police officers to come in the door.

Detective Wade proceeded with the reading of Cole's Miranda rights and escorted Mr. Steele out of the building in handcuffs.

Luc slapped Carson on the back and said, "And just like that, you're the boss."

Carson tilted his head and straightened his shoulders. "Well, sir, I'll do the best I can to make you proud."

Luc strolled over to the window before glancing over his left shoulder. "I'm sure you'll do fine. It's not calculus or physics. Just open your ears and listen. Do what I tell you to do and we won't have any problems." He paused and held his hand in the air. "Wait for it— Cole has left the building." Luc did a fist pump and turned to Walt and then Hammer. "Do either of you have a problem with my decision today?"

"No, sir, damn glad to be here," replied Walt.

Hammer cracked his knuckles and said, "Makes no difference to me, boss."

"Great. I'm glad everything can proceed as normal. I have to pop to New York for a few hours before I return to Arrington. Secure the perimeters of the farm's property. Baldric will come for his missus, and I want to be ready for him." Luc dematerialized.

RUBY RACED TO ANNA'S CLINIC on Main Street. She burst through the door to find a full waiting room of patients. Anna's receptionist, Kris, glanced up and said, "Ruby, Dr. McDaniel is with patients. You're going to have to wait."

Ruby cocked her head to the side, pursed her lips, and pushed the door open toward the exam rooms. She shouted, "Anna, Anna. Where are you?"

Kris caught up with Ruby as Anna opened the door to the exam room on the right. "Good grief, what's going on out here?"

In exasperation, Kris said, "I tried to tell her you were with a patient. Like that ever works."

Ruby touched Kris on the shoulder and said, "Sorry, kiddo, but this can't wait. A moment, Anna."

Anna gave Kris a smile and said, "It's okay, honey. We all know Ruby. She's a freaking force of nature." She turned and motioned Ruby into her office. Once inside the private office, Anna closed the door and blew out a breath. "For crying out loud, I have patients. What's the problem?"

Ruby broke into a sob. Several choppy breaths had escaped her lips before she said, "The Dragon has Sandy. It's not a dream—it's freaking for real. I've already called Reed and Mom. You have to call Jerry and come to Everglade Farms ASAP."

Anna grabbed Ruby's shoulders and said, "Calm down and talk slowly. What do you mean? How do you know?"

Ruby stomped her foot on the ground several times. "Dad-blame it, Anna. I'm not joking. Luc is The Dragon. Sandy is the person in my dream. She's the one. I told her to come to the store. Sandy should've been at the store thirty minutes ago. I had an overwhelming need to check, so I went to her parents'. There was a struggle inside the Cothran's home. Broken glass and furniture were tossed all over the place. I'd bet my life Luc has her."

Anna hit her forehead with the palm of her hand. "Have the guardians been notified? And where's Baldric?"

"How the heck do I know? Mom is summoning the guardians. Let's go. Call Jerry and I'll see you at the house." Ruby left as fast as she came in.

Opening the door to her Jeep, Ruby slid into her seat and cranked the engine. She looked both ways before pulling onto Main Street. She drove straight to Everglade Farms. Little Joe had spent the night with Lee and Harry because she'd been on schedule to open the store. She met Rose, the store manager, and waited for Sandy, but Sandy never showed up. Reed was going to meet her at her parents' house.

Ruby's mind raced, and her insides twisted, thinking about Sandy in the dream with Luc. "Seneca, I need you."

Seneca materialized in the passenger seat. Ruby tossed him a glance and noticed he seemed frazzled. She said, "Oh, it's bad, I've never seen you upset. Tell me like it is. Don't sugar coat it."

Seneca leaned back in the seat and turned to face her. "Baldric and Sandy were paired last night by the Spirit of Man." Simultaneously, Ruby's mouth dropped open; her brows rose, and her eyes widened. He said, "Don't interrupt. Listen, Michael summoned Baldric. After their meeting, Michael escorted Baldric to the throne room. There's no communication with the outside once you enter the holy place."

He swiveled in the seat and crossed his legs. "Well, while they were still in the waiting room for The Creator, Sandy's parents' property was overtaken by an elite demon angel force led by Caiojezeal, their commander. Evidently, Luc developed this new weaponry that blocks our warriors' powers and any transmittal for help to the AFF control room. We have our research team on the scene to develop a counter weapon. Sometime later, Sandy's voice broke through the ethereal plane to the AAF command center, screaming for Baldric. Luc's using Sandy as bait to get Baldric. Our generals are working on an evacuation plan. We'll meet in the barn later. I'll be back soon." Seneca vanished.

Ruby began to hyperventilate. She'd had The Dragon Dream so many times. Why couldn't she see something, anything to help? What good was her power if she couldn't stop bad things from happening? "Oh, God, please watch over and protect Sandy. Please."

An hour later, the wards and the guardians met inside the Everglade Farms barn. Lee set up a banquet table in the center of the barn. Angels sat in the rafters as Erinelle and Ralph spread out a map of Luc's Arrington Estate to develop a plan for Sandy's escape.

Erinelle's voice rose. "Baldric doesn't know Luc is holding Sandy prisoner. He'll need restraining until he can get his emotions under control. He'll be highly volatile. Raizeal and Samian, come forth."

Raizeal and Samian appeared in front of Erinelle. Each warrior angel was at least Baldric's size. Ruby doubted two would be enough to subdue Baldric.

Erinelle said, "Wait for Baldric and Michael at the throne room gates. Bring Baldric here. I'll have the calming chair ready for him in one of the horse stalls." The two warrior angels disappeared.

Erinelle looked at the wards and the angels. "The rumors are true. Baldric paired with Sandy." The room erupted in an uproar. She continued, "Please, settle down and listen. He's meeting with The Creator to plead his case regardless of the outcome, in his heart Sandy is Baldric's mate for eternity. When he finds out Luc has Sandy, it'll take all of us to convince him we go into Luc's compound as a team, or we don't go at all."

Ruby had noticed the way Sandy looked at Baldric on several occasions but never fathomed the growing romance between the two. Ruby whispered to Reed, "Just Sandy's luck to fall in love with an angel."

Reed nodded and said, "I know, right?" Erinelle narrowed her eyes at Ruby and Reed and frowned. They shut up fast.

Ralph took center stage in the middle of the barn. He threw his arms open wide and said, "Love is what lights our way. Our brother is in love, and we'll help him. Our ward is in trouble, and we'll help her. My earth angel contact told me Cole is no longer in charge at the compound. He'll serve out a sentence in the human jail before Luc sends him to hell. The new human commander is Carson Jones. He's weak."

Lee stepped over next to Ralph and asked, "What do you want us to do?"

Jerry raised his hand, and Erinelle nodded approval for him to speak. "Nelson Doune's farm connects to Luc's Arrington Estate. I know the layout of the farm well. I'm sure Nelson will cooperate with us if I asked him for help."

Reed shook his head and said, "Are you sure? I mean, you did jilt his daughter."

Anna frowned and placed her hands on her hips. "We saved Rachel. She was possessed by three demons. Now she's engaged to Jack, my old boss. From what I hear, they're crazy for each other. I agree with Jerry. We can penetrate Luc's estate from Nelson's farm."

Luwenia pointed to the map on the table and drew a large circle around the house. "Luc has supernatural sensors to detect and track the AAF. The sensors were wired into the estate's electrical panel box. We need a human to bypass the security panels."

Ruby walked over to her mom and whispered in her ear, "George can do it. He is a master electrician."

Lee squeezed Ruby's hand and said, "Ruby's right. George is a master electrician. Jerry, any chance Nelson could have one of his men mess around with Luc's panel box so Arrington Estate needs an electrician?"

"Anna and I will head over to Nelson's now. Y'all can fill us in on the specifics when we get back." He grabbed Anna's hand, and they rushed out the side door.

Walking around the table, Erinelle traced the diagram of the house and the outbuildings. "If you think George will agree to work with us, he needs to be brought into the meeting." She turned and pointed to Simon, Reed's combat trainer. "Simon, go to Celina. Tell her to bring George to the barn. I'll take it from there."

Lee placed her hand on Erinelle's forearm. "You must protect George. Bestow a power on him so when he walks into the Lion's den, he'll have protection."

"Of course. As George's guardian, Celina will gain access to the estate with him. She'll be our eyes and ears. Luc's human chef, Estevo, is on our side, too, and he's working diligently to find the cavern's entrance. We've worked for some time to gain access. We believe Luc has several wards in the caverns in addition to Sandy. Our mission is to rescue Sandy, but if we can help any other wards to escape, we must extricate them, too."

Ralph said, "The informants, Estevo, George, and Celina, need to get us a head count of the human and demon angel guards on the compound. It's imperative to find the entrance to the caverns and its layout to carry out any rescue attempt. Baldric is our best weapon.

He and Sandy are linked through their pairing. Baldric may reach Sandy through the cords of light and telepathy. However, the AAF uses memory cleansing, and Luc's army uses the same techniques. Sandy may not remember Baldric, but his DNA link that made his mark the night they paired should lead us directly to her."

Lee ran her fingers through her hair. "Those assigned to Luc's compound will face incredible risks to smuggle the captives out safely once we have confirmation of the entrance to the cavern and Sandy's location. We must confirm everyone is on board with those risks before we proceed."

Reed placed the tips of his fingers on the table and leaned in toward Erinelle. "I know I'm the new kid on the block, but the military strategy is crucial. I suggest we continue training for battle while the plan is under development. Working together as a team to save Sandy needs to be as seamless as possible to prevent loss of life and injuries. Luc and his Arrington recruits aren't going to let us just waltz in without a fight."

Seneca chuckled and said, "Ruby, your husband is as smart as he is good-looking." The other angels began to laugh.

Reed straightened his shoulders and said, "Not funny. My wife, her mother, her brother, and her best friends could die."

Ruby wrapped her arm around Reed's waist. "Seneca was only trying to break the thick cloud of dread in the barn. I'm sure combat training is a part of the plan."

Erinelle extended her wings and flew up in the air. "Reed's right. Break into your groups. Let the combat training begin."

BALDRIC STOOD ON THE STEPS of the AAF command center. The Angel Armed Forces headquarters was a massive, rectangular, white structure. Precious gemstones such as bloodstone, topaz, rubies, hiddenite, amber, and amethyst adorned the magnificent building. Enormous fluted columns with rosette necking and ornate moldings went around the building in two rows. AAF Warrior angels guarded the exterior and interior building with weapons developed by The Creator.

The AAF headquarters housed all of the maps and coordinates of the universe. The divisional leaders met with Michael on a weekly basis to develop and hone their military strategy regarding Luc and his army. Baldric entered the building and strode toward Michael's office. He had worked out his plea for sanction.

The warrior angels standing guard parted, and Michael greeted Baldric at the door.

"Good morning, Baldric. Please come in." Michael allowed Baldric to enter before closing the door behind them. Michael waved his hands in the air. "Have you completely lost your mind? I pleaded with Seneca to separate you and Sandy, but no, he assured me you had it under control. Now you've paired with Sandy and brought the Spirit of Man into the mess." Michael didn't sit down, nor did he offer a chair to Baldric. He folded his arms over his chest and raised a brow. "What say you?"

Baldric held his head high and squared his shoulders. "I'm paired with my other half. To the female I love, and she loves me. I'll not let Sandy go. You may disengage me from her care, but I'll never leave her side. Assign me to earth, but I demand you sanction this union. I've served the AAF faithfully for thousands of years and heaven before that."

Baldric splayed his fingers out with emphasis. "In my youth, I agree I was unstable. But I'm a warrior who is willing to lay down his life and his last breath for his mate. Sandra Daireann is my partner, my wife. She's my life, Michael. What say you?" Baldric stood with his feet apart and clasped his hands behind his back.

Michael blew out a breath, making Baldric's hair stand on end. "I say we go to the throne room. The Creator is the only one who can sanction a human and an angel's pairing. It's been nice knowing you. Let's go."

The two warriors' boots slapped loudly and echoed on the white and gray marbled floor along the Great Hall of Moses. Several angels openly stared. The hushed whispers swirled around Baldric as they walked out the side door, down fifty steps, and onto the spring green grass that felt like a soft carpet underfoot.

Baldric and Michael entered the portal to heaven from the In-Between's Garden of Life, which teemed with new and exotic plants and animal forms of The Creator's experiments.

Appearing in front of the Palace of Gold, Baldric hesitated. He closed his eyes and said a silent prayer to the Spirit of Man for guidance and for the right words to use to bend The Creator's ear in his favor.

The palace doors opened automatically, and the Spirit of Man ushered them into the Hall of Light. She said, "Baldric, I stand with you this day, my son."

Baldric bowed before her, and with reverence, he said, "Thank you, gracious one."

Bathed in warm golden light, the room and its double-tiered stained glass reflected The Creator's journey of life and the making of the universe.

The beauty of the room filled Baldric with great peace. He knew once the next doors opened, the answer already waited for him. The Creator had an all-seeing eye. He had a knowledge of everything all at once because everything in existence was of His creation.

Michael let out a sigh and said, "Whatever happens, my old friend, it's for the best."

Time stood in the balance as Baldric fidgeted nervously, and he began to pace about the chamber. Baldric thought his beautiful bride and their pairing ceremony. It had been perfect in his eyes. The Throne Room opened, and Baldric took a deep breath before following Michael through the golden doors.

The Throne Room décor was simple in comparison to the exterior. White columns ran the length of the room on both sides. Chandeliers of light hung from a ceiling painted with murals of life in all forms, shapes, and sizes. The high throne was made from the oldest trees of time and space. The Creator watched Baldric approach. Baldric fell to his knees, then prostrated himself on the floor as a sign of humility.

The Creator wore His white tunic and linen pants. His golden sandals laced across His ankles. He reached down and stroked Baldric's blond hair. "Rise, my son. Come, sit by my side and we'll talk."

Baldric wiped the tears from his eyes and followed The Creator, who motioned for him to sit next to the throne. The Creator said, "Tell me of your great love and why I should sanction a union forbidden for thousands of years."

Baldric looked into The Creator's eyes and began to weave his story of great love. "From the moment I looked into Sandy's, or, well, Sandra's eyes, I knew she was different. As you know, I have held my position as a guardian for thousands of years and for thousands of humans. But from the first look in her eyes, as an infant, I loved her. When she was a child, my heart broke for her when the human male breached her innocence. I became fiercely protective of Sandy after that incident."

Baldric fiddled his thumbs and looked at The Creator. "I've always loved Sandy's quirky sense of humor and her tough-as-nails attitude. But underneath all of her steely composure lay a soft and compassionate heart scared to fall in love."

Baldric cleared his throat and ran his fingers through his hair. He said, "The first time I realized I had a problem was during Sandy's college years. In front of her friends and family, she tried to be the strong one. But on this day, she danced around and sang some silly human song on the radio then the song changed to a sad tune. Sandy stopped and listened to the words full of longing and despair. Tears rolled down her cheeks, and my pairing scent released. She went into the kitchen and opened a cookie jar and took a sniff. The jar was empty. She'd inhaled my pairing scent and something shifted in my chest."

Baldric took another deep breath and held onto his knees. "I tried to push the implications of my chemical reaction away, but it seemed every time I witnessed the soft side of Sandy, my scent released, and I couldn't control it. The smarty pants finally figured it out last summer in Florida while she partied with her friends on the beach. Sandy knew the scent was me. The need to pair with her continued to increase, but I fought against it."

Baldric closed his eyes in pain, and The Creator placed His hand on his shoulder. Baldric turned to Him and said, "Watching her have sex with other males was the worst. I'd get so jealous and want to kill the men. But she knew my scent. She didn't look at the men but searched the room for my scent, and she began to perform for me. I'll tell you it was rough."

Baldric glanced at Michael, who smiled back at him. He turned back to The Creator and said, "After the Carson Jones attack, I made myself known to Sandy, and she tempted me. Oh, Lord, did she tempt me." The Creator chuckled, and Michael laughed out loud.

Baldric looked between The Creator and Michael. "I fought it, I did. Then last night, at St. Timothy's, you heard her prayer. You heard mine. I couldn't deny my love for Sandy any longer. I knew it was against the rules, but honestly, I couldn't stop myself, and I asked Sandy to be my other half for the rest of eternity. I love her."

The Spirit of Man and The Prince materialized before Baldric and The Creator. The Spirit of Man said, "I paired them, Lord. Their love is not ordinary; it is extraordinary. I search for signs of love throughout the universe, and when I find true love I want to light the world with it. I'm at fault for breaking the rules. Baldric and Sandy's love is the rarest of all loves I have ever witnessed. I believe Sandy to be Baldric's true love and the other half of his soul." She bowed before The Creator.

The Creator stood from the throne and then sat on the step next to Baldric. The look in His sapphire eyes made Baldric's chest tighten. He couldn't breathe. The Creator placed His hand on Baldric's knee and looked into his eyes. "Son, I know you love Sandy. I have seen the love the two of you share. Be that as it may, we have a much bigger problem at the moment to discuss. Luc holds Sandy prisoner to trap you."

Baldric paled. Arching his back, Baldric threw his head back and roared, "No! No, God!" He ripped his armor from his chest and screamed, "I've failed her. I failed!"

The Creator held onto Baldric's shoulder. "Listen to me, son. You're the only one who can save her. Your marking on Sandy is a direct link to help pinpoint her location." Baldric tried to shake The Creator's hand loose and couldn't. "I can't allow you to go off half-crazed. You have to control your emotions and work with your team to rescue Sandy. Luc holds other wards captive at Arrington Estates in the underground caverns. Are you listening to me?"

Baldric heard The Creator, but every fiber of his being wanted to dematerialize to Luc's compound. Breathing hard, Baldric said, "I have to rescue my wife."

The Creator's hands bore down on Baldric's shoulders. "Luc is using Sandy to trap you. It is you he wants, not Sandy. He uses many techniques to break his prisoners. She was taken this morning, not an hour after Michael summoned you. Don't give Michael that look. You did the forbidden, but I'm not dwelling on your breach. I want Sandy back."

Baldric gritted his teeth as he imagined choking the life out of Luc. "I vow to rescue Sandy and the others."

The Creator looked at Michael and said, "Escort him to Everglade Farms. The guardians are making plans for a special operation to rescue Sandy and any other wards."

Michael nodded and said, "As you wish, my Lord."

"May love light the way." The Creator vanished.

Baldric hit a dead run for the golden doors and pushed them open. Raizeal and Samian were waiting for him and cast a net over Baldric, knocking him to the ground. Baldric screamed, "Let me go, damn it. I have to save my wife. Let me go." Baldric punched Raizeal in the mouth and did a roundhouse kick to Samian's ribs before they secured him.

Michael, Raizeal, and Samian created a circle and ported Baldric to Everglade Farms through the Campbell Ridge Cave portal. Inside the barn, Baldric fought to get out of the net. He yelled, "I'm going to kill anyone who stands in my way and don't think I'll forget who's doing this to me. Let me go."

Erinelle knelt down beside Baldric and placed her hands on his shoulders. "Place him in the calming chair. His anger is dangerous to us all. Until he can converse with us calmly, we'll proceed without him." The pressure Erinelle placed on his neck made him sleep.

AFTER WORKING FOR TEN YEARS with a commercial outfit out of Nashville, George took his state contractor's test and opened Champion Electric. The Middle Tennessee area grew so fast that he owned a fleet of trucks and had twenty-five employees on his payroll. He could've doubled the size of his business but made the decision to turn down work when he and Lizzie started having problems.

Then Lizzie moved to her mother's in Florida because she said she needed some space or some shit. He called numerous times and pleaded for her to come home, but she only turned him away.

George opened a large manila envelope from Brock Rogers, attorney at law. He stared at the documents and couldn't believe his eyes. Lizzie filed for divorce. He thought they'd grow old together. He thought they shared a once-in-a-lifetime kind of love. George was wrong.

Lizzie wanted children and blamed him because they didn't have any. Little Joe's birth in December sent her over the edge. George went to the doctor and found out he wasn't shooting blanks. He never told Lizzie, but she must've known. Real relationships don't always end in a happily ever after.

After Lizzie had moved, George hired a part-time bookkeeper and receptionist. Debby was only nineteen, but she had excellent organizational skills and wasn't hard on the eyes, either. He glanced out his door as she bent over the filing cabinet. *Dang.* He shook his head. The thought of being single again made him sick. He loved Lizzie. She just didn't love him enough, and he was tired of calling her. If Lizzie wanted a divorce, then by God, he'd give her one.

George pushed away from the desk and had every intention of marching into the other room and asking Debby out on a date when the door slammed shut by itself. A boy appeared before his eyes, and George thought he was losing his mind. Lizzie had finally driven him insane.

"Get a grip, George. I'm Simon. I'm an angel, and the angel to your right is Celina. She's your guardian. I mean, come on, George, the stories are real. Don't you remember Hugh's hospital room?" Simon looked at Celina.

She shrugged and said, "Memory cleanse."

Simon sighed and said, "Angels are real. Look, I don't have time to walk you through this gently. Sandy was kidnapped by one of Lucifer's men this morning. You're an electrician, and our team is in the process of screwing up Luc's compound's panel box. Your sister seems to think you'll help us. I need an answer, George." Simon looked like a ten-year-old kid as he jumped up and waved his hand in front of George's face.

Celina placed her hand on George's forearm. "It's all right, George. Do not be afraid because I am with you."

George blinked and rubbed his eyes. "What in tarnation? I'm not dreaming you." He pinched Simon, who punched George in the gut. George let out an *ooof* and doubled over, gasping for air.

Celina narrowed her eyes at Simon. "You have the finesse of an alley cat." She turned to George and placed her hands on his shoulders. "George, are you with us?"

George nodded and came to an upright position. "You little shit. Hit me like that again and I'll knock your ass out."

Simon laughed and said, "I like you, George. Will you help us? We need to go to the barn. Um, your mom and sister have inducted you into the Campbell Ridge wards. Let me see. Erinelle said I had to give you power. I got it. The power to appear and disappear." Simon vanished, reappeared behind George, and tapped him on the shoulder.

George nearly jumped out of his skin. "Jesus, you want to give me a freaking heart attack? I'll do anything for Sandy D. She's like my little sister, too."

Simon said, "Great. No time to waste." Celina grabbed one of George's hands, and Simon grabbed the other. Seconds later, they materialized inside the barn.

George looked around the barn, stupefied. He'd been in his office and, like magic, he was in his parents' barn. Angels were everywhere. He glanced over and saw his mom, Ruby, and Reed.

Ruby ran over to her brother and grabbed his hand. "I knew you would come. Look, we're going to give you a crash course on our powers. It's okay, Georgie, breathe." Ruby spoke so swiftly he wondered if he should take notes.

Lee draped an arm around his waist. "I tried to keep one of my kids out of the loop for purely selfish reasons. But you're smart, and I know you won't do anything stupid like be a hero. We work as a team, or we don't work. Got it?"

George turned to Reed and said, "If y'all are a part of this incredible other world, why in the heck did you wait so long to include me? Sign me up. I'm all in. Oh, and by the way, my wife is divorcing me."

All eyes turned to George. Lee said, "I'm sorry. I prayed Lizzie would have a change of heart. Don't be hard on her. She left to give you a chance at having a family. I tried to talk her out of it. But you're so crazy around Joe, and she didn't want you to suffer."

"If she truly loved me, she'd never have left in the first place. Look, I don't want to talk about Lizzie. Take me to your leader. I'm ready to kick some demon ass."

Chapter 10

Greatest Love of All

DRIVING ALONG THE WINDING COUNTRY road, Jerry rolled his window halfway down to breathe in fresh air. Springtime was less than a month away, and the burst of warm air would have the buttercups and tulips on the verge of blooming before March. This time last year, he'd been engaged to Rachel Doune, Nelson's daughter.

Ruby's grandfather, Joseph Campbell, had died. His death brought Anna home to him. He remembered the moment he set eyes on Anna at Ruby's house. Anna stood at the door with her suitcase, and they'd locked eyes. They spoke no words because none were needed. He knew he still loved her and couldn't marry Rachel. *Boy, what a whirlwind those few days had been.*

He and Anna ran away to her condo in Florida and Rachel followed. Rachel had been possessed by demon angels and pulled a gun on Anna. Anna risked her life to save them all. Anna emitted an incredible glowing light around her physical form that he later learned was the light of love. Demon angels seek the light of love, and Baldric sliced the demons to ash, to the Eternal Darkness.

Baldric, the bad-ass warrior, married Sandy. He didn't know if he should congratulate Baldric or tell him he was sorry. Sandy continually placed herself in danger for her news stories. Luc kidnapping Sandy seemed unreal. But the guardian training they'd received would prove very useful in their attempts to rescue Sandy.

Anna looked at Jerry and said, "Do you think about Rachel?

Things happen for a reason. I believe it. Rachel and Jack are getting married, and we need Nelson. Everything that happened last year has led us to this moment in time to save Sandy."

Jerry squeezed Anna's hand. "Yeah, thinking about last year and thanking God daily for having you in my life. I believe things happen for a reason. I know we're not supposed to question the Almighty. But why didn't He warn us Sandy was the catalyst in the coming battle that the encrypted message revealed? Maybe I read it wrong."

Anna slid next to him in the truck cab. "Sandy's free will lead her to Luc's book and exposed all those terrible facts about Cole. Good and evil sometimes go hand and hand. I don't understand the whys. I gave up trying. I concentrate on making decisions which are proactive in the fight against the darkness and the coming battle." She pointed and waved. "Look, Jerry. Nelson has some new colts in the front lot."

Jerry turned onto the pebble stone driveway of Nelson Doune Farms, stopped at the gate, and rolled down the window.

Zeke opened the door to the gatehouse and grinned. "Hello, Missy. How's this ole boy treating you?"

Anna waved and leaned over in the truck cab. "He's the best. Life been treating you right?"

Zeke took the toothpick out of his mouth. "Ain't got no complaints."

Jerry interrupted Anna and Zeke's chitchat. "Hey, man, hate to cut to the chase, but we're in a bit of a bind. Is the big man home? We need to see him. It's urgent."

Zeke waved him through the gate. "I'll telephone Hazel. She'll be glad to see you. Oh, and Rachel is up there, too." He sniggered.

Anna rolled her eyes and waved goodbye. "Zeke is a mess. Does it still bother you to be around Rachel?"

"Nah, I just wonder sometimes if she still hates me." He pulled into the circular driveway and put the truck in park.

"We're getting ready to find out. She's coming out the front door."

Rachel ran down the front steps of the plantation house and opened Anna's door. "Look, Anna, look. Jack went all out and bought me a three-carat diamond."

Anna held Rachel's hand and inspected the rock. "It's simply gorgeous, sweetie. Are you as happy as you look?"

Rachel pinned Jerry with a look and said, "Much more thrilled than I was with him. Jack *loves* me, and he's wonderful." Anna slipped out of the truck and tossed Jerry a glance. She shrugged her shoulders and followed Rachel inside the house.

Jerry didn't think Rachel would ever cut him any slack. He turned off the truck, jumped out, and closed the door behind him. Jerry followed the two women inside Nelson's home, and Hazel met him at the door.

Hazel leaned into Jerry's shoulder and quietly said, "Zeke called. Mr. Doune is waiting for you in the study."

Jerry picked the older lady up, hugged her, and set her back down. "Miss Hazel, I've missed you."

Hazel blushed and said, "Aw, Mr. McDaniel, I've missed you, too."

Walking into the study brought back memories. Not good ones, either. Unfortunately, this visit wasn't social. The room was still full of Nelson's taxidermy trophies. The mahogany secretary and leather chairs sat on deep crimson and gold handmade rugs. Nelson sat at the elaborately carved eighteenth-century American desk writing out checks.

Jerry walked over and extended his hand, and Nelson reached out and shook it. "You need to let me hook you up with one of my computers. It'll save you time and automatically tracks expenses. Just sold a new line to the Bank of Eagleville. Hey, thanks for meeting me on short notice. I need your help."

Nelson looked over his reading glasses. "You always do. Let's have a drink next to the fire, and you can lay it on me. Did you see Rachel?"

Jerry followed him to the bar. "Yeah, she's still pissed."

Nelson chuckled and raised a brow. "That's my girl. Whiskey?"

"Sure. Just one shot. I need to keep a clear head." Jerry sat in the leather chair, holding the cocktail glass in his hand. He filled Nelson in on the information he had on Sandy's abduction. He didn't refer to Luc or the demon angels. "We're fairly confident Cole has Sandy somewhere on his estate. Would you allow us access to your farm to scope out the place? And, um, think Zeke and the boys could mess with the electrical panel box? It's our only way inside the main house. Ruby's brother, George, is an electrical contractor."

Nelson drank his shot and set it down on the side table. "Are you sure you didn't work for the mob? And did you contact the police?"

Jerry crossed his boots at the ankles and leaned back in the chair. "I know you have dealings with the man. I'm pretty sure you're aware he has important people in high places, including the police. We need to confirm he has Sandy. Then we'll make a plan."

Nelson placed his elbow on the arm of the chair. "Interesting. Jackie, his assistant, called, and he wanted a meeting. Then she called back an hour later. Cole's in jail and Carson Jones has taken control of the business and the estate. I think something a lot bigger is going on than you want to tell me, am I right? But I guess I could get the boys to mess with the panel box. They typically play cards with Cole's guards after hours."

Jerry took a deep breath and let it out. "Great. Nelson, you asked for it." Jerry gave Nelson the shortened version of the angelic war, the wards, and the coming battle. "That's why Sandy was kidnapped. I'm fairly sure the angels in the room with us will wipe your memory of this event after we gain access to Luc's estate."

Luwenia appeared in her armor before Nelson. She knelt on one knee. "Sir, we need your assistance. I'll make a vow neither you nor your family will suffer any consequences for our actions."

Nelson stared at Jerry's breathtaking guardian angel. "You have my cooperation. You're stunning. Jerry, you sure know how to pick 'em."

"Luwenia was assigned to me, and she's in love with Anna's angel." Luwenia cut her eyes at him, and his lips curved into a smile. "True."

Nelson threw his head back and laughed. "How appropriate."

Luwenia reached out and clasped Nelson on the forearm. "We must take our leave. Thank you for your help."

"Um, okay. You're welcome." Nelson rose from the chair.

Jerry reached into his coat pocket, pulled out a card, and handed it to Nelson. "Here's a few numbers to call me when the panel is compromised."

Jerry walked with Nelson into the main foyer. He caught Anna's eye, and with a nod of his head, he motioned for her to come to him.

Anna reached over and gave Rachel a hug. "I can't wait to hear all about the wedding. Jerry, Rachel and Jack are eloping to Aruba."

Jerry nodded to Rachel and said, "I wish you all the happiness in the world."

Rachel rolled her eyes at Jerry. "Oh, you're still so full of shit. Bye, Anna. We'll do lunch when I get back. Maybe the four of us could go to dinner one night." Rachel cast Jerry a weak grin as he left with Anna out the door.

They ran down the steps, and Jerry helped Anna into the truck. He went around to the driver's side and got in. "I had to tell Nelson the truth. Luwenia, why did you clasp his arm?"

Luwenia didn't materialize but replied, "I had to see if Nelson spoke the truth. He's on the naughty list."

BALDRIC WOKE A FEW MINUTES later in the calming chair. The chair emitted an electrical charge, zapping him anytime he fought to get out. The chair zapped him if he tried to scream. His mind raced as he thought what Luc could be doing to Sandy, and the chair zapped him. The electrical shocks continued until he was near tears when Ruby approached him.

Ruby pulled a chair in front of Baldric and sat down. She proceeded to tell him the plans the Campbell Ridge wards and the guardians had developed to rescue Sandy. George agreed to go undercover, and Nelson Doune decided to allow access to his farm so the wards and guardians could enter Luc's compound. Nelson's boys stripped some breakers from the panel before the estate called an electrician. The guardians intercepted the call and redirected it to George's company, Champion Electric.

George scheduled a morning appointment to access the damage and scope the interior of the compound. Celina would use her faze to infiltrate the humans for a head count and try to get a sense for the number of demon angels on the premises.

Ruby said, "Baldric, we need you to remain calm and use your marking to pinpoint the cavern's entrance and find where they're holding Sandy. You'll compromise my brother's life if you do something stupid. Erinelle and the other guardians are developing a military strategy for the battle. Then you can unleash your anger on the demons and Luc. But first, you have to assure me you will remain calm. Will you allow me to ask Erinelle for your release? Are you ready to plan and execute Sandy's rescue?"

Baldric closed his eyes and nodded. "Yes. I'll need help standing because this damn chair has zapped me too many times. Calming chair? They need to call it the limp noodle chair."

Ruby went to him and touched the side of his face. "My friend is very blessed to have you as her husband. I'm happy for both of you."

His head dropped, and tears fell onto his lap. "I'm not worthy. I failed her as a spouse. I didn't protect her."

Ruby stomped her foot. "I will not have that kind of negative crap coming out of your mouth. Sandy had Luc's book. She knew he would come for her. She just didn't expect it so soon. They were watching her every move. Cole and an elite group of demon angels struck as soon as you left the ethereal plane, and they overwhelmed the warriors that were in place for her protection. Stop the bullshit and let's get my friend home. I mean, I need to plan her a wedding shower."

Baldric's lips turned upward ever so slightly. "I'm ready. Get Erinelle." He'd battled Luc many times and prayed for a miracle. Baldric didn't know how they would penetrate Luc's compound without significant injuries and possibly casualties.

THE GUARDIANS OF CAMPBELL RIDGE along with several divisions of the AAF trained in the barn and out in the back lot. The double doors at the front and back of the barn, and every side door was open to allow the breezy, warm air to circulate.

Ruby pulled her mom off to the side, next to the stall where Baldric had been in the calming chair. "Mom, I need to go to the hospital and tell Hugh and Sally about Sandy. What should I tell them?"

Lee began to straighten the bridles, reins, and bits along with the other tack that had fallen to the ground during Baldric's struggle. "You have to tell them the truth. I spoke with Erinelle before the meeting this afternoon. She agrees. Baldric is their son-in-law and needs to go with you. Reed's practicing with the warriors in the barn lot, so take Daddy's truck. Your Jeep is blocked in."

"Where's Baldric?"

Lee laughed and said, "Eating me out of house and home."

"Gotcha. Oh, what about her boss? She's off for a few more days. Should I call him?"

Scratching an eyebrow, Lee said, "What a mess. Let's wait a day or so before calling her boss. The fewer people that know about Sandy's kidnapping, the better. The angels will have an enormous cleanup regardless. I don't see another recourse but to fight for Sandy. Ruby, please be careful. Little Joe needs his mommy."

Ruby kissed her cheek. "I'll do my best, Mom." She left out the side door and ran up the hill in the backyard to the kitchen door. The kitchen looked like a war zone. Baldric and Harry had devoured several pepperoni pizzas and two apple pies. Little Joe was in his playpen sound asleep.

Ruby opened the fridge and pulled out a pitcher of sweet tea. After she had poured a glass, she sat on one of the bar stools because the table looked disgusting. "Baldric, when you're finished eating, we need to take a drive to the hospital. It's time you officially met your in-laws."

Harry choked and coughed before taking a drink of tea. "I forgot Hugh is still in the hospital. What are you going to tell them?"

Baldric tore off a paper towel and wiped his mouth. "The truth. They deserve it. Hey, Harry, I hate to leave the mess and run."

Harry scooped up another spoon of pie. "Go on. Joe has another hour of sleep. Besides, that's why I bought a dishwasher. Might as well use it. I called in more pizza from Rose. She's bringing them with a case of Cokes in a bit. I figured it would be the easiest way to feed everyone. Give Sally and Hugh our love."

Ruby grabbed the truck keys off the hook next to the back door. "My Jeep is blocked in, so Mom said to use yours." Harry nodded with a mouth full of pie and waved Ruby out the door.

On the drive to the hospital, neither Ruby nor Baldric said anything until Main Street. He looked at Ruby, and she glanced at him. In a quiet voice, she said, "I dread telling them. I don't know what to say."

Baldric stared out the window. "It needs to come from me. I'll tell them."

"This isn't your fault." Ruby turned into the hospital parking lot and found a spot close to the entrance.

"It is my fault. I should've done my job. But I'll never regret marrying her." Baldric's armor mysteriously changed into human clothes.

It was the first time Ruby had ever seen Baldric in street clothes. He wore blue jeans with a navy crewneck sweater and a pair of Timberlands. Ruby teased, "Sandy would flip out seeing you in jeans. Has she ever seen you in clothes? Oh, you know, something besides your armor gear."

Baldric's green eyes seemed dull, and he replied, "No. I rarely wear street clothes. I'm going to deliver a major shock to her parents, so I just thought it might be easier looking a little more human."

Baldric walked in his physical form toward the entrance. Ruby noticed his typical swagger was gone, replaced by a slower gait. Her heart ached for Sandy and Baldric. They took the elevator to the second floor. Every female, civilian and hospital staff alike, stopped and stared openly at the hunk walking by them. He was oblivious to his effect on the women.

Stepping out of the elevator, Ruby and Baldric walked several doors down and stopped at Hugh's room. Ruby knocked softly and said, "Is it okay to come in?"

Sally replied, "It's okay, Ruby." Hugh was sitting up in a reclining chair, and Sally lay on the bed thumbing through a *Town & Country* magazine.

Hugh wore a pair of blue-and-green plaid pajamas with black slippers. "Hey, girlie. I'm glad you came to see us. We've been trying to call Sandy. Have you heard from her?"

Ruby shut the door and pulled the blinds. "Hugh, Sally, this is Baldric. He is, well, he is…"

Baldric interrupted and said, "I'm Sandy's husband." Hugh's eyes went wide with surprise, and Sally's hand went to her mouth. With respect, Baldric said, "Please hear me out before you ask questions."

Baldric started from the beginning, at Sandy's birth, and did a chronological account of his relationship with their daughter. He explained Sandy's divine calling and power. Her parents were struck silent and appeared to be in shock.

In a flash of white light, Baldric appeared in his armor, and his beautiful, shimmering wings expanded. "The evening of your car accident, Sandy and I were married at St. Timothy's by the Spirit of Man. It's forbidden for a human and angel to get married. But Sandy and I belong together. I was summoned to appear before my commander and archangel, Michael, and The Creator. No outside communication is available during closed-door meetings. The Creator delivered news to me about Sandy's abduction."

Baldric paused and went on one knee before Hugh and looked up into his eyes. "Sandy was kidnapped by Cole Steele, who works for Lucifer. Sandy possessed Luc's Testament, a very powerful book containing the souls of the damned and incantations, along with personal entries of Luc's existence on earth. He wanted the book back, and he's using Sandy to get me. Our pairing left him an opening to take her without me for protection. The angels sent to relieve me were overpowered by the demon angels. Some of our angels are still recovering in The Treatment Center from the injuries sustained during the attack. I vow to you, her father and mother, I will get Sandy back."

Ruby nearly rubbed the skin off the pads of her fingers from nerves. Hugh looked at her and said, "Is this true?"

Ruby stepped over and placed her hand on Baldric's shoulder. "Yes, sir. I know it must seem like something out a fairy tale or movie, but I tell you the truth. There's supernatural warfare going on around us every single minute of every day. You all are members of St. Timothy's. The stories, the Bible classes, it's real, not something abstract you read in the Bible and then go about your everyday business."

Hugh reached over and gently placed his hand on top of Baldric's head. "It was you. You're the one who whispered to me about Ben Salinger hurting Sandy."

Baldric nodded and folded his arms over his knee. "Yes, sir. That's the day I started breaking the rules. Every human has free will. Ben's free will inflicted abuse on Sandy. I wasn't supposed to interfere, but I did."

Hugh broke down and cried. Sally jumped off of the bed and placed her arms around his shoulders. "It's going to be okay. Baldric will bring her back to us. He'll save Sandy." She turned to Baldric and asked, "You will save her?"

"Yes, ma'am. I will. I vow to you both I'll not stop until I get Sandy back."

Ruby watched Baldric with Sandy's parents. She prayed silently to The Creator to give them strength. She had a bad feeling. A memory from a dream long ago flashed across her mind. People were injured and screaming. Was the coming battle the same as her dream? Would she lose people she loved? Destruction and darkness were coming for them all, but they would fight for the light.

Chapter 11

Human

LUCIFER ENTERED SANDY'S CHAMBER THROUGH his adjoining door. He walked over to her bed and looked down at the human female. The light of heaven shone on her face, and he became jealous and homesick. He sat on the bed and brushed the hair away from her face.

She rubbed her eyes, stretched, and yawned. "CJ?"

Luc frowned and raised a brow. She had to be referring to Caiojezeal. "No, it isn't CJ. I was just checking to see if you were comfortable."

She sat up on the bed and pulled the covers to her chin. "You shouldn't be in my bedroom. It's not proper."

Luc chuckled and said, "Who are you?"

"I'm Dee. It's what CJ called me. I can't remember who I am or where I am. But the room is beautiful, and I love the mountains."

Luc looked around the dark chamber with only a few pieces of furniture and a stone fireplace. No windows and certainly no mountains were in the caverns. Caiojezeal had outdone himself with the memory cleansing and had given Dee a pleasant image to ease her mind. *Whatever.* "What have you and CJ been doing while I've been away?"

"He took me for a walk in the caverns to the blue pools. It was super fun."

Luc didn't know if he liked the juvenile Dee, but he decided to play along. "Would you like to swim in the pool?"

With excitement, she replied, "Would I ever. I have a closet full of clothes. I bet there's a swimming suit in there."

"Hmmm, a whole closet of clothes, you say? Why don't you look for a suit and I'll wait for you."

Dee jumped from the bed and ran into the closet from the bathroom. She emerged later wearing a white halter top swimsuit, making Luc adjust his jeans. She said, "This is the only suit I found. I don't feel old, but when I looked into the mirror, I had boobs, big ones."

Luc threw his head back and laughed. "You certainly do." There was something about this human he couldn't wrap his head around. Usually, all humans revolted him. This human had a feisty spirit, and she made him laugh. Sandy would be furious when she figured out about the memory cleanse. He couldn't wait. Luc reached for her hand, and she took it. He chuckled to himself. Luc liked Sandy all hot and bothered. Not like some giddy schoolgirl.

Luc and Dee walked through the caverns, and she looked up at him with a curious expression on her face. "It must've cost a fortune to run electricity down here, but the different colored lights reflecting off the stalactites are phenomenal."

He leaned next to her ear and said, "What if I told you it was magic lighting the caverns? Would you believe me?"

"Aw, you're trying to pull my leg." She giggled and followed the natural stone steps down to the pool. He watched her as she descended to dip her toes in the water. "The water is warm. Is it deep enough to jump in?"

Luc waved his hand and said, "Jump away."

Dee submerged herself into the clear blue water. Luc watched as she rose to the top and broke the water's surface. "Wow, it's very deep. I couldn't touch the bottom." She swam over to the edge and placed her chin on top of her hands. "Aren't you getting in?"

Luc began to undress, and Dee screamed, "Aren't you going to get your suit?"

"No, darling, I prefer to skinny dip." Luc dropped his jeans, and Dee turned her head. He entered the pool and swam to her and turned her to face him. The blood rushed into Dee's cheeks.

Dee playfully splashed water on him. "Keep your distance, mister."

Luc shook his head in disbelief. He looked up to the cave's ceiling and then said, "I can't take another minute of this bullshit. The school-aged kid routine doesn't do a thing for me." He snapped his fingers and said, "Daireann, wake up."

SANDY NERVOUSLY GLANCED ABOUT THE cave's chamber. She slowly backed against the stone wall of the pool. She gritted her teeth and shouted, "How in the hell did you get me into the pool and who put this swimming suit on me?"

Luc chuckled and treaded water, inching closer to Sandy. "Now that's more like it. Caiojezeal must have a thing for little girls. I told him to give you a memory wipe, not make you a kid. I'll talk to him. Music, cocktails?" Soft jazz bounced off the walls, and a frozen margarita materialized in Sandy's hand.

Sandy pushed herself up on the stone ledge to climb out of the pool. But Luc flipped her around to face him using his powers, not his hands. "I'm not through playing with you in the pool."

A lithe female demon angel sauntered into the pool room. Her bronze skin shimmered in the reflective light. Her short black hair was slicked back behind her pointy ears. Her *Bambi* eyes were a deep azure. She reached down and took the drink Sandy had discarded. Something about the female reminded Sandy of a magical fairy in the storybooks. She ran her fingers through Sandy's hair with care. "What's she doing here? I didn't think you were into humans."

On the opposite side of the pool from Sandy, Luc sat on the stone ledge, kicking his feet back and forth in the water. "I've never been into humans. But there's something about this female that intrigues me. Are you jealous, Sazae?"

Sazae stripped off her clothes and dove into the pool. She swam over to Luc and ran her hand between his legs. "No, I don't have to be jealous. The human female hates you."

"Hate is such a lovely word." Luc turned to Sandy and asked, "Please, tell me you hate me, and we'll be moving in the right direction, love."

Sandy's lips thinned over her teeth, and she clenched her jaw. "I despise you."

Luc clapped his hands. "Oh, happy day." He grabbed Sazae and crushed her with a kiss. "Sandy, watch. I want you to see what you're missing. But, most important of all, I want to smell your arousal when I take Sazae." He jumped into the pool and entered the female demon angel, and Saze arched her back in response while emitting moans of pleasure. He shouted to Sandy, "I said look, human."

Sandy went wild with fear when Luc made Sazae appear in Sandy's image. Luc crooned, "See yourself as I enjoy the ride." He grabbed Sazae, who looked like Sandy, by the head of her hair and pushed her under the water.

Sandy retched onto the stone floor.

He laughed and said, "Do you taste me in your mouth?"

Caiojezeal entered the pool room and saw Sandy giving Luc underwater oral and frowned. He glanced across the pool, and another Sandy was throwing up on the stone floor. Caiojezeal swiftly reached down and lifted the real Sandy into his arms. He glared at Luc and hissed, "You are one sick bastard."

"Yeah, well, what's new? Into kiddies, CJ? What's up turning my Sandy into a little girl? Just leave her with the memory of me in the pool. I want the image burned into her brain. Erase everything else."

Sazae emerged from the water. Luc had returned her appearance. "What's wrong with her?"

Caiojezeal gritted his teeth and replied, "Ask your husband." Sandy glared at Luc before burrowing her face into Caiojezeal's neck.

Luc threw a stream of greenish, glowing fire swirling around Sandy and Caiojezeal that bounced off the walls of the cavern as they walked away. Laughing, Luc yelled out, "You can run, Sandy, but you can't hide." Luc laughed again and yelled, "Hey, great idea, let's play hide and seek later."

Caiojezeal held Sandy in his arms as she shivered. "It's okay. He was playing mind games with you. You must stay strong, or you'll not last here. He didn't touch you. He just made the illusion seem real. Look at me. Come on, look at me."

Sandy lifted her head and cried, "Where's Baldric? Why hasn't he come for me? He's supposed to protect me. That vile thing in the pool. I hate Luc. Help me, Caiojezeal. Please help me escape."

Caiojezeal walked into her bedroom and sat her down in a chair next to the fireplace and draped a blanket over her shoulders.

"You're in shock. Your emotions will change from one minute to the next. Anger and then fear one minute, and then next you'll be in denial, and the next after that, you'll be overcome with anxiety."

He crouched down next to her. "I know Baldric. He'll come for you. Based on my experience with the AAF, they probably restrained him. The AAF needs him thinking clearly, not busting down the doors getting you killed. That's what Luc wants. He's deliberately using you to get to Baldric. Don't help him do it."

Sandy's hands trembled as she held herself tightly. "I...I was abused as a child. What Luc just did to me in the pool, well, he abused my mind. I have to get out of here. Help me."

Caiojezeal stood and placed his hands on the mantle. He stared into the fire. "I'm trying to find a way to assist you without going against a direct order. Under Luc's authority, if I go against him, I'll get thrown into the Eternal Blackness, and you'll be alone."

Caiojezeal knelt back in front of her and held onto her thighs. "Do what you must to survive, whatever you must. There are other prisoners in the caverns. Other wards like you. They're doomed because Luc has lost interest. Once he possesses your power and the essence of your soul, you'll no longer hold his favor. Play his game. Become an award-winning actress and just maybe, when the AAF infiltrates the compound, you'll still be alive."

Sandy closed her eyes and said, "I need to sleep if I'm to fight that wretched being. Make me sleep."

Caiojezeal lifted Sandy from the chair and placed her on the bed. He put his hands over her eyes and Sandy slept.

NIGHT FELL QUICKLY, AND ONE by one the AAF angels, guardians, and wards retreated from Everglade Farms. All except the Legion left to protect the exterior boundaries of the farm. Baldric placed his hands on the doorframe as he stared up at the sliver of a moon and the twinkling stars. He waited for what seemed to be an eternity, and when the coast was clear, he ported to the edge of Nelson Doune Farms.

In the top of a hundred-year-old oak tree, Baldric watched and listened for any signs his position had tripped Luc's sensors, but no alarms rang out, and no demon angels appeared. The outline of Luc's

Arrington Estate was impressive. The main house set on a hill with open lots in the front and back of the property. Any human could detect encroachment from all angles of the main house. A half dozen human guards stood atop the main roof with automatic weapons. Only two guards watched the outbuildings and barn. The enemies' weakest flank. He made a mental note.

Baldric wasn't scouting weak links tonight. He had to see if Sandy was here. He had to try to find her through their pairing cord of light. He settled himself in the sturdy branches and allowed his mind to travel out of his body and along the pairing chords of light.

Mental images flashed across his mind. Sandy had been brought in through the side door of the main house. He saw Caiojezeal carrying an unconscious Sandy in his arms. Baldric's pairing scent flared. His scent became stronger the further he traveled along the cord. He centered his emotions so he wouldn't set off an alarm among the demon angels stationed around the estate.

After a few minutes, Baldric relaxed and picked up the image of Sandy with Caiojezeal. He walked through the kitchen, past the main foyer, and down a long hallway to the back of the house. Caiojezeal pressed his hand on a hidden wall panel in what appeared to be the TV and entertainment room. A large television, movie projector, and pool table were in the dark hunter green room with dim lighting. The room had only one window with dark gold, and green drapes pulled together.

The hidden panel opened the wall to manmade stairs. As Caiojezeal descended with Sandy, Baldric noticed what looked like compassion in Caiojezeal's eyes. *Aw, hell, the poor son of a bitch.* Baldric had seen the same look on enough men to last a lifetime. Caiojezeal was hooked. That could work in the AAF's favor. Turn the demon to the cause, offer leniency, and maybe Caiojezeal would help with the escape plan.

On the second landing, Caiojezeal placed his hand on a rock wall that barely opened wide enough for one person, much less two. Caiojezeal turned sideways and continued down the natural stone steps, and the chamber opened up to reveal the caverns. Magic spells lit the vast underground caverns. Except for the stalactites, the underground caverns resembled a stone palace from antiquity. Baldric's pairing cord took him deep inside Luc's lair.

Caiojezeal entered a room with Sandy, and she awoke. She looked confused, and it didn't take a rocket scientist to know Sandy had undergone a memory cleanse. Baldric listened and watched Caiojezeal turn the dark stone room into a chalet in the mountains. Her bedroom made of stone transformed into an illusion of a rustic pine bed with brightly patterned quilts and soft pillows.

Baldric didn't know if he wanted to kill Caiojezeal or hug the bastard. Sandy fell asleep, and Caiojezeal left the room. After what seemed like hours, The Dragon walked into Sandy's chamber. Baldric ghosted to the door when Luc entered, and his chest tightened. Luc placed Sandy in the room next to his own. *Dear Lord, help me.* Luc woke an innocent Sandy, a little girl in a woman's body, and took her to the cavern's pool.

Baldric's cord began to burn bright red as he watched the scene unfold with Sandy and the female demon angel. He had to get his wife out of here fast. Luc never slept with humans, but Baldric read his mind. Luc was thinking about having sex with Sandy. Baldric remembered Luc's vow from a time in heaven, thousands of years ago. Luc's words came back to haunt him. *I will lay with any female I choose, especially if she's promised to you.*

Thankfully, Caiojezeal rescued Sandy before Luc made good on his promise. Baldric listened as Caiojezeal pleaded with Sandy to do what she must to survive. Baldric had to get Sandy out of there before Luc took her. It would break their pairing and their bond, forever. Infidelity in any form wasn't tolerated and would split a pairing whether the act was intentional or not. Luc knew the rules. He knew it would destroy Baldric if he slept with his pairing partner.

Caiojezeal left the room and planted his ass outside of Sandy's door. Baldric only had a few minutes before his pairing scent raised alarms.

"Sandy. Wake up. It's Baldric. Please, honey, wake up." Baldric looked over his shoulder. He was in his ethereal form, but his scent was overpowering in the room.

Sandy sat up groggily in the bed and recognition lit her face. "Thank God, you came. I knew you would come for me." She frowned and narrowed her eyes. "Why has it taken you so freaking long?"

"I'm sorry, honey. I didn't know what happened. I had no communication with earth while I was in the command center or the throne room. Once I found out, I ran to you, and the AAF subdued me in a calming chair. Not pleasant, to tell you the truth. Listen to me. I don't have long. I have to follow the AAF protocol because you aren't the only captive down here. We're coming for you and the others. I love you. I have to go before they catch me. I'll be back. I promise." Baldric leaned over and kissed her gently on the lips. Even in his ethereal form, he could feel her sweet, full lips.

Frantically, Sandy reached for him and cried, "Baldric, don't leave me here. Please take me with you."

"I risk your life and the others if I try to act alone. I promise I'll be back soon, and that son of a bitch is going to pay for kidnapping you. I promise you, my Daireann." Baldric dematerialized to the barn.

Erinelle waited for him. "You're the most stubborn angel I've ever known. You placed the entire operation in jeopardy."

Baldric roared into the night air. He picked up a square bale of hay and threw it into the outside lot. "I didn't get caught, and I know where she is. We have to work fast. Sandy doesn't have much time. With or without the AAF's permission, I'm going back for her either tomorrow morning or tomorrow night. You decide. I saw Luc's plans for Sandy. He plans on taking my bride." Sandy's look of distrust and disbelief ripped out his heart.

Erinelle sat on the metal gate leading out to the cow pasture. "It's too soon. We'll place the Campbell Ridge wards in harm's way. I need at least one more day of training before we execute retrieval of the captives. Well, did you get a layout of where Luc's keeping Sandy? How many human guards? How many demon angels? Anything that'll be of use to our military strategy?"

"One more day. Or I'm going in by myself and don't try to pull that trick again with the calming chair. I swear I'll strap you to it."

Erinelle chuckled. "You were limp as a dish rag when we took you out of it. I'm sorry. You weren't thinking clearly. I had to do something. You'd have done the same thing, and you know it."

Baldric propped his forearms on the gate and looked up at Erinelle. "All right, the estate has roughly a dozen human guards with automatic weapons. A half dozen on the main house roof. The house sits on a hill, and the guards can easily pick off anyone who tries to enter. Two additional guards for the barn and one guard for the outbuildings. The north left flank is where we should enter."

Baldric flew up and sat on the front tire of Harry's tractor. Pulling from thin air, he produced a screen and began to draw an outline of the buildings, using Xs to mark the guards. "There's a tree line, and if we attack at dusk or dawn, we'll have sufficient cover to knock out the human guards at the outbuildings and barn. We can take positions in the barn and then eliminate the remaining boys on the roof. I'd say that'll give the division, oh, about five to ten minutes to scale the yard and enter the main house. I'll need two dozen AAF, skilled soldiers. I didn't get a head count of the demon angels, but I do have a suggestion."

Erinelle hopped on the other side of the tractor to make notes on Baldric's screen. "So, what's the suggestion?"

"My wife has turned the eye of Caiojezeal. Let me approach him. He may consider working as a spy if we offer him leniency. Maybe allow him in the AAF reconditioning program. He's a talented messenger and has many contacts."

Erinelle placed her finger over her mouth as she entertained his proposal. "How do you know Caiojezeal likes your wife?"

Baldric laughed and shook his head. "Come on, Erinelle. I've been Sandy's guardian and unfortunately seen her in action. The demon angel is smitten with her. I swear while I was replaying the events, part of me wanted to kill him, and the other part wanted to kiss his ass."

Erinelle waved her hand, and the screen disappeared. "Very well. But be sure before you offer him any deal. It could be a trap. Bringing down Baldric the Warrior would be a shining star on anyone's résumé, and that's exactly what Luc wants to do."

"At this point, I'm willing to take the chance because time is ticking. The longer Sandy stays in the cavern, the more her soul is at risk. Luc's twisted, and you've seen it firsthand." Erinelle winced at his reference. "Sorry." There had been few beaus in Erinelle's life since Lucifer broke her heart in heaven. Baldric thought for a second. No, Luc trampled Erinelle's heart with one of her best friends.

Luc's demon angels would work double time on Sandy's weaknesses. What made matters worse, Luc's private chamber adjoined Sandy's. He knew what the S.O.B. had on his mind, and sleeping wasn't it. "I want Sandy out of there before she can't remember me at all and before Luc brings her into his bed. I'm praying Luc is still vain. He'll want Sandy to come to him willingly."

SANDY SWUNG HER LEGS OVER on the side of the bed. Caiojezeal returned the illusion of the mountain chateau. Sandy knew it wasn't real, but the illusion kept her calm. Sleeping had helped her regain some strength. But seeing Baldric as a hologram left her with mixed feelings. He found her, and the son of a bitch left her here. She knew he couldn't just walk into Luc's compound, but damn it. Baldric left her here.

The door to Luc's chamber blew open, and he strode into her room. "Where's Baldric? I smell the son of a bitch." He stepped over to her and yelled, "Tell me, human whore."

Sandy took a deep breath and calmly replied, "You're delusional."

Wrong answer. *Whack!* Luc backhanded her. "Answer me, now."

Sandy should've cowered, but she hated abusers in any form, including Satan. "Screw you."

Luc raised Sandy into the air and slammed her against the uneven rock wall of the cavern. Caiojezeal's mountain chalet illusion shattered. The room became cold and smelled of dank earth. Luc said, "I can go all day." With his mind, Luc raised her up the wall about three feet off the ground, making her arms and legs spread-eagle. He materialized a cat of nine tails from thin air into his hand and cracked it loudly in the air. Caiojezeal rushed into the room, and Luc cut his eyes toward him and said, "Out. Now."

Caiojezeal pleaded, "But sire, you don't want to do this to Baldric's wife. You know there are rules. Pairing partners of any angels are off limits on either side of the war. You'll have to answer to The Creator." Caiojezeal looked back and forth between Sandy and Luc.

Luc ran his hand along the whip cord. "Caiojezeal, you can be next if you like. You can even watch, but shut your mouth or I'll rip out your tongue. Got it?"

Caiojezeal's opalescent wings jutted up while he planted his feet on the ground. "You may do what you like to me, but let her down. Don't torture her."

"Fine."

Caiojezeal exhaled as Sandy hit the stone floor. In a flash, Caiojezeal replaced Sandy and was splayed out on the wall. Luc said, "Looks like you've snared another admirer, among many, I'm sure. This is your fault, Daireann." Luc began to flog Caiojezeal, ripping and tearing out his flesh, lash after lash until Caiojezeal's head hung low.

Sandy watched in abject horror. She couldn't tell if Caiojezeal was alive or dead. She screamed, "Stop it. Please stop it. I'll tell you what you want to know. Please stop hurting him."

Luc's eyes glowed red, and his skin shimmered with sweat. He turned slowly, and an evil smile crept across his lips. "Well, I'm waiting." He cracked the whip in the air, barely missing Caiojezeal's face.

From somewhere down deep in her soul, Sandy pulled off the performance of a lifetime. "I dreamed of Baldric. I dreamed we were making love. I dreamed of him taking me from every position, over and over. You were smelling his scent because I came. His mark is on my body. Not Baldric's physical form, but his essence."

Luc walked around Sandy, inhaling and sniffing like the beast he was. He cupped her privates and held her stare. Sandy tilted her head back slightly, parted her lips, and stared at Luc with heavy lids. In her mind, Sandy thickened the multicolored cords of light to block her real thoughts, praying it was enough, praying Luc believed she wanted him.

Luc went from maniac to charming in less than a second. "Darling, I would've accommodated you had I known you were in need of release." He raised a brow. "Are you in need of release?"

Sandy never wavered her gaze from Luc's eyes. "No, I'm quite weak-kneed at the moment."

"Tomorrow evening, I shall take you on a trip. I'll show you what I can lay before your feet if you join my side." Shaking his head, Luc chuckled and said, "You're proving to be a delightful distraction from the humdrum." He dropped Caiojezeal to the floor. "Clean up your friend. I'll see you tomorrow night." Luc dematerialized.

Sandy rushed to Caiojezeal. He was covered in blood, or what she thought was blood. "What can I do to help?"

Caiojezeal pulled his upper body upright and leaned against the wall. "Look in your fridge and bring me wine. The wounds will heal by morning. I need to get drunk. How about you? I've seen Luc flog others, but he's never laid a hand on me. I've faithfully served Luc since our fall to earth."

Sandy rummaged inside the fridge and then through the cabinet doors, opening one after the other. "Eureka, I found a bottle." She brought the bottle with a silver goblet to him.

Caiojezeal grabbed the bottle, pulled the cork out with his teeth and guzzled it. He said, "The wine has dulled the pain, but I'm afraid there's not much left. You want some?"

Sandy shook her head and slid down on the floor beside him. With her back against the wall, she asked, "Why did you do it? I'm grateful, but why did you do it?"

Caiojezeal ran his fingers through his hair and drew his right leg up to rest his forearm on his knee. "Beats me." He laughed and said, "We're stupid fools. Luc sees weakness as a challenge. Our compassion for one another, he'll use against us. I guess I did it because you reminded me of the warrior angel I used to be. The part of me still belonging to The Creator. And partly, because I'm sick of this war." He took a deep breath and exhaled, then winced with pain. "I've less than twenty-four hours to teach you ways to thwart Luc's come-on."

Sandy drew her knees up and wrapped her arms around them. "Why does he want me? He hates humans."

Caiojezeal turned up the bottle and drank. "One reason is you're Baldric's pairing partner. He made a vow to Baldric long ago that he'd sleep with any female Baldric was promised to. Luc sees humans as a blight on the earth. I don't think he desires you. Luc wants you to submit to him, and he wants your divine power."

Caiojezeal rubbed his jaw and with hesitation, he said, "Luc had around nine or ten wards in the Arrington's caves, below in his lower earth. Three turned to the darkness and were released to work both sides of the war. Three were tortured and died, keeping their souls intact. Three more are being worked over daily, and then there's you. He's placed a spell on you. Outside of this room, you won't remember much. If Baldric returns, you won't remember him. You won't remember your friends. I have no clue what the counter spell is. You may want to use your cords of light to find one in the book. I unbind you, Sandy. Oh, was Baldric here?"

Sandy didn't know if she could trust Caiojezeal, but she needed his help. "Ever since I was a little girl, Baldric and I have carried on conversations with the cords of light. He was in my mind, but he was real. He's coming for me."

"I hope, for your sake, he doesn't wait."

Chapter 12

Live To Tell

AFTER BREAKFAST, BALDRIC WAITED IMPATIENTLY for the AAF soldiers and the Campbell Ridge wards to arrive in the red barn. He worked out feverishly and still had energy to burn. He wanted to sever The Dragon, but The Creator kept waiting for the final battle of the war.

Erinelle appeared behind him and knocked him to his knees. "Thought you were ready, huh? You're thinking with your heart, not your head, soldier. The Creator waits for Luc to admit defeat. To humble himself and repent. To ask for forgiveness. The irony is Luc waits for the same thing. I can't imagine what it must've felt like to create something so beautiful and have the creation stab you in the back. Admittedly, even before the fall, The Creator saw how Luc treated the other angels."

Baldric draped an arm around her shoulders. "It's not our right to ask even though we think it. He'll end the war when it's His time, not ours, not the humans, and certainly not Luc's. Did you find me warriors?"

"Only the best. Me." She shoved Baldric away. "And more are arriving now."

The barn filled with warrior angels of varying sizes and shapes armed with weapons of mass destruction, Creator-style. Baldric watched Ruby and Reed, Jerry and Anna, Lee and George enter the area set up for sparring in the barn. The soldiers were ready. The wards were not. Each ward would be spotlighted in the center of the arena to fight an angel who wasn't their guardian, and the AAF warrior angels didn't play.

Erinelle walked up to Lee and said, "You up to the challenge?"

Lee placed a hand on her hip and raised a brow. "You asking?" They both laughed. "So, George doesn't have to go to Luc's compound?"

Erinelle said, "Yes, he does. Baldric has the vicinity of the captives. I need George to place bugging devices around the interior of the house. Any intel is better than what we have now. We attack at dawn tomorrow."

Lee stretched and said, "Place me in the arena first. Allow the kids to see what they're up against. They have to know going into a supernatural battle they may not come out."

Erinelle nodded and whistled. The roar in the barn became silent. "Lee has volunteered for the arena. Who will be her challenger?"

"I will." Raizeal stepped forward and bowed in front of Lee.

Lee and Raizeal stepped inside the arena, and the spectators shouted from both sides. Then the lights went out. Flashes of light from the blade on blade contact lit the room. Thumps and bumps, grunts and sighs filtered in the air. The lights came back on. Lee and Raizeal were in full-fledged combat mode. Blood oozed from the side of Lee's head, and flesh carved out of Raizeal's leg. Neither Lee nor Raizeal held back. They fought as if their lives depended on it. That was the point.

Baldric watched as Ruby held Reed's forearm, white-knuckled. He didn't know if Reed was holding Ruby back or vice versa. Seeing her mom battle for the first time had to be a shock. The AAF had been training the wards, but not like this angel-on-human combat. That was what the wards would face in the morning.

Lee did a back somersault into the air, knocking out two of Raizeal's teeth, and scissored her legs around his neck while she tried to claw his eyes out. The human was a fierce fighting machine. Lee had seen her share of battles since she was fifteen. Lee held on until Raizeal's knees hit the straw-and- dirt covered floor.

Erinelle whistled and yelled, "Time. The winner of this battle is Lee." The wards were jumping up and down. Lee and Raizeal walked to the triage set up by Ralph and Anna. Anna ran to Lee to heal her wounds while Ralph went over to treat Raizeal. Once they cleared the arena, Erinelle turned to the wards and said, "This isn't a game. This is not practice. You must fight to the death. I will stop the final blow. Your very life tomorrow depends on it. Are you ready?"

Ruby started to step up, but Reed held her back. He said, "Ruby, watch me fight. I'll use the spheres of light. That's your best fighting skill."

The roar went up, and Erinelle said, "In the pasture. I promised Harry not to burn down his barn. Who will challenge Reed?"

Kaduntz, the earth angel, said, "I know I'm party crashing, but my division of warriors wants to fight. We've been waiting years to get our shot at our former boss."

Baldric remembered the look on Kaduntz's face when the worship angels were cast with Luc out of heaven. She'd broken off with one third of Luc's army and set up the earth angel division. Her command had worked with the AAF ever since. Most major battles were strictly AAF soldiers, but Baldric could see her point. Why should she miss all the fun?

Baldric shouted, "Let her fight." The chant went up, and Erinelle relented.

Reed and Kaduntz squared off in the lowland pasture, away from anything flammable. Erinelle had her fire fighter angels ready to douse flames that got out of hand. Each sparring partner had four blue energy spheres. The spheres' chemicals were altered to give pain, not annihilation. The spectators watched from the split rail fences.

Baldric had watched Reed play baseball years ago. He had a mean left curve.

Erinelle whistled, and the fight began. Reed whizzed his curveball and made contact on Kaduntz's shoulder that knocked her off balance. He didn't stop until Kaduntz was on the ground. Reed straightened his shoulders and raised his hands, turning around in victory. The wards shouted and whistled for Reed, but Kaduntz wasn't down for long. She hit Reed in the middle of the back, propelling him face-first. He nearly landed in a fresh pile of cow dung. She was on Reed in less than a heartbeat, and she pummeled Reed with subsequent hits.

Erinelle whistled and shouted, "The winner of this round goes to Kaduntz, the earth angel."

Reed rolled over onto his butt and pulled himself off the ground to a standing position. "Man, I thought I knocked you out." He arched his back and Ruby ran to him.

Kaduntz replied, "And that's what you get for thinking."

Reed and Kaduntz suffered minor injuries and went over to the triage in the barn. Reed shrugged and said, "So I got my ass handed to me by a girl."

"Correction, human, you got your ass handed to you by a female warrior angel."

Anna raised Reed's shirt, and he yelped. She said, "Nasty burns. I saw the spheres turn demon angels to ash last summer. You have to make sure your opponent is defeated before you turn your back on them."

Each ward had their chance to battle a warrior angel. Only Lee and Jerry triumphed during their bouts, but Ruby and Anna fought valiantly. The wards proved to their guardians and themselves they were ready for battle. After the combat training had ended, the wards and the angels met back inside the barn.

With a sweeping motion of her hand, Erinelle said, "Excellent work, everyone. We have a plan ready to execute. If you turn your heads to the barn wall on the other side, I will lay out our plan of action."

Baldric listened to Erinelle as she laid out their plan of attack. Two divisions along with the wards would attack from the north border near the outbuildings and barn. Once they secured their position, Baldric would take a dozen seasoned, battle-hardened warriors across the field leading to the back entrance of the main house. Luwenia and Jerry along with skilled archers would take out the human guards on the roof.

Once Baldric led the initial charge, two additional AAF divisions would follow in waves, attacking the estate from all angles. In theory, the plan was solid. The AAF warriors selected were the best of the best.

Baldric would approach Caiojezeal on becoming a turncoat later in the evening. Having a warrior on the inside would help keep the trains running on time. If Baldric read Caiojezeal correctly, he'd help him, and his warriors get into the caverns with the least amount of resistance.

The image of Sandy's hurt expression made his insides twist into knots. Would it be too late?

GEORGE AND CELINA PULLED INTO the Arrington Estate. Celina said, "Remember, I'm with you. If you need me, just call out using your mind, and I'll materialize in seconds." She disappeared as George parked his work truck next to the detached garage.

George opened the side toolbox and strapped on his tool belt. He grabbed an extra voltage tester. George had obtained several different types of bugs to plant inside the house. Planting the bugs and going unnoticed had him jittery. He took a few deep breaths and said a quick prayer.

George wore a Champion Electric shirt with a pair of khakis and held a clipboard with the call-in form requested by Luc's house as he walked up to the front door. He rang the doorbell and stepped back. Within minutes, a tall man with brown hair and mustache opened the door. George held back a chuckle because the man could've been Magnum, P.I. and he worked undercover.

The man said, "Yeah, whatcha want?"

George handed him the request form. "Someone from this address called about electrical problems."

The man opened the door and said, "Yeah. Come in. I'll get the boss. You wait by the door."

George glanced around the main house while he stood in the large foyer. A winding, white staircase with plush, dark gray carpet led up to the second floor. No signs of life up there. On the left, two men sat in the dining room. Both were packing heat. The great room was empty. George's blood pounded in his veins. He was ready to lay his life down for his friend, but he just wasn't in a hurry to do it.

A fierce-looking man walked around the corner of the dining room and into the foyer. He had a handsome face with a long scar running along his jawline. He wore a tan suede jacket with black pants and black Caiman belly boots. He reached out his hand and said, "Hi, I'm Carson Jones. I run the estate. The panel box keeps blowing fuses, and it's compromised our security system. You think you can fix it?"

George nodded and said, "Well, sir, if you'll show me the panel, I'll take a look-see. Oh, I may need to test the outlets, with your permission, of course."

"Sure, of course. Before I give you access, you have to sign a confidentiality agreement not to disclose anything you may see or hear while on the property. Agreed?"

"All right, where do I sign?" George took out a pen and signed the non-disclosure agreement between Champion Electric and Arrington Estate.

"Great, please follow me." Carson folded the contract and slid it into his coat pocket.

George made a few mental notes of each room and how many guards and staff were present. He walked down a long hall and passed a den with a pool table and television. It had to be the same room Baldric had referred to in the meeting. In the kitchen, Carson opened the door to a utility room with a washer and dryer unit.

Carson said, "Behind the door is the main panel. The meter base is located at the rear entrance, next to the garage door. I'll be in the kitchen if you need me."

"Okay, I'm going to test the breakers and then test the GFIC outlets. I'll come find you when I have it repaired." George watched Carson walk away. George took off the panel and quickly found the burned-out breaker.

George repaired the damage caused by Nelson Doune's boys. He went through each room of the house planting bugs in the wall outlets. George located the security system in a study next to the den. His fingers trembled while he made some minor tweaks to disengage the alarm along the north perimeter of the property. George wanted to disconnect all the entry points but thought it would raise red flags.

After George had completed his tasks, he walked through the house and overheard a conversation in hushed tones.

"The boss is taking her on a trip tonight."

"Yeah, where to?"

"Who knows, but my guess is he'll be banging that piece of ass before midnight."

"Wanna bet? She's pretty damn tough."

"I'll betcha a hundred dollars and a bottle of Hennessey."

"You're on."

A tap on George's shoulder made him jump. He turned and started to explain the eavesdropping.

The man said, "I'm Estevo. I'm on your side. Carson sent me to get you. He's waiting for you in the great room."

George exhaled, and his knees went weak. "You scared the shit out of me. That's the room next to the front door, right?"

Estevo nodded and said, "Do you need some water? A drink perhaps?"

Shaking his head, George replied, "No, thank you. I'll just go on and meet with Carson so that I can get the hell out of here. Have you seen Sandy?"

Estevo had looked both ways before he whispered, "Luc permitted her to go on a walk with Caiojezeal. Physically she looks fine. I didn't approach. Can't blow my cover. Best of luck." Estevo strode past George and went back into the kitchen.

In the great room, George handed Carson the invoice. "I repaired the burned-out receptacle and replaced your breaker. I tested the outlets and didn't find any tripping the box. So you should be good to go. Here, you can pay me now or mail a check to the address on the invoice. Call me if you have any problems."

Carson reached into his back pocket and opened his wallet. He peeled off a couple of bills and handed them to George. "This should cover your expenses. Thanks for coming."

George looked at Carson and said, "I don't have change."

"Please keep it." Carson walked George to the door.

Minutes later, George was hauling ass out of the driveway and heading to Everglade Farms. He had to report his findings to the guardians. George wondered if the men in the dining room had been betting on Sandy sleeping with Luc. He wondered if Luc was taking Sandy on some trip. Celina appeared in the passenger seat of the work truck. *Damn, it was going to take some time adjusting to angels and demons popping up out of nowhere.*

Celina said, "I counted twenty human guards around the exterior and another dozen or so on the inside. Only a few demon angels were in the main house. I sensed more and assumed they're with the captives. The ones inside the house watched me carefully. I couldn't take a chance of porting into the caverns. I pray Baldric has better luck with Caiojezeal."

131

George twisted the hair in his eyebrow and then placed both hands on the steering wheel. "As long as nothing trips the back entrance sensors between now and morning, the AAF and the wards should enter the Arrington Estate before anyone knows the alarm's deactivated.

SANDY STOPPED WALKING AND TILTED her face to the sun. With her eyes closed, she said, "We take many things in our lives for granted. A simple walk outside and the sun on your face." She opened her eyes, and Caiojezeal was staring at her. *Oh no, not him, too.* "Don't look at me like that, please. I need your friendship. I need you to think clearly. I don't need you fantasizing about us." Sandy read his thoughts. He pictured them together, walking on the beach holding hands, and in this dream, he kissed her.

"I hate you reading my thoughts," Caiojezeal said. "It sucks. Do you have any idea how long it's been for me to have positive feelings toward anyone or anything? And you burst the bubble."

Sandy tripped on a loose stone in the pathway and fell into Caiojezeal's arms. "I'm sorry on both counts." She straightened up and pushed herself out of his arms. "I have no idea. Do you have any idea how many men have flirted with me for this face without even knowing who I am? I'm sick of it. This face has only caused me pain. I married an angel with it, for crying out loud. Now, the lord of all darkness is taking me on a trip." She rolled her eyes and kept walking.

A few strides and Caiojezeal caught up to her. "Let's forget about my fantasy and Baldric for the moment. Luc plays an excellent game of chess, and you're the pawn in a much larger game. He'll try to woo you at first, and if it doesn't work, he'll torture you. You need to answer his every question with a question. Never admit one way or the other when confronted with a choice he gives you."

He said, "For example, Luc will play on your success as a reporter. I'll be Luc and you, well, will be you. Sandy, I can offer you the keys to earth's kingdom. Picture yourself sitting as evening anchor to one of the major networks, or better yet, as owning a major network. You could control the media. You could possess power and influence over the masses. Whip them into a frenzy and bend them to whatever your will chooses. Join me."

Sandy thought about the implications of Caiojezeal's statements. The media truly held the keys to the kingdom. She had just read where the National Science Foundation was going to fund a supercomputer network. Opening that can of worms would stretch the media's hand across the globe. Luc would use the information to help sway her decision. Controlling the media was a beast. "It's an intriguing prospect. Global domination through the use of media. What else do you have to offer?"

Caiojezeal laughed and then turned serious. "Don't overplay. But you have the right idea. Keep it simple and move him in another direction after each offer he proposes. Stay sharp. Did you access the cords of light into your memories of Luc's book? Have a couple of spells in your arsenal and only use them if your life depends on it. Just a reminder, every spell you use propels you into the darkness. Once the darkness gets inside, it's hard to get rid of it. Darkness is like cancer. It spreads and destroys."

Sandy walked into the winter garden of the estate and sat down on a wrought-iron bench. Cheery pansies, English daisies, and snapdragons filled the landscape borders. Several containers overflowed with variegated vines and elongated Laurel with white flowers. *Southern Living* could shoot a cover in Luc's backyard. She crossed her feet at the ankles and gripped the lip of the bench. "I have a favor to ask."

"Anything." Caiojezeal sat down on the bench next to her.

Sandy swiveled around to face him. "If I turn to the darkness...when I return to the estate, if I'm no longer the person you see before you—kill me. I don't want to help further Luc's army, and I don't want to hurt my family and friends. I want you to tell Baldric that he made my life beautiful. Tell him he fills me with joy and happiness and our brief but glorious encounter during our pairing, well, I—I..." She wiped the tears away from her eyes. "Just tell him that I love him."

Caiojezeal looked at the ground, then reached over and squeezed her hand. "It will be as you wish."

Chapter 13

Invisible Touch

THE ILLUSION OF THE CABIN retreat returned to her chamber, thanks to Caiojezeal. Sandy walked across the cabin's great room through the bedroom and into the lavish bathroom. She took off her borrowed clothes and folded them into a neat pile. Old habits died hard.

Sandy had turned on the water faucet before she stepped into the shower. The double shower heads pulsed steaming water onto her skin. She poured shampoo into her hands and lathered her hair. After rinsing the shampoo and conditioner, she reached for the soap, and a washcloth from the bronze metal stand sitting on the fresco tile. Sandy scrubbed her skin nearly raw and still felt dirty living among Luc and his demon angels.

Horrific images flashed brilliantly into Sandy's mind. Pain seared her temples as she focused on bits and pieces of information from the other captives held in the caverns under Arrington Estate. She could see one female and two males humans held captive on the floor beneath her chamber.

The female human ward succumbed to Luc's charms. Luc wouldn't touch her, and his rejection drove the female insane. Flashes of Luc flirting with the woman filled Sandy's mind with images that she wished she could erase. Luc crooned a headful of compliments in his velvety voice to pump the woman for information.

Sandy couldn't quite grasp her name. The woman constantly begged Luc to touch her, kiss her, and sleep with her. Sandy cringed and cranked the water hotter. She couldn't decipher if the thoughts were plants from Luc or the woman. Her cords were a little fuzzy and frayed at the edges of light.

Down a few stone steps, two male wards with nerves of steel tried to hold their ground until Luc began to torture them. Sandy reeled with nausea and grabbed for the stainless steel shower bar so she wouldn't fall to her knees. She threw up from her visions when she entered the cold chamber. Like a page out of an ancient history book, the stone room was windowless with wet rock and earth for a floor. Next to the door, only one torch dimly lit the area and secured to the wall with metal brackets. The grim depiction of Sandy's fellow captives plunged her into dark despair.

One male chained against the wall was a victim of a recent beating or flogging. The man's face was unrecognizable, and feces and urine ran down his legs. His name was Jason. He was conscious, and for a second, Sandy thought he tried to lift his head. Jason was near death. She tried to make contact with the man's light, but it was too dim. His cords of light were fading. Locked in her room, she felt hopeless.

The other man in the cell with Jason lay strapped to an ancient rack, ropes fastened around the man's arms and ankles. The handle of the rack cranked to the point where the man's bones dislocated, and he lay unconscious from the pain. Sandy tried to find his name on the cords of light, but nothing came to her mind.

Sandy teetered under the showerhead until the water ran cold. The cold, hard water pelleted her until she came to her senses. Were her visions real? Sandy was going into battle with the devil tonight, and the last thing she needed was to be off her game.

Stepping out of the shower onto plush bathroom rugs, Sandy dried off with a white, soft, fluffy towel and then wrapped the towel around her dripping shoulders. She reached out for another luxurious towel and wrapped her hair up, turban style.

Had the other captives been given the royal treatment before being cast into the pit of pain? Was this phase one? Would she be strong enough to stand up to The Dragon? Would Baldric save her before she fell? She punched the mirror hard. It didn't break, but her knuckles bled profusely. Sandy looked at the back of her right hand. The injuries healed before her eyes.

Staring at her reflection in the mirror, Sandy looked at her hourglass body, a body women coveted and men desired. Her gentle, rounded shoulders were in perfect proportion to her hips. She turned to catch her rump in the mirror. Yeah, that too was well rounded. Sandy looked inside the bathroom sink drawers. Caiojezeal had filled the drawers with every conceivable amenity and cosmetic. Could she play Luc like she'd played so many men in her life?

Sandy reached for a hairbrush, the kind with teeth, and unrolled the towel, allowing her hair to tumble over her shoulders. Starting from the bottom, just the way her mom taught her, she brushed the tangles out and blow-dried the strands. Sandy didn't need big hair curlers for extra body. It was funny how so many women she knew strived for perfection. No woman was ever perfect. She had the physical attributes but struggled with why she was born with them, always trying to prove to people she had brains, instead of just beauty.

Sandy went through the motions of getting ready. She brushed her teeth and then applied a little brown eyeshadow and black mascara. On the bed, Caiojezeal had laid an outfit she wouldn't have been caught dead in. A tomato-red maxi dress made out of jersey fabric that would cling to her curves and shout, "Take me, Dragon." The dress straps tied at the shoulders, and it was unlined. Sandy cringed when Caiojezeal suggested she shouldn't wear undergarments. They had argued, and she'd won. She wasn't going into battle without a strapless bra and underwear.

Caiojezeal chuckled and said, "You're trying to slay a dragon."

Ha, ha, hilarious. Sandy slid the dress over her head and felt the silky fabric glide against her skin. She opened the small purse and found a tube of red lipstick and a note. *May love light the way.* Caiojezeal risked more torture and the Eternal Blackness if Luc knew he was helping her. Sandy walked over to the fireplace and threw the note into the fire.

On the floor, next to her bed, was a pair of red sandals with tiny encrusted diamonds in the center. Sandy slipped them on and waited on the sofa for her date. She closed her eyes and allowed her mind to travel along the cords of light. Her first stop down memory lane was her wedding night. Sandy needed Baldric foremost in her mind. She replayed Baldric appearing in the church sanctuary. It had been the happiest moment of her life. Sandy wanted to imprint every detail of the evening to take on her journey with Luc.

The second stop of her cords of light trip was Luc's Testament. Sandy mentally flipped to the section on spells and turned the pages while she read incantations of protection. She tweaked one into a prayer and began to chant mentally:

Great Creator of day and night, protect me with all your might. In my dire hour of need, send Baldric to me with great speed, bind my heart and close my mind. I bind Luc from my soul. I pray, oh, Creator, please keep me whole.

Sandy repeated the prayer as many times as she could until the adjoining door to Luc's chamber opened. Luc had come to play. Sandy held her breath as he walked over to the sofa, dripping sex appeal. He wore tight, black leather pants and a white, long-sleeved silk tunic accenting his metallic golden skin. Luc's shiny jet-black hair was pulled back into a long braid held together by a black leather strap. Luc was a living, breathing sex god, and cockiness rolled off him like water on a duck's back. Sandy held in a laugh. She thought of Ruby and her colorful Southern language. Sandy missed her friends.

Sandy tried to appear aloof, uninterested, making Luc laugh out loud. She mentally worked harder to weave and thicken the color bands of light and visualized a two-inch braided rope she'd seen in the red barn the night Baldric taught her to fence. Her heart began to pound as she lifted her chin in defiance.

Luc bowed in front of Sandy. "Ms. Cothran, you're a true vision of loveliness. Shall we go?" He extended his hand, and she took a deep breath and placed her hand on his.

Sandy stood and said, "Where are we going? Do I need a coat?"

Luc's eyes roamed over her body from head to toe, and the upturn of his lips revealed a dimple in his right cheek. She needed sunglasses from his blinding white teeth. "I promise to keep you warm." Luc's chuckle made her want to scream. Two points for the visiting team.

Sandy flipped her hair off her shoulders. "Let's get this over with."

"Tsk, tsk, tsk, my sweet and sexy miss. Tonight's adventure will be heaven's bliss, and I count the seconds to taste your kiss."

Sandy narrowed her eyes at Luc and placed her hand on her right hip. "So how long have you been at my door?"

"Long enough to catch you casting a spell." He laughed again and said, "You can't bind me in my own home. That's the number one rule of spell casting. Number two, every time you cast a spell you slide closer into the darkness and closer to me. By all means, cast away. Oh, and I assure you Baldric will come for you. But by the time the AAF allows him the freedom to pursue his quest of rescue, will you want to go? We shall see." He squeezed her hand and circled her waist with his other arm.

A thick mist filled the room, and Sandy realized they were traveling on the ethereal plane. Her journey had begun. Would she return as the person her family and friends loved? Or would she return as a despicable human like Cole?

BALDRIC'S LEFT FOREARM RESTED ON the mantel in the large great room at Everglade Farms as he gazed into the blazing flames of the fireplace. The place was officially deemed by the AAF as the central command center until the completion of the SEU (Special Exfil Unit). Tonight, all of the guardians and wards of Campbell Ridge were in attendance, and the conversation was beginning to get on Baldric's last nerve. He didn't want to hear about the what-if scenarios. He wanted the green light to haul ass to Arrington and rescue his wife.

Last night, traveling on the cords of light, he had found Sandy. She was being held in an underground cavern chamber next to Luc's bedroom at Arrington Estates. Baldric was a powder keg of dynamite waiting for someone to light the damn fuse.

"Baldric, hey, Baldric, anyone home?" Michael, the commander of the AAF, had popped into the meeting to go over the last-minute details before the dawn invasion.

Baldric lifted his head and turned around slowly. "I've heard everything at least twice. Why do we have to wait? We have the numbers. We have the equipment and the element of surprise. Waiting until morning could mean the difference between life and death. Don't tie my hands. Let me go."

Lee walked over and wrapped her arms around Baldric's waist and leaned against his bulky bicep. "We love Sandy, too. The waiting is brutal, but I agree with Erinelle. Dawn is the best time to attack. The fog will roll in from the river, which will give us cover."

Reed and Ruby sat on the couch while Anna and Jerry lounged on the loveseat. Ruby and Anna were both writing feverishly in their diaries. The Ditch Lane Diaries had originated over ten years ago when the girls were in college. It had been the first night the girls realized they were chosen to fight in the angelic war over the earth and the human species. The girls, now women, were Sandy's lifelong friends. Each loved Sandy as a blood sister—sometimes friends were closer than blood relations.

George looked around the room and locked eyes with Baldric. He nodded toward Baldric as a sign of respect. Southerners were known for their genteel hospitality and manners, not always found in other parts of the country.

George's Southern accent was drawn out, but the man was sharp as any human he'd ever met. George said, "I placed bugs in every receptacle on the first floor. I didn't get clearance to go upstairs. I tweaked the security panel and disengaged the alarms to allow us access to the northern border of the property. I went down the hall to search for the opening to the caverns when Estevo caught me. Scared me half to death. From a security standpoint, the team can attack now or in the morning." George hadn't been given clearance to fight in the battle. But his moral support was with Baldric. He folded his arms over his chest and winked at Baldric. Baldric smiled and nodded in reply.

Erinelle began to walk about the room. "Excellent job, George. The intel that's coming in from the plants seems reliable. We found out two of our wards passed away, and three of the captives remain Luc's prisoners. After lunch, we learned from Carson that Luc was going out of town. It's good news for us. Our special forces will overtake the compound and rescue with fewer injuries and casualties if Luc is away."

Baldric's nerves were shot, and he needed fuel. He strode over to the bar laden with food and drink. He piled on a plateful of carbs and grabbed a glass of Lee's sweet tea. He glanced out the window and noticed several of the AAF guards flying to the end of the driveway.

Baldric left the plate on the bar, made a mad dash out the front door, and ported to the end of the road.

Surrounded by six well-trained AAF guards, Caiojezeal stood dressed in a dark brown habit tied at the waist with a leather belt. Caiojezeal's hands were in the air when Baldric broke through the guardian circle.

"What are you doing here?" Baldric's chest tightened, and he swallowed hard. "Is she dead?"

Caiojezeal asked, "May I put my hands down? We need to talk, alone."

Baldric addressed the guards and tossed a glance over his shoulder at the warm golden light coming from the windows of the house. "Leave us."

An AAF warrior guard, Troy, released a guttural growl and said, "This is one of the demon angels who tied me up at Sandy's parents. Are you sure you want us to leave?"

"I fight my own battles, Troy. I'll be along soon. Take the others and return to your post." Baldric turned to Caiojezeal and said, "Speak the truth, demon. My patience is running thin, and I don't need mind games."

Caiojezeal leaned toward Baldric and whispered, "I come with information, but I need cover. Demon angels run the lines of the faze looking for a weak link to break the barrier into Everglade Farms. In another minute, they'll know I've crossed enemy lines."

Baldric grabbed Caiojezeal's arm, and they ported into the red barn. The AAF military maps and coordinates had been moved into the big house, leaving only combat training equipment in the barn. Baldric shouted, "Tell me about my wife. Is she well?"

Caiojezeal pushed the hood off his head. "Luc took Sandy on a trip tonight. They left before dusk, traveling to his penthouse suite in Manhattan. I came as soon as I could get away. Luc knew you were in her room last night. Sandy lied to him, and he nearly flogged her, but I pleaded The Treatment of the Angel Prisoner Act in regards to pairing partners. I took the flogging in her place."

Baldric reached for one of the training spears and forcefully threw it into the neck of a scarecrow. Shaking his head, Baldric ran his fingers through his hair in frustration. "The son of a bitch. Damn the AAF rules of engagement. I should've tried to get Sandy out. I shouldn't have left her there. She begged me to take her." Breathing heavy and near to his breaking point, Baldric said, "I'm grateful for your sacrifice. But I've seen the look in your eyes. You love Sandy, don't you? Tell me why you're here, and speak true."

Caiojezeal crossed his arms over his chest and stared straight into Baldric's eyes. "And what's not to love? Sandy is most infuriating, but she struck a tender chord within me I haven't felt since I was cast out of heaven. Besides, Luc would've sent you to the Eternal Blackness. Luc kidnapped her to get you. Or, well, at least in the beginning that was his plan. He wanted retribution for you kicking his ass eons ago."

Caiojezeal's hand motions moved simultaneously with his words. "Luc's plans have changed. He's intrigued by Sandy's feisty spirit. Previous ward captives, he took their power or turned them to fight for the dark side. Luc seeks not only her divine power and beauty but also the light of the Campbell Ridge wards which burns bright. Dark creatures are drawn to the light of love. His failed attempts to take Anna last summer have made him erratic in behavior. Failure isn't an option with Sandy."

Caiojezeal shifted his feet and clasped his hands behind his back. He looked to the ground and then back up to Baldric. "And I'm sick and tired of the war. In less than a hundred years, the earth as we know it will change. Luc has instigated civil unrest and rebellion across the globe. His goal is to incite another World War. One that will annihilate civilization as we know it. Luc uses human faith and religion. He uses wealth, poverty, greed, and the destruction of natural resources to pit not only nation against nation but brother against brother. He's taken Sandy to New York to persuade her to join his army. I believe he intends on mating her."

Baldric rubbed his fingers down his jawline, his face reddened, and he lowered his voice. "Luc only mates with purebred angels. To my knowledge, he's never taken a human female."

Caiojezeal let out an exhale of breath and said, "True. But Luc will bed her to avenge himself from the humiliation you brought upon him. I had told Sandy before she left with Luc tonight I would help her escape. I told her I would come and find you. I can't get her out of the compound without help. I need the AAF and the AAF needs me."

Baldric trembled with anger but held his sharp tongue in check.

He said, "I need to know if you're willing to renounce Lucifer and work as an operative for the AAF. I can't promise The Creator will offer leniency, but if you help me get Sandy away from Luc, I'll do everything in my power to initiate negotiations to place you in the AAF reconditioning program."

Caiojezeal clasped Baldric's forearm. "May love light the way."

Chapter 14

True Colors

LUC STOPPED AT A RANGER'S station on Mount Mitchell's lookout tower over the Appalachian Mountains. The snow-covered mountains at dusk were one of Luc's favorite spots on earth. In the hills, away from most humans, the earth seemed peaceful. He held onto Sandy's waist and inhaled the sweet smell of her shampoo. He hated humans. Why had he brought this person to one of his most sacred places? Luc glanced at Sandy out of his peripheral vision. She was awestruck by the majestic mountains. He held his tongue from making witty quips and took in the scenery.

Time in this graceful spot did not tick. No need to rush to and fro to tasks requiring his attention or the constant plotting and planning while attempting to stay one step ahead of The Creator and his warriors.

Luc held the human female in his arms and felt the warm blood pump through her veins. He pictured a different world. The world where he and The Creator were friends. The world where The Creator consulted him on the creation of the earth and its inhabitants. A world where this gorgeous female was neither human nor angel, but his mate. A partner for eternity. Never before had the thought even crept into his mind.

Fat snowflakes began to fall, and Luc waved his hand, so the snow fell on everything but them. He whispered, "I've never brought anyone here with me. I'm questioning the sanity of it."

Sandy turned to him, and with a frown, she said, "Why did you bring me here?"

Luc shrugged and said, "I was taking you to New York, we were passing through the mountains, and I haven't been here in a long time." He chuckled. "Well, to be accurate, it's been decades. Time for me doesn't hold the same relevance as it does for humans. One day, one year, a thousand years makes no difference."

Sandy asked, "Makes no difference for what?"

"For anything. No schedules, no clocks ticking, no time. Einstein was a ward and figured out time and space were woven into a single continuum with his theory of relativity. He hit the nail on the head, so to speak. Close your eyes for a moment and try to visualize no time, no space. No right, no wrong. How does it feel?" Luc traced his fingers along the soft skin of her arms. He was inclined to kiss the exposed part of her neck. Curious as to the taste of her. Baldric marking her—would it repel him or drive him to possess her?

Sandy followed his instructions without an argument. She played the game well, and he wondered what it would feel like to be inside this human. Sandy opened her eyes and swiveled around in his arms to face him. What was the look in her eyes? Curiosity? Or something else?

She replied, "I believe you're describing heaven. As long as the earth rotates on its axis, time will tick for humans. I read H.G. Wells' *The Time Machine*. To be honest, I've always wondered if time travelers existed until I met real angels and demons. All the UFOs humans report seeing. They're seeing angels or demon angels. The Chariot of Fire taking Elijah into heaven was angels. The burning light of The Creator, the light of love, has no time and space."

She searched his eyes and said, "It amazes me how a person of faith scoffs when you tell them you've talked to angels. But they do. You ask anyone of faith if they believe in angels. They'll reply, 'Oh yes. I believe in angels.' But tell the same person you see angels and carry on conversations with them, and, well, they'll lock you up and throw away the key."

Luc laughed so hard his shoulders shook. "You amaze me. Humans make me sick. But you make me laugh. I won't lie or try to convince you to think I like humans, or that I consider humans as having redeeming qualities. I don't. I never have. But once in a long while, I'll meet an exceptional person who gives me pause to reflect. You're one of those humans. The thing is, your life span is short in the big scheme of life. So, exceptional or not, humanity will not change until the end of an age and that day is coming sooner rather than later."

Luc said, "I want to show you, New York, as night falls over the city. It's quite spectacular."

Luc and Sandy materialized to a high-rise building in Manhattan. Even though it was still considered winter, the opulent patio of his penthouse suite had an array of blooming flowers in exotic-looking planters. Full-grown trees grew out of the concrete floor with plants and vines intertwining up their trunks.

Luc encircled Sandy with his arms and leaned close to her cheek. "The sunset glistening on the Hudson River is one of the reasons I love New York. I love everything about New York with all the excess, glitz, and wealth. One of my top ten cities. Why should you live unceasingly unsatisfied? Do you want to live an average life in an average world when you can live with me in splendor?"

The wind from the river blew Sandy's hair off her shoulders, and he inhaled her sweet, peach-ripened scent. She held onto the rail of the patio as he held onto her waist. With a tilt of her head, Sandy replied, "My life is beautiful. I'm deeply satisfied. Material things without love are empty. The convenience is nice, but it doesn't warm my soul."

Ignoring her comments, Luc rubbed his cheek next to hers and said, "Our view faces south toward lower Manhattan. I prefer to be close to the water while I'm here. I want you to see the city the way it was before the revolution."

Luc snapped his fingers, and all of the modern buildings disappeared. The streets below reflected an eighteenth-century New York with dirt streets and horses and buggies. Wooden-hulled hundred-foot ships driven strictly by sails anchored in the harbor. The people below were oblivious to the time travelers. "See? Time travel does exist. I control earth and at my discretion may manipulate time. You are different, aren't you? Most humans would've passed out or screamed in fear. But look at you. Daireann, the wonder in your face is quite refreshing indeed. I see why Baldric is interested in you."

Sandy shrugged out of his arms and walked along the patio wall. He watched as she took a glimpse into the distant past of America. "I'll say you have some cool tricks. I admit, I'm awestruck. However, I wouldn't want to live here. It's bad enough today the lack of respect women get, but back then women were the property of the fathers and husbands, and I'd miss indoor plumbing."

Luc chuckled and walked over to Sandy and grabbed her face with his hands. He leaned close, nearly touching her lips to see if she would take his kiss. She didn't. Scruples in humans were rare indeed. "Come inside. Let's drink a cocktail."

Luc had purchased the penthouse in the 1920s and everything about the suite carried the elegance of what it looked like living at the top of the heap. The views were breathtaking from his penthouse at night with the lights of the city. Sandy followed Luc inside the penthouse. She looked around and traced her fingers along the back of the white sofa sitting on top a rug made of thick white shag carpet. Two mohair club chairs were positioned close to the twenty-foot white marbled fireplace.

The combined living and dining areas had dark hardwood flooring that offered a grandeur the average working class only saw in the movies. The sleek black dining table held a silver candelabra along with fine china settings. A Parisian-inspired screen separated the dining room, with a long, black onyx bar fully stocked with any cocktails one might desire. Luc stepped over and out of thin air produced two cosmopolitans and offered one to Sandy. She took it from him and sipped. He was making slow progress.

Sandy sipped her drink and sat down in one of the club chairs. "You live well. I'm sure the other women and men you've brought to this suite went gaga. I grew up in a house that didn't have expensive furniture or china. We didn't live extravagantly. While I love beautiful things, beautiful things cannot love you back. Living to excess, having the best of everything the world offers, does it make you happy?"

Luc was taken aback by her question. He couldn't remember anyone ever inquiring about his happiness. Sandy touched a part of his soul no one ever had, except The Creator. Most humans and demon angels wanted something from him. It didn't take long in most cases to figure it out, and he used their desires to lock them into a contract he recorded into his testament. "Ever the clever one. Happy, what does it even mean? Can you honestly say you've lived your life happy? Baldric finally had the balls to admit his feelings, and it was the happiest moment of your life. Well, what have you been doing the other twenty-eight years? I'll tell you. You've masked happiness with power. You've used your quite enticing body to bring men to their knees, sexually. But how many of those men wanted to marry you outside the throes of passion? Maybe one lovesick moron. And your lifelong best friends. You resent their happiness. You resent their constant judgment over your lifestyle choices. Well, I say, celebrate who you are. Celebrate your sexuality. Don't allow society to dictate how you're supposed to feel."

Luc walked over to the bar and pulled out a bottle of tequila and said, "Drink with me, Daireann. Celebrate who you are. Celebrate with me." The slight change of her expression and the twitching of her upper lip gave him an indication he was close to sealing the deal.

Sandy stepped over to the bar and drank a shot of tequila. "I used to think that way. The old saying, if it feels good do it. God, it was my motto for years. I've slept with many men and satisfied my sexual hunger. I loved the rush of the power I held over the men in my life. It took your thug, Cole, nearly killing my dad before I realized why I used my body."

Sandy ran her finger around the rim of the shot glass, then sat it down on the bar. "It was because of my child abuse, which you were probably behind anyway. I sat in St. Timothy's and poured my heart out to The Creator, and Baldric appeared. The Spirit of Man paired us. I know the difference now between sex for the hell of it and what it means to make love to your soul mate. I'd rather have one night with Baldric than years of meaningless sex. Sex without love is like watching two dogs go at it."

Luc got mad and threw his shot glass into the fireplace, sending shards of glass across the floor. "Damn it, woman. Don't you think Baldric lusts after you? It's because of his honor and respect to The Creator he paired with you because he was your guardian. He was sworn to protect you. Do you have any idea how many human females Baldric fucked? If you don't believe me, ask him. Don't you see the possiblities we could have together? All that you see and don't see on earth belongs to me." Luc grabbed her face between his hands and he leaned in close to her mouth. With barely a whisper, he said, "You're the first human female since Cleopatra I've wanted to mate. I've never made love to a human, and I want to make love to you. I desire you."

Luc caressed her cheek and then rubbed the top of her lip with his thumb while he stared into her hazel green eyes sparkling with specks of gold. He took in her beauty and released a moan of desire. "I'm giving you choices I've never offered another human. Mate me, bear my children, and we'll create a superhuman race."

Luc released her and went over to stand at the floor-to-ceiling windows. With his back turned to her, he said, "Baldric thinks he loves you, but he'll never leave The Creator or the AAF, not even for you. Don't delude yourself. Your one night will have to last an eternity because it's all you'll ever get from him." He turned toward her. "Before you blurt out an answer you'll live to regret, sleep on my offer tonight."

Sandy ran her fingers through her hair and walked over to stand in front of Luc. She took in a deep breath and exhaled, then said, "Just so we're clear, I'm paired with Baldric. He is my soul mate. As miraculous as this trip has been with you, I wouldn't trade my life with him for anything you have, real or imagined. If I only get the one night with Baldric, it was worth it. You don't have the capacity to love."

Sandy opened her arms with her hand's palms up. "I have no idea why The Creator keeps you alive to wreak havoc on the whole world. The only thing I can fathom is you are His creation. You were once a part of His inner circle. It's like the prodigal son parable in the Bible. You're his lost son. He waits for your return to admit and repent your wrongs against him and the earth. He still loves you. But judgment day comes to all, and you're not the exception to the rule."

Luc's eyes glowed red, and his wings extended. He threw his head back and screamed so loud it shattered all of the windows in the penthouse. How dare she speak to him about The Creator. Luc grabbed Sandy by her hair. The next second, they were back in the caverns in Sandy's chamber. Luc threw her on the floor and yelled, "You have twenty-four hours to submit before me. I want you willingly. But if you feel you can't, then I will take your soul.

You'll lose everyone you love. Remember this, pretty fades, but stupid lasts forever." Luc disappeared in a whirlwind, sending Sandy flying against the stone wall.

SANDY SAT ON THE COLD stone floor and cried. Had Baldric slept with many human females? He had lusted after her. She hadn't read his come-on signals wrong. Had Baldric only paired with her out of respect for The Creator?

Sandy shook with fear and drew her knees up to her chest, wrapping her arms around them. By the grace of the Almighty, she'd survived the trip with Luc. She closed her eyes and prayed for help. Sandy prayed for deliverance.

Twenty-four hours to choose between her everlasting soul or the people she loved. The Prince sacrificed himself for humanity. The Prince prayed for deliverance. Sandy complained many times growing up about going to church every Sunday. The countless drills of memorizing Bible verses in Sunday school paid off. On her knees, she closed her eyes and prayed. "Father, if you are willing, take this cup of suffering from me. Yet, I want Your will to be done, not mine." Sandy repeated the verse aloud several times.

Pain and suffering had plagued Sandy for most of her life. Why did some suffer more than others? Her choice would affect many lives. She thought about her soul. The inner spirit never dies but lives on forever. How could she give up her spirit to live an eternity with Luc?

Luc had many bad qualities, but on the turn of a dime, he oozed charisma. One moment he was tender and the next manic. Sandy thought about the look in Luc's eyes on Mount Mitchell. If Luc loved anything, it was earth. But his manipulations of humanity were destroying the very thing he held dear. Sandy thought of the legion of angels, including Caiojezeal, who loved Luc so much they pledged allegiance to him and were cast out of heaven. Maybe Caiojezeal found Baldric. Maybe they would rescue her before her soul was damned.

People were clueless to the supernatural warfare waging around them as they went about their lives. The earth was held in a fragile balance of good and evil. Sandy curled into a ball on the floor.

Baldric had committed to her in front of the Spirit of Man. He was her husband whether their union was sanctioned or not. Sandy wouldn't hold it against Baldric if what Luc told her was true. She'd used enough men in her life. Sandy was a mere blip on the radar of life. As she drifted in and out of sleep, she decided on her answer and would give it to Luc in the morning.

A warm, glowing light filled the cold chamber. "Sandra Daireann, you will not fail The Creator, your husband, family, or friends. You have my inner light within you. Keep your faith and hold it dear. Your divine soul is not yours to give up. Rise, my daughter."

Sandy opened her eyes. She wasn't dreaming. The Spirit of Man levitated before her. "He said he would take my soul if I didn't submit."

The Spirit of Man waved her hand over the top of Sandy and filled her with great strength. The Spirit of Man said, "Luc's been using that old chestnut since the beginning of humanity. He cannot take your soul unless you give it to him. Luc also is extremely manipulative when he doesn't get what he wants. Baldric loves you, dear. He and you share a rare love. Love is the strongest power in the universe. Stand strong and be brave, for I will be with you until the end of an age."

The light faded, and Sandy knew the spirit was right. Love was the answer, and she would fight for Baldric and their love unto her death.

RUBY LAY IN BED WITH Reed spooning her. She'd set the alarm for three thirty. Reed was still sound asleep as she stared at the digital clock radio on the nightstand next to one of her wedding photos. Behind the wedding picture, a larger silver frame held a picture of Ruby holding Joe with Reed's arm around her waist. Ruby knew The Creator had blessed her beyond measure with the man of her dreams and their bouncing baby boy. But in a couple of hours, her happy little family might be destroyed in spiritual warfare. Knots twisted in her stomach at the thought of losing Reed.

They'd spent the night with her parents. Anna and Jerry along with the guardians were meeting at four o'clock in the kitchen to launch the SEU rescue mission. Harry was babysitting Joe during the battle. Ruby tried to talk her mom out of fighting, but Lee wouldn't budge. She explained she'd fought in battles before, and the team needed her experience.

Frightened but determined, Ruby would give her life for her family and friends. She knew they felt the same about her. Love sometimes meant sacrifice. Her heart fluttered wildly as if summer butterflies were having a party. Her mouth was dry as a bone.

Reed stirred and nuzzled her neck. "Were you able to sleep at all?"

Ruby rubbed his hands and flipped around to face him. His beautiful chiseled face and whiskey brown eyes reflected the love he felt for her. Reed volunteered for the mission. Tears welled in her eyes and she said, "I want you to know you've made my life." He started to say something, but she pressed her finger to his lips. "Please let me finish. If I die today, I know my son has the best daddy in the whole world. I know how much you love me, but I want you happy. I want you to celebrate this miracle we call life. I want you to move on and find someone who will love and take care of you. We'll meet again in a place where there are no tears."

Reed wiped her tears away and held her face in his hands. "Ruby Jane, I love you more than my life, and I will not let you die today. The guardians trained me well, and, Jellybean, I'm a lethal machine. So get the thought out of your pretty red head." He kissed her slowly and moved away slightly to kiss each cheek before grazing her lips again. Ruby breathed him in, and as their kiss lengthened, they touched each other's shoulders, trailing their fingers over each other's arms until they clasped hands. His soft sensual touch was delicate as a feather, and when he made love to her, it was as close to heaven as she wanted to be.

After they showered and dressed, Ruby and Reed checked on little Joe. Joe slept soundly with drool slipping out of the corner of his lips. Ruby lightly ran her fingers through his curly red hair. She carefully lowered the rail of the baby bed. She bent down and kissed his soft, chubby cheek, and Reed leaned over and kissed Joe, too. She returned the rail to its former position and tucked Joe's blanket around his body. Ruby straightened her shoulders, lifted her chin, and with an intake of breath, she said, "I'm ready. Let's go see who's here."

Reed held her in his arms again and kissed the top of her head. "Let's rock, baby."

They held hands walking down the stairs, past her dad's den, down the hall, and through the great room into the kitchen. Inside the kitchen, the guardians of Campbell Ridge stood battle ready in full armor, packing a multitude of weapons.

Ruby noticed the love in the air between her parents, and Jerry and Anna. She could only assume everyone took the opportunity to get a little extra loving before they went into battle.

Harry hugged Lee so tight and kissed her like no one was watching. He released her and said, "I'll hold down the fort. Come back to me, Tootie." Harry and Lee had called each other Tootie for years as a sign of affection. Ruby fought hard not to cry. She couldn't eat or drink anything because she didn't think she'd keep it down.

Seneca stepped over to Ruby and held her arms. "You're ready, and I'll be with you. Just remember, when the battle starts, never look back. Go for the kill. I'll give you armor and weapons at Nelson Doune Farms." Seneca kissed her forehead and said, "I love you." He dematerialized.

Ruby glanced at Baldric. She understood why they called him Baldric the Warrior. He looked like a slayer of dragons. He would get Sandy back. Baldric said, "Before I leave, I want to say I owe each of you a debt of gratitude I'll never be able to pay back." He bowed and dematerialized.

One by one the guardians left on the ethereal plane to Nelson Doune Farms. Jerry and Anna, Ruby and Reed, Harry and Lee stood together in a circle. Without being told, they grabbed hands and bowed their heads as they recited the King James version of Psalm 23:

The Lord is my shepherd; I shall not want.

He maketh me to lie down in green pastures: he leadeth me beside the still waters.

He restoreth my soul: he leadeth me in the paths of righteousness for his name's sake

Yea, though I walk through the valley of the shadow of death, I will fear no evil: for thou art with me; thy rod and thy staff they comfort me.

Thou preparest a table before me in the presence of mine enemies: thou anointest my head with oil; my cup runneth over.

Surely goodness and mercy shall follow me all the days of my life: and I will dwell in the house of the Lord forever.

Chapter 15

Sledgehammer

TRAVELING ON THE ASTRAL PLANE from LA, Lucifer entered the northern border of Arrington Estates shortly after four a.m. Walking past the two aluminum outbuildings, he sensed a change in the air. It prickled his built-in what-the-fuck sensor. Something just didn't feel quite right. Luc looked at both buildings storing farm equipment along with a varying array of weapons for the human guards in his employ.

Luc strode from the outbuildings to the large barn and went through the main double doors down the center alley. Stalls held his prize-winning Tennessee Walkers. The main barn also had a tack room and grooming area. Luc stepped over to his black beauty, rubbed his nose, and materialized a carrot in his hand. "Good boy. You're a magnificent beast." He flew up to the massive loft holding hay bales and straw. Nothing was out of place or seemed out of order.

Luc shook his head as he left the barn and ported across the back lot to his garden. He'd drawn the design from his memory of the Rose Garden in heaven and hired the best landscape developer in the South. It was one of the few areas which gave him contentment. Luc took the side entrance through the state-of-the-art kitchen with black appliances and opened the microwave. Estevo left him a plate of spicy lime chicken with a side of Spanish rice and corn on the cob. The personal chef worked miracles with herbs, sauces, and peppers. Luc had a sophisticated palate that loved spicy food and the hotter, the better, but he wasn't hungry for food.

Walking down the hall, he stuck his head in the living room. Carson had fallen asleep on the couch in front of the fire. A demon angel stood by the front entrance door. Luc nodded and proceeded to the TV room and waved his hand, opening the false wall panel.

The underground cavern was Luc's playground for various pursuits. He'd been unable to keep the encounter with Sandy out of his mind. Determined to bed her, Luc jogged down the manmade steps of the first floor to the second underground landing with a suite of rooms designed by him with spectacular formations and colorful lighting enhanced by his powers.

Caiojezeal stood in front of Sandy's room with his back against the wooden door. Luc tilted his head and inhaled. The demon angel cared for the human female. "I don't need you anymore. Take a load off, go down to the club and hook up with one of the new demon females. Some very tasty tail."

Caiojezeal stepped away from the door. "I don't want to go to the club. I prefer to stand my post."

Luc narrowed his eyes at the demon and said, "Just so we're clear. I came back to bed the female. Are we going to have a problem?"

"Does the female want to bed you? Or do you plan to rape her?"

Luc backhanded him across the face. "Are you defying me?"

Caiojezeal rubbed his jaw and said, "I've served you without question from the very beginning. I've traveled this earth over since its existence carrying out your bidding even when I disagreed with some of your methods because I believed in you. There are humans I despise, but I've seen firsthand their compassion and love, their kindness and generosity. I understand why The Creator loves them and wonder why we continue to fight this war."

Luc took a deep breath and said, "Come into my room. Let's talk." The white, marbled walls against the black stone of the cave created a fantastical grotto complete with stalagmites and stalactites. He had a king-size onyx bed with diamond embellishments of stars and angels. Elaborate tapestries hung on the walls along with gilded mirrors. His bedroom reflected romanticism to entice the female demon angels who begat him children.

"Sit down. I'm going to have a drink. What about you?" On the far left side of the room, hot springs ran under an arch in the rock ceiling. Next to the steaming waters, Luc opened a door with a pull down latch and revealed a crystal bar with colorful prisms. "Beer or cocktail?"

Caiojezeal replied, "Beer."

"Sounds good to me." He grabbed two out of the cooler and stepped over to the two chairs next to the end of the bed. He handed off the beer to CJ and sat down and popped the top of the can.

"Los Angeles is thriving. Our numbers have tripled in less than a year. It rivals New York with the glam. Ah, here's to vanity and greed." He raised his beer and Caiojezeal did the same. "Tell me why the sudden change of heart when everything we've worked so hard to accomplish is unfolding before our eyes. At this rate, the humans will destroy themselves with little effort on our part. We just have to sit back and watch."

Caiojezeal sat down and sipped his brew. With a turn of his head, he said, "I like Sandy. Please don't sleep with her."

Luc chuckled and said, "I knew it. I knew you fell for her. Sandy is different, isn't she? I'm sorry, old boy, but I can't make that promise. I intend to make her mine as soon as you leave. Get over it or get out. Those are your choices, my man."

"Will you give her a choice?"

With a sideways grin, Luc replied, "Yeah, she can make love to me, or I can fuck her. She's going to bear me a son. A hybrid, half demon angel, and half human. He'll go to the best schools and meet the right people until he's placed in authority over this planet."

"What happens to Sandy after you've used her?"

Luc turned up his beer and belched. "I'm going to kill her. I need her body, not her mind."

Caiojezeal stood and threw the beer can against the wall. "I can't let you do it. You have the book. You made your point to Baldric. I'm taking her home." He turned and in three strides was at the adjoining door to Sandy's room.

Luc flew into the air and lunged for Caiojezeal as he entered Sandy's room. They tumbled to the floor and rolled into Sandy's bed. "I don't want to fight you, son. Repent and I'll let you live." Luc straddled Caiojezeal and held him down by his shoulders.

Caiojezeal screamed, "Run, Sandy. For the love of God, run!"

Sandy bounced out of bed wearing a pale yellow nightgown. Luc snarled and said, "Stay where you are, human."

Sandy ran over and kicked Luc in the face, giving Caiojezeal the momentum to throw Luc off. Caiojezeal punched him in the gut. Sandy glanced between Luc and Caiojezeal. Her door was blocked, so she ran into Luc's bedroom.

Luc roared and flung Caiojezeal against the wall. He turned toward Sandy and yelled, "Sandra Daireann, do not move." Luc immobilized her as Caiojezeal jumped on his back.

Caiojezeal screamed into Luc's ear, "I don't want to fight you, but you've given me no choice. You're out of control. Your actions are going to make it impossible to reconcile with Father."

Luc stomped on Caiojezeal's left foot and elbowed him in the ribs. A wheezing sound escaped from Caiojezeal. Luc reached over his right shoulder and grabbed Caiojezeal by the head, then flipped him over onto the floor. Before Caiojezeal could regroup, Luc pounced on him and locked Caiojezeal's arms behind his back. Caiojezeal jerked back and forth to get away, but Luc threw a punch into his jaw, making Caiojezeal's head snap right. Luc lost control and beat Caiojezeal until he lay bleeding and unconscious on the floor.

Breathing heavy, Luc's lips tightened in a curl as he walked back into his bedroom. Still as a statue but wide awake, Sandy glared at him. The bitch wasn't afraid even in her quiescent state. He paced slowly around Sandy, watching her chest move up and down in a steady rhythm.

Luc leaned next to her ear and whispered, "I need you to do something for me." He ran his hands gently up and down her arms. He stared into her eyes and placed Sandy in a trance. "Nod your head if you can hear me?" She nodded. "I want you to walk over and get into my bed. I'm going to make love to you. I command you." He stepped away and placed his forefinger and thumb on his lips. Sandy did as he commanded. "Good girl."

REED STARED OUT THE SUBURBAN'S backseat window. Jerry volunteered to drive to Nelson Doune Farms. Anna sat upfront with Jerry while Ruby and Lee joined him in the backseat. Reed's mind raced as his adrenaline pumped. College was the last time he'd been in a real fight and not against demon angels and paid assassins. And not with his wife and mother-in-law.

Reed thought back to the first time he'd laid eyes on Ruby Jane at Everglade General Store. He and Brent had stopped by to check out George's little sister. Reed fell hard and fast for the red-haired spitfire. They'd married six months later, and it seemed like a lifetime ago.

In the beginning, Ruby's dreams seemed cool, but lately, more often than not she'd wake screaming or crying. Ruby blamed herself for not being able to see Sandy in The Dragon Dream.

They'd argued about Ruby's training with the AAF for the special ops mission. Harry intervened to get Reed in the AAF's front door. Ruby's stubbornness and loyalty wouldn't allow her to sit idly by while her friends fought the devil. That in itself seemed unreal at times. The spiritual war consumed them every minute of every day. Reed didn't dwell on it but accepted it as fact. After seeing how the wards were saving humans lives, he wanted to join the team.

Reed worked out on a regular basis to keep in shape, but it was nothing compared to the workouts with Simon, the little boy angel who wasn't a little boy at all. Reed was ready to fight to get Sandy back. He wasn't willing to lose anyone in the process. But he knew no amount of training prepared you for the real battle or its consequences.

Ruby squeezed his hand and leaned her head on his shoulder. Reed inhaled her sweet scent. He wanted to keep her safe. He prayed for strength.

Lee glanced at him and said, "It's okay to be scared before a battle. It's called self-preservation."

Jerry chuckled as he gripped the steering wheel. "So that's why I feel like I'm going to shit myself?"

Everyone laughed. Reed knew laughter released fear. He'd heard his uncle describe Vietnam, and he'd said soldiers during war cracked jokes all the time.

Ruby said, "The skin on my head is as tight as a tick. It feels like it's going to split open."

Anna turned around and said, "It's your nerves. My fingers are tingling with energy, and my stomach is in knots. I get like this before a major surgery. The guardians wouldn't put us in this position if they didn't think we could do the job."

The velvet night sky began to turn a shade lighter as they pulled into Nelson Doune Farms gatehouse. Reed remained quiet and focused on keeping his mind clear.

Zeke stepped out of the gatehouse door and walked over to the Suburban as Jerry rolled down his window. Zeke said, "Hey, kid, the boss said y'all were heading to the hunting cabin, but my gut says something's up. I smell it in the air. If you need me, I'll jump in the Jeep and follow you back there."

Jerry leaned his arm on the windowsill. "Zeke, you're a good man, but are you a praying man?"

Zeke twirled the end of his handlebar mustache and replied, "I don't hit the church doors often, but I know how to hit the floor. I'll pray until I see you again."

As Jerry pulled down the long pebble driveway over the stone bridge, they passed rolling hills and black split rail fences. The old brick plantation-style house sat on a hill overlooking a small lake. Jerry took a right, bypassing the main house driveway, and turned toward the horse barn. Around the back of the barn, a metal gate was open, and the back trail became rougher, bouncing them in the seats.

The hunting cabin was at the back of Nelson's property. Last spring, Jerry took Reed to the cabin to get hammered, right after Anna found out about his engagement to Rachel. Ruby and Sandy had flown to Pensacola to spend the weekend with Anna. The cabin nestled in the thick woods was the closest access point to the Arrington Estate property from the map the guardian angels revealed.

Pulling to a stop, Jerry said, "Nobody's here."

Lee leaned forward and said, "They're waiting until we get out of the truck. Let's go."

They exited the Suburban, and the angel faze lifted. The sight before Reed took his breath away. It was like something out of the Old Testament. The Legion before the wards was of biblical proportions. At the front line were the guardians of Campbell Ridge, but behind them, it looked like there were thousands of warrior angels dressed in armor with weapons strapped to different parts of their bodies.

Jerry muttered, "Holy moly, now that's something you don't see every day."

The guardians parted, and Michael walked through the crowd of angels. The angel wore illuminating golden armor with a dark crimson sash across his breastplate. He bowed before the wards and said, "Wards of Campbell Ridge, the Angel Armed Forces is at your service. Your guardians will escort you inside the cabin to change into your military uniforms. The suits will protect you from injuries sustained at the hands of the human guards and will help to repel injuries from the demon angels. When your guardians have you prepared for the battle, we'll meet here. Since Erinelle has chosen to fight this day, I will execute the official orders of engagement. Our spies were unable to determine how many demon angels are in the caverns, so I decided to come prepared for a major battle. Keep in mind, the humans driving along the roads and neighbors with properties adjacent to Arrington Estates are protected with warrior angels and faze. They will not see or hear anything. Now hurry, dawn approaches."

Inside the cabin, the guardians set up an area for Jerry and Reed and another one for Ruby, Lee, and Anna. Reed pulled on the golden uniform, a bodysuit that fit like a second skin. Then he slipped on a pair of golden military boots. Simon quickly secured straps and two belts holding an array of supernatural weapons as well as Reed's sword sheath at his right hip.

Simon smacked him across the face, and Reed glared at him. "Just wanted to get your attention. You make me proud today, human."

Reed nodded, took a deep breath, and waited at the front door for Ruby while Jerry waited for Anna, his energy field cranked on high as he flexed his fingers. When the women exited their side of the cabin, Reed's eyes went wide. Ruby in the skin-tight golden suit with her flaming red hair had the fierce look of a fighter. Her jaw set and her shoulders straightened, she was resplendent. Reed went to her and grabbed her hand.

The wards of Campbell Ridge were solemn as they walked alongside their guardians to the front line. Baldric glowed from head to toe, and his nostrils flared, reminding Reed of a bull ready to charge.

The night before, Erinelle went over the battle strategy again.

Luwenia would take Jerry and a division of archers through the woods of Nelson Doune Farms and set their positions to take out the human guards on the main house roof and grounds. They would meet Baldric's charging army as they entered the estate to take out any obstacle to retrieve the prisoners. Based on Caiojezeal's description, they'd open the false wall panel in the TV room and enter the cave.

The SEU mission was to retrieve the captive wards held in the caverns below Sandy's floor.

The first tactic was to overtake the outbuildings and barns. Once accomplished, and at the sound of the charge, Baldric would lead the surprise attack with Erinelle and two dozen battle-hardened warrior angels, while Luwenia's division wiped out the human guards.

Baldric's group would cut through the front line of the demon angels' defense through Luc's gardens and into the main house. Michael would use the barn's vantage point to calculate how many divisions to send once the demon angel floodgates opened. After Baldric's initial wave, the demon angels would begin to materialize in seconds on the battlefield. Simon would lead the second division of warrior angels along with Reed and Lee, and Seneca would lead the third line with Ruby.

Raphael and Anna, along with other healer angels, would quickly set up a triage in the barn with all the doors and windows open. Any AAF soldiers who fell on the battlefield, the healer angels would try to repair the damage, but if injuries were too severe, the healer would immediately portal the soldier to The Treatment Center in heaven. No demon or human could kill a heavenly angel or send them to the Eternal Blackness except Lucifer.

Shouts and whipping wind filled the air when Michael waved to his trumpet blowers, and the sound of the horns made the earth shake. The AAF warriors descended on Luc's foothold in Arrington in waves to thunder rolls and lightning strikes. Luwenia and Jerry's division ripped flaming arrows of energy in rapid succession with synchronized precision, dropping the human guards on the roof and grounds, then proceeded to join Baldric's group at the front battle line while protecting each other's backs. Simon's group with Reed joined the charge on Luc's compound with Lee, and Seneca and Ruby's team closed in behind him.

The surprise attack gave them the advantage as the AAF ripped through the unsuspecting demon angels. Baldric's division made it inside the house. The demon angels regrouped and formed another line to protect the compound. Demon angels began to appear in the back lot, and chaos unleashed. Some demon angels resembled humans, and others looked reptilian. The demon angels' cry revealed sharp, pointy teeth and something slimy oozing from their mouths.

Reed, Erinelle, and Lee fought the demons with supernatural weapons of varying swords and daggers, weaving in and out of the demon angels, cutting them down to ash. As Reed's division gained ground to the back entrance of the house, he noticed several AAF soldiers fall and dematerialize. As mayhem ensued, Reed was cut off from Erinelle and Lee.

Three to one, not a fair fight for the demon angels. Reed's divine gift was a superhuman strength, speed, and agility plus the gift to dematerialize at will, and he reappeared behind the three demons and sliced and diced them to ash.

Ruby and Seneca's division fought behind Reed. Propelling the blue energy spheres with blinding speed, Ruby nailed the demon angels point blank in their faces, blowing out the back of their skulls and disintegrating them into ash.

Reed materialized to the gardens. He glanced over his right shoulder, to find that Ruby had fallen in the field. Lee saw her, too, and they both materialized beside Ruby. Reed at her head, and Lee at her feet. It was then Reed realized, too late, that the demon angels had used Ruby to set a trap.

THE TRUMPETS BLEW, AND THE battle cries and swordplay fell on deaf ears. Baldric was in the zone with Sandy as his only goal, his only objective. As an expert swordsman and a battle-seasoned veteran, Baldric cut through the demons as they attacked him from every angle. He and his blinding blade of light weaved and dodged in an age-old, sacred dance, searing each demon to the Eternal Blackness.

With lightning speed, Baldric traveled to the outbuildings and barn. His team secured the area before moving on through the open back lot directly behind the main house of Arrington Estate. Baldric crossed over Luc's immaculate gardens resembling the Rose Garden in heaven as he entered through the patio's double doors. His pairing senses flared, and everything went red. Sandy was in imminent danger.

Baldric closed his eyes and allowed his pairing cord to link with Sandy's. Then multiple shots fired from an automatic weapon hit his chest. He opened his eyes and glared at Luc's human guard, who continued to unload another cartridge of ammunition. The bullets deflected from Baldric's chest. The human male just pissed Baldric off further.

With his mind, Baldric made the weapon disappear. Looking into the frightened man's eyes, Baldric levitated the human before catapulting him through the living area's window, shattering glass over the furniture and floor.

From the false wall panel in the TV room, Baldric ported to the underground caverns and materialized in front of the door holding his bride. Baldric blew the wooden door into a thousand splinters. As he crossed the threshold, he nearly tripped over Caiojezeal, who lay unconscious on the cold, dank floor. The adjoining door to Luc's chamber was open, and he flew into the room. Luc held Sandy down on the bed with his hand over Sandy's mouth, and she bit him. Then Luc punched her with his fist, and Baldric lost all control. His blade levitated in the air.

Luc's pairing scent filled the room, making Baldric heave. Luc was so absorbed with the intent of taking Sandy he seemed oblivious to the war going on above ground and inside the estate. Baldric attacked Luc from behind with his wings extended, and the light of love radiated with its blinding white energy. Right before he sank his teeth into Luc's trapezius, Sandy looked up into Baldric's face with tears streaming down her cheeks. He didn't know if it was real or his imagination but Sandy's face seemed to blur in and out between the nine-year-old girl and the woman he married.

Baldric went wild as he grabbed Luc in a chokehold and bit into his neck right above the clavicle, the weakest point on any angel. Baldric tore into Luc's muscle, his gray blood filling Baldric's mouth, cutting off Luc's life force line.

Out of nowhere, someone attacked Baldric's back, clawing and biting him until all three fell backward, crashing into the rock wall.

Seconds later, Sandy entered the fight as naked as the day she was born. She too glowed with the light of love and held the sword he'd given her in the barn. He watched Sandy attack the female demon angel with a vengeance.

Baldric and Luc paired off, the warrior angels circling each other. Luc growled, "You're fodder for my army now, my old friend. My blood runs in your veins."

Baldric shouted, "Good because I'm destroying The Dragon once and for all." The blade of light materialized in Baldric's hand. Luc held his own as they clashed swords, grinding and pounding blade on blade.

Luc spat at him. "I fucked your wife."

Baldric didn't fall for Luc's mind games. His sole purpose was to destroy The Dragon. He concentrated on his blows to send Luc to the Eternal Blackness in a battle that he prayed would change humanity for the better.

A GROUP OF DEMON ANGELS attacked Ruby and Seneca. Blades of fire ripped through Seneca's torso, and he dematerialized. The demon angels hit Ruby with an invisible power source, rendering her useless as she lay on the ground. Seconds later, Reed stood at her head, her mother at her feet. Ruby watched in horror as the demon angels ran their blades through her husband and mom.

Another division of the AAF descended and destroyed the demon angels in her sight. Ruby yelled for Anna and Raphael. Anna appeared as Ralph was busy healing a blow to Luwenia's head.

Anna looked at Ruby with a face of stone and said, "Your spouse or your mom. You have seconds or they're both dead."

Lee reached for Ruby and said, "I love you," and closed her eyes. Erinelle flew down and picked up Lee into her arms and dematerialized.

Anna swiftly placed her hands on Reed's injury, and a blue sphere of light materialized around them. The demons who tried to enter into the area turned to ash the instant they hit the blue energy field.

Ruby cried her eyes out as she thought of her mother. Gone. As she reached for Reed, tears rolled down her cheek. Reed's eyes were a blank stare. Ruby prayed aloud, "Save him, Father, please save him."

Anna shouted over the noise of battle, "He's alive, but we have to get him to a hospital. He needs blood before he slips into a coma or worse. Get Jerry now. He's fighting in front of the house. This battle is over for us if we're to save Reed. Don't just stare, Ruby! Wake the hell up and get Jerry before we lose Reed, too."

Ruby ran as fast as she could around the corner of the house, jumping over Luc's dead human soldiers, and up the front sidewalk, hysterically screaming Jerry's name. He ran to her and grabbed her arms. "What's happening?"

"Hurry, Jerry, please hurry. Reed's dying, and Mom's dead." Ruby turned and ran back to Reed and Anna in the battlefield. "Anna, is Reed dead?" she cried.

"No. Reed's unconscious. His pulse rate is dropping. Where is Jerry?"

Anxiously, Ruby pointed and watched Jerry sprint over the fence to retrieve the Suburban. Seconds later, Jerry drove the Suburban through fences and plowed over shrubbery to get to them. Jerry jumped out of his truck and ran to Reed and picked him up. Ruby opened the back door so Jerry could place Reed in the backseat. She slid into the truck and put Reed's head in her lap. Anna ran around the other side of the vehicle's backseat, opened the door, lifted Reed's legs, and sat down. Anna placed her hands on the open wound near Reed's chest. Jerry smashed the gas pedal and jerked them in motion down Arrington Estate's front drive.

Ruby's fingers trembled as she brushed the hair away from Reed's face. She prayed silently. *Please God, don't take him, too. We need him. I need him.*

SANDY THOUGHT SHE'D IMAGINED BALDRIC when he looked into her eyes. There had been this weird flashback of being a kid again, and Ben Salinger was on top of her pulling her panties down, and then she looked into Luc's face. He was trying to rape her when suddenly Baldric appeared. Baldric's eyes locked with hers in an embrace and their pairing chords linked.

Baldric went crazy as he bit into Luc's neck. Sandy saw fear in Luc's eyes and she wanted to go in for the kill. Sazae appeared out of nowhere and latched onto Baldric's back. Luc, Baldric, and Sazae fell back into the rock wall.

Sandy could feel Baldric's pain. She could read Baldric's thoughts. Sandy called on her cords of light and utilized the powers from Luc's book to save her husband. Her sword materialized in her hands, and she jumped off the bed and went for Sazae.

Sandy lunged for Sazae and lashed the demon across the face with her sword, which freed Baldric to fight Luc.

Looking confused and wild-eyed, Sazae met Sandy in a battle-ready stance holding a jagged dagger in her left hand. "I am going to gut you like a fish, human."

In the initial blows, Sazae sliced Sandy across her left bicep and punched her in the face. Sandy allowed her mind to focus on Baldric's training. She allowed her muscles to relax and settled into the rhythm of the fight.

Sandy laughed as she pressed the demon into a corner. "Ha, I can read your thoughts, demon. I'm more than your equal. You will meet the Eternal Darkness today." The singing of her blade rang out.

Sazae fought for her life and lunged in the air to come down on top of Sandy's back. Sandy swiveled in the air and thrust her blade into the demon's sternum. Sazae exploded into gray ash, which disappeared before hitting the floor.

Sandy turned quickly to the fight between Baldric and Luc. They were chest to chest in a battle to the death. Sandy slipped on the bloody floor before getting her balance. She rushed to join her husband's side. Sandy's left arm touched Baldric's right arm, and a blinding spectrum of light burst forth from the palms of her and Baldric's hands. They pointed the light toward Luc, raising him into the air. Luc hung lifeless in the air with his head bowed forward, and his wings disappeared. They had done it. They were killing The Dragon.

A flash of light entered the room and flew to Luc. It was the Spirit of Man. She looked at Baldric and said, "Release him, Baldric. It's not your will to be done but The Creator's. I am here on His bequest. Lower your arms."

Baldric lowered his arm, and his voice quivered with anger. "He was going to rape my wife. He deserves to die."

The Spirit of Man held Luc in her arms. "Luc has lost his way, but he belongs to The Creator just like you and Sandy. The Creator knows all and everything will be revealed in His time, not ours. I'm taking Luc to The Creator in the Garden of Eden. He will deal with Luc. You must abide by the rules in our agreement. Understood?"

Baldric let out a deep breath and said, "Understood."

The Spirit of Man looked at Sandy, nodded her head, and clothed Sandy in a radiant white gown. She turned back to Baldric and said, "Take Caiojezeal to Michael at the cabin. You and Sandy need to talk. The battle is over, and the cleanup crew has arrived. It's time to leave." The Spirit of Man vanished with Luc in her arms.

Baldric turned to Sandy and said, "We have to leave. They're going to blow the place up. You know, make it look like an accidental fire for the humans. I have to get Caiojezeal. He's received redemption."

Sandy wrapped her arms around his waist and said, "I love you. Thank you for saving him."

"Oh, Daireann, don't thank me. I love you, too. We'll talk soon. We have to go, okay?"

Sandy nodded, and they walked into the other room. Baldric slung Caiojezeal on his shoulder, and they left the main house. There were angels in white spreading a low mist on the grounds of the estate.

Sandy, Baldric, and Caiojezeal ported to the last outbuilding as Arrington Estates engulfed in flames. Sandy wanted to ask questions, but those would come later when she and Baldric were alone. Walking toward the hunting cabin, they saw a legion of angels waiting for them. She wondered if the other captives made it out alive.

Chapter 16

There'll Be Sad Songs

LEE PRESSED HER HEAD INTO Erinelle's neck as they flew to Everglade Farms. She and Erinelle had talked last night about the possibility of her dying. Giving life to Reed in exchange for her own had been a no-brainer. He was Ruby's mate and Joe's father.

They materialized in her bedroom upstairs, and Erinelle laid her on the bed. "I'll get Harry." Lee nodded weakly.

Minutes later, Harry entered the bedroom pale and frightened. Lee lifted her hand, and he joined her on the bed, placing her hand over his heart. "Harry, be brave. We both knew this day had to come eventually. I'm not afraid of dying, but I hate leaving you."

Harry broke into tears and said, "Don't leave me, Lee. Please fight to stay with me."

She closed her eyes and swallowed as the fluid filled her lungs, making it hard to breathe. "Erinelle will fill you in on what happened. I don't have the strength. In my bottom dresser, I have the love letters and photos of our life. You read those and remember I wait for you. You've been my light in this world, my darling. My true love. Kiss me."

Harry leaned down and held her face gently in his hands then kissed her. "You have made my life, too."

Lee looked at him with half-lidded eyes, and a smile crept across her face. "You're a granddaddy now. You take care of our boy and girl and our grandbaby. You tell him about me."

Harry wiped the tears away with his forearm. "I will, I promise."

An incandescent light filled the room, and Lee turned her head. "Not now, please."

Gabriel's messenger, Arlene, hovered in the corner of the room. "Lee, you're a faithful and loyal servant. Heaven awaits, and Harry is left in good hands." Arlene extended her right arm and the beam of light covered Lee as her soul left her physical body.

Lee glanced back at her husband one last time before taking her journey home.

RUBY SAT IN THE EVERGLADE Hospital ICU waiting area. She glanced down at the buffed hardwood floors and up to the hall door as she waited for Anna to come in with news. Outside in the corridor, a tech rolled a deck of food trays toward the elevators.

Nurses wearing scrubs rushed to and from the ICU. There was a doctor in scrubs speaking with another family at the table in the back next to the vending machines. Ruby had sat in here a few days ago after Hugh's car accident. Cole Steele's actions had set events into motion that changed her life forever.

Anna had told her before the surgery that Raphael placed faze over the surgical team. Anna, along with Raphael, was in surgery with Reed.

Ruby pushed the thoughts of her mother to the back of her mind. She would deal with her grief later. Reed needed her. Jerry walked into the room with a bag of food from McDonald's. He handed her a Coke and offered her a burger. "I can't eat. I'm numb all over. I wish Anna would come out and give us an update. Hold my hand."

Jerry placed the bag of food on the side table and gently nudged her over on the couch to sit down. He put his arms around Ruby and rubbed her back. She wouldn't cry. She had to stay strong. As if Jerry read her thoughts, he said, "It's natural to cry. Don't hold it in. It'll make you sick. You can be strong and cry."

Ruby glanced up and said, "I can't start crying. I'm afraid I'll go bonkers if I do. Have you heard anything from Luwenia? Did Sandy and the captives get out?"

Jerry pointed and said, "Luwenia is here. Baldric has Sandy, and the other prisoners are free. Seneca is recuperating at The Treatment Center. Erinelle took your mother to Harry."

Ruby let out a cry of pain and a river of tears began to fall. "Is she gone? Really?"

"Yes, my sweet girl. Lee is with The Creator." He continued to hold Ruby until the tears began to subside.

Ruby thought of her poor daddy and Joe. "Should I call Rose to take care of Joe?"

"I already thought of that, and Rose is with Joe at Everglade Farms." Jerry leaned against the couch and Ruby leaned against his shoulder.

Ruby held Jerry's hand, and her words came out choppy. "Do you think The Creator knew all this would happen when he gave us the power of the angels? In less than a year, I've lost my grandfather and my mother. Sandy's kidnapping, the battle, and Reed fighting for his life don't seem fair. Somehow deep down in my soul I always thought things happened for a reason. Do you think there's a reason for all of this suffering?"

Jerry rubbed Ruby's right arm and said, "I asked the same thing to Anna the day of Hugh's accident. She told me, sometimes good and evil go hand in hand. I don't understand the whys. I gave up trying. I concentrate on making decisions that are proactive in the fight against the darkness. As a doctor, Anna has seen so much suffering. We need to look at the big picture. Life is a blink. Then, when our human suit expires, we'll have all the answers we need."

Ruby straightened up as Anna came through the ICU doors. Her chest tightened as she stood on shaky legs. Anna looked as though she'd aged ten years.

A small smile crept into the corners of Anna's lips. "Reed made it, honey. He's going to be all right."

A loud cry of relief escaped, and Ruby said, "Thank you, sweet Jesus. Can I see him?"

Anna draped her arm around Ruby's shoulder. "Come on. I'll get you back to him." She tossed a glance over her shoulder at Jerry and said, "Then you and I are going home. I need some serious loving."

Jerry chuckled and said, "I'm all about the love, baby."

BALDRIC CARRIED SANDY THROUGH THE ethereal plane to the hidden room at Campbell Ridge Cave. He placed his hand on the symbol of the sun and went through a portal. They materialized on a beach paradise with no hotels or humans in sight. Baldric set her down. Crystal blue waves of an endless sea lapped up onto shore, breaking at his and Sandy's feet feeling like warm bathwater.

Sandy stood on the beach and lifted her face to the sun. Then she looked left and right at the palm trees lining the pristine beach for miles. "Where are we?"

Baldric stripped into a pair of turquoise blue swim trunks that hit right above his knee. His golden chest shimmered in the sun. He looked at Sandy and waved his hand, so she wore a red and white striped bikini. "Let's go swimming and then I'll explain." He dove headfirst into the water, and she followed him.

They swam out to the second sand bar and sat down on the exposed beach. The water healed his wounds from the fight and hers.

Sandy looked at the injury on her arm disappear and then looked at him. "Are these healing waters? And where are we?"

"Yes, the water is from heaven. When a soul goes to heaven, it experiences a transformation. After a period of adjustment, a soul must make accounts for their life actions and choices, both good and bad, before the Prince. The soul takes a training course for assessment and atonement is offered for any wrong doing. After the course is complete, the soul is allowed to create its own version of heaven. The soul may take the ethereal form or a physical form. It is up to the individual. And if you think something, it happens. For example, if I think I want a piña colada, then *voila.*" Baldric held a piña colada and handed it to Sandy. "Angels have the same opportunity. This is my place. How do you like it?"

Sandy took a sip of her drink and said, "Not bad. Are we alone? Have you ever brought anyone here?"

Baldric chuckled and shook his head. "Yes, we're alone, and you're the only person who's seen my place. You're my partner, my wife, and I wanted you to see it. Sandy, will you forgive me? I failed you when you needed me. I couldn't take you the night you begged me. My superiors wouldn't allow me. Did he hurt you?"

Sandy took another sip and handed Baldric the cocktail. "I was mad at you. I was mad at myself. There's nothing to forgive. I took the book and placed myself in a dangerous situation, and it nearly cost me my life. What happened to Caiojezeal? And what'll happen to Luc and his people? Are the other wards okay, the prisoners and my friends?"

Baldric gently placed her hand into his hand. "The demon angels who fought us at Arrington Estates reside in the Eternal Darkness. The human guards are currently making accounts for their life choices and actions before the Prince. Luc is with The Creator, and I'm not privy to that conversation. Caiojezeal is in the reconditioning program with Michael. The AAF recovered the prisoners, and they're with their families. Your friends..." He blinked and took a deep breath.

Baldric continued. "Reed's in surgery. He'll recover. Anna, Jerry, and Ruby are all right." He paused again, looked out at the ocean, and turned back to her. With sadness, he said, "I hate to tell you, but Lee passed away a few minutes ago. She was one of the best examples of humanity I ever met, and I'm so sorry, honey."

Sandy dropped her face into her hands and cried. "Lee died?"

He draped an arm around Sandy's shoulders and drew her next to him. "No one dies. They move on. Lee is with her mother and father. She is at peace."

Sandy sobbed, and her shoulders shook. "Oh my God, Ruby and Harry and George. Oh, little Joe will never know his beautiful Mama Bear. She died for me, Baldric. Why do I consistently cause pain in the lives of people I love?"

"Humans are born into the world, and humans pass on. Lee served The Creator well, and a celebration is going on in heaven in her honor. The one thing I know with certainty is The Creator will never fail you. He will always bring you through the storms of suffering. When you love greatly, you grieve greatly. Angels aren't immune to suffering. I suffer, too."

Sandy searched Baldric's eyes. "You're not telling me something. What is it?"

"I have to give you up. After today, I'll no longer be your guardian, and I must do penance to The Creator for breaking the rules."

Sandy placed her hands over her ears and screamed, "No, no, no. I don't want to live if I can't be with you."

Baldric removed her hands from her ears and drew her into his lap. "I placed you in grave danger by pairing with you. I almost didn't make it before Luc did the unthinkable. When I entered his chamber, Luc was oblivious that I was in his presence. He was going to take you and make you bear him a son and then he was going to kill you. I can't place you in danger any longer. A guardian will be assigned, and you won't remember me at all."

"No, Baldric, no. You can't take my memories. I won't allow it. You're the only one for me. The Spirit of Man paired us for eternity. Please don't leave me again." He winced in pain from her words. She dove into the water and swam back to shore. He swam behind her. Baldric ran after her, turned her around, and crushed her with a kiss.

A rush of heat spread throughout his body as Baldric held her in his arms. His lips on hers, moving alternately between rough and smooth. She kissed him back and then jumped up, locking her legs around his waist. "I love you, Baldric. I love you." He made a bed materialize behind them as the palm trees swayed back and forth in the warm, balmy breeze.

Baldric moaned as he pulled and sucked on her sweet lips. He lightly traced his tongue around the smoothness of her teeth. Then he plunged inside her mouth circling his tongue with hers. Sandy sighed, and his heart soared.

As Baldric made love to her, golden sparkles released in the air and fell onto her lovely skin. His fingers brushed out her long tresses to fall over her shoulders. Baldric stared into her eyes and then memorized every line of her face. Their paring cords linked and held no secrets, connecting them on a higher plane of consciousness. He let out a growl that echoed in the air. His cry was one of love, passion, and loss.

Baldric held Sandy in his arms, loving her and kissing her. Their time was running out. He had to plead his case, ask for forgiveness, and take whatever punishment was deemed appropriate to keep his wife safe. Baldric made a deal with The Creator to return after the battle. He would atone for the broken rules, so he had added one more to the list by taking Sandy to his paradise.

Sandy looked up into his eyes and said, "Remember, you told me not to give up on you. I'm not. I'm going to fight for us. I'm going to petition the Spirit of Man for help. I'll pray so much they'll want to send you back just to shut me up. I'll not give up what we have. Do you hear me?"

He chuckled and rubbed his cheek next to hers. "I love it when you're feisty. But I have to make atonement for breaking the rules. So, you'll behave while I'm gone? Promise not to get into any trouble?"

Sandy cut her eyes left and then right. "I never try to get in trouble. It just seems that trouble finds me. I know I need to check on my friends and my parents. But I don't want to let you out of my sight. And you must make me a promise." She propped her elbows on his chest and laid her chin on the palms of her hands.

"Anything. I will promise you anything." He brushed a strand of hair away from her eyes and tucked it behind her ear.

"Excellent. You cannot take my memories. Absolutely no memory cleansing. Deal?"

Baldric took a deep breath and exhaled. "I thought it would be easier on you if you didn't remember me. What if I can't get back for decades? I don't want you to be alone."

Sandy stretched her body out over his and held onto his biceps, then laid her face in the crook of his neck. "You will always be with me. In my heart and my soul as I will be in yours. You made me whole, warrior. I don't need anything else."

He growled low and whispered, "Make love to me again, wife."

LATER IN THE EVENING, SANDY and Baldric ported back to her parents' home to pick up her car. Sandy squeezed his hand and said, "I haven't been here since Cole kidnapped me. Go inside with me, please."

Baldric held her hand as they walked up the front steps and he opened the door. "Let me go in first. I don't think we have any worries. But I'd rather be safe than sorry." He walked inside and then came back for her. "The coast is clear."

Sandy stepped inside the house. Someone had come in and cleaned the place up.

Sally yelled from the kitchen, "Who is it?"

Sandy grinned at Baldric and said, "It's me, Mom."

Her mother ran in from the kitchen with tears in her eyes. "You're home. Oh, thank God. You're home." She wrapped her arms around Sandy. "I love you so much, baby." Sally released her and looked at Baldric, then hugged him. "Thank you for bringing her back to us." She yelled out, "Hugh, honey, come downstairs. Sandy's home."

Hugh ran down the steps and into the den. He picked Sandy up and twirled her around. "You're a sight for sore eyes, little girl." He sat her down and extended his hand to Baldric, who picked Hugh up and hugged him.

Sandy said, "Be careful."

Baldric's eyes widened. "Sorry, got caught up in the moment."

Hugh laughed and said, "No apologies needed. So what happened?"

Sandy looked at the ground and tears formed in the corners of her eyes. "Mom and Dad, I have to go to the hospital. Reed was hurt trying to rescue me." Then she sobbed. "And Lee was killed."

Sally released a cry and held Sandy in her arms. "Oh, honey, I'm at a loss for words. Hugh, we need to check on Harry and see if he needs anything."

"Mom, it just happened today. Let's give Harry some time and we'll go together. I have to go to the condo and get some clothes. I'll call when I have news."

Sally reached for her hand. "I went to your condo. You have some clothes upstairs."

Sandy's voice filled with emotion, and she replied in broken words, "Okay, I'll walk Baldric out. He has to go to a meeting."

Baldric bowed before Sandy's parents. "I will try to return as soon as possible. Take care of my girl while I'm gone?"

Hugh nodded and said, "Baldric, you've saved my girl twice. I look forward to seeing you again soon."

Sandy and Baldric walked out on the front porch. The afternoon sun warmed her skin as she squeezed his hand. She straightened her shoulders and lifted her chin. "I love you, Baldric. I love you so much, and I'll be here waiting for you."

Baldric leaned down and held her face in his hands. "The AAF has sent warriors to watch over you while I'm away. The research team figured out the properties of the gelean wire, and demon angels will never threaten your life again. I love you more than my life." He kissed her and dematerialized.

Sandy slumped against the porch door. Her heart sank as she wiped tears out of her eyes. She had to stay strong. Ruby needed her, and Baldric would come back to her—someday.

Chapter 17

These Dreams

SANDY QUICKLY SHOWERED AND CHANGED into her jeans and a sweater. She slipped on a pair of loafers and went downstairs. Her purse and keys lay on the table in the foyer. She stuck her head in the den and said, "Mom and Dad, I'll be back later. I love you guys."

"Be careful," her parents said at the same time, then looked at each other and smiled.

"I will." Sandy went out the door and walked down the steps to her Corvette.

She cranked up the engine and turned on the radio to WKDF Rock before she pulled out of the driveway. Listening to music occupied her mind as she drove to the hospital. Her friends had sacrificed much to save her. The prophesied battle came to fruition. Sandy never wanted to waste another precious minute of her life on things that didn't matter. It didn't matter what kind of clothes you wore, the car you drove, or the place where you lived. It was the people she loved the most who mattered.

Had it only been days since her news story about Cole had aired? It seemed like an eternity. Life changed in a split second. Sandy pulled into the parking lot and stopped her car. She took a few deep breaths as she walked toward the entrance of the hospital. When the automatic doors of the ER opened, Sandy experienced a sense of déjà vu. She stepped over to the nurse's station and inquired about Reed Jackson.

The nurse looked up from her computer screen and said, "Are you, family?"

Sandy nodded. "Yes." Ruby and Reed were part of her family.

The nurse replied, "Mr. Jackson has been moved to the fourth floor, Room 422. Take a right at the hall, and you'll find the elevators on the right."

"Thanks." Sandy walked down to the next hall, took the next right, and then hit the button on the elevator. She rode to the fourth floor and stepped out. Glancing at the sign on the wall, Sandy took another right to Room 422. Sandy began to tremble as she knocked on Reed's door. The door opened, and Ruby burst into tears. Sandy enveloped her in her arms. They both cried until a nurse came over and quietly requested them to go inside Reed's room.

Reed slept in the bed with an IV. Thankfully, no other monitors were hooked up.

Sandy swallowed hard, and her voice cracked. "Ruby, I'm sorry about Mama Bear. I should've left Cole alone. It's all my fault."

Ruby wiped her eyes with the back of her hand. "Don't. It wasn't your fault. If anyone is to blame, it's Luc."

Ruby took another deep breath, and there was a hitch in her voice. "You put Cole behind bars. The battle ended Luc's foothold in Nashville, and Mom knew the risks. We all did. Sandy, as bad as it hurts, you should've seen my mama fight. Even in battle, she was graceful but lethal. The fight was unlike anything I've ever seen even in the movies." Ruby swiveled in the chair and leaned in closer to Sandy.

In a quiet voice, Ruby said, "We fought with the warrior angels. We fought as soldiers. Erinelle pegged the demon angels correctly. They worked together, and I got caught in a surprise attack. They immobilized me. Reed and Mama came back to help me. It was a trap. The demon angels ran them through with their blades. Erinelle swooped in and took Mama to Daddy."

Ruby shook her head and said, "Anna, man, she saved Reed's life. Her healing power stopped Reed's internal bleeding. She and Jerry saved my husband."

Reed's eyes opened, and he said, "Sandy, don't let her fool you. Ruby fought like a madwoman. You should've seen her blow out the skulls of the demon angels with those blue energy spheres." Ruby and Sandy moved to either side of Reed's bed.

Ruby brushed the hair off his forehead and bent over to kiss him. "How are you feeling?"

Reed frowned and said, "I'm sorry Mama died, honey. I wished I could've seen those bastards before they tricked us." He winced and placed his hand just under his chest.

Ruby gently put her hand over his and said, "Does it hurt bad?"

"Only when I move." He snickered and winced again.

Sandy held the rail of the bed and looked at Ruby. "Have you talked to your dad?"

With sadness, Ruby replied, "Yes, I plan to go over in a little while. I just couldn't leave Reed."

Reed squeezed her hand and said, "Honey, I'm going to be all right. Go to your father." He turned to Sandy and asked, "Will you take her? I'm going to click on the tube and see if I can find a basketball game to watch."

"Of course, I will."

Ruby's shoulders slumped, and she sagged down into the chair next to the bed. "Part of me dreads going into the house without Mom. I still can't believe she's gone. George and Rose are staying until I arrive. Jerry and Anna stopped by to check on Daddy, too."

Sandy walked around the bed and held out her hand to Ruby. "Come on, sister. We'll do it together."

Ruby nodded and stood. She looked around the room and shook her head. "I forgot we came here from the battle. The weirdest thing I remember is we had on these golden, armored angel suits, and when Jerry pulled onto the highway, our street clothes materialized. Isn't that weird?"

A slow smile came to Reed's lips, and he said, "You looked fierce and awfully sexy in that angel suit. Hey, come give us a kiss and I'll be here when you get back."

Ruby leaned over the bed and kissed Reed on the mouth, then caressed the side of his face with the palm of her hand. She took another deep breath and turned to Sandy. "Let's ride, Clyde."

Sandy and Ruby walked down the hall to the elevators.

Ruby looked at Sandy and said, "Oh, Sandy, I've been blubbering and didn't even ask how you were. What happened the day after we talked on the phone?"

Sandy began to tell Ruby on the elevator about the terror she'd experienced at the hands of Cole and Luc. Once they got inside the car, Sandy paused and stared out the windshield. "I'm still afraid Luc will come back for me. Baldric said the AAF assigned several warrior angels to guard me, but I'm still afraid without him."

She turned toward Ruby and said, "Baldric and I had Luc. We were killing The Dragon, and the Spirit of Man stopped us. I wanted Luc to explode into ash like Sazae, his demon wife. I don't understand why we couldn't finish him off. During my captivity, I saw a glimpse of something in Luc, a potential of something still good, for a brief moment. Then he'd go all crazy on me. Do you think that's why The Creator saved him? The potential of what Luc could be instead of the malevolent being he is?"

Ruby shrugged and said, "I don't know. I don't know anything anymore. I'm afraid to fall asleep. I'm scared of the next dream. Will it be about death or life? It's going to take time for us to heal from this ordeal. Like Anna said to Jerry, we need to quit trying to figure it all out and work proactively to make the right decisions in our lives."

Sandy turned on the ignition and the engine varoomed. "You're so like Mama Bear."

Ruby smiled and said, "Well, Mama wouldn't want us wallowing in sorrow. She'd want us to celebrate her life, and that's what we're going to do."

EVERGLADE FARMS HAD A HOUSE full of people when Sandy and Ruby arrived. Jerry, Anna, Rose, and her friend Haley were in the kitchen. Harry sat in the living area watching little Joe as he rolled over onto his stomach from his back and tried to push up with his hands. Everyone seemed to talk at the same time. It was a nervous kind of chatter that comes when there's death in the family. But there was laughter too, and plenty of tears as each person told a story about Lee's life.

Sandy went upstairs with Ruby and Anna. They needed to pick out what Lee would wear for her burial clothes. Ruby pulled out several dresses and one pink pants suit. Lee loved the pink suit and wore it frequently to social gatherings in the community. They agreed on the pink suit and paired it with a light gray blouse with little pastel pink flowers.

Lastly, Ruby put together some undergarments and accessories. "Did you know my parents already picked out their caskets and made arrangements for their funeral service years ago? The only thing left to do is take her clothes and call Pastor Logan. Will you girls go with me to the funeral home tomorrow?"

Tears rolled down Ruby's face, and she sniffled. "It's just like Mama to choreograph her death, too." Then Ruby chuckled. "I feel like I need to sleep but feel wired at the same time. You know what I mean?"

Sandy and Anna both nodded. Then Sandy said, "Oh, I get what you mean, Jellybean. I feel the same way. But we have to try to get some rest. The next couple of days is going to be tough. Are you going back to the hospital?"

Ruby sat on the edge of Lee's bed. "No. Reed called and told me to stay with Daddy. I'll head over in the morning to check on him. Then y'all can meet me at the funeral home around ten o'clock. I don't think I can do this without you two."

Sandy and Anna flanked Ruby's sides, and they linked arms. Sandy chuckled, remembering a time long ago, and said, "The Three Mouseketeers." Ruby and Anna both laughed out loud.

THE EVERGLADE COMMUNITY CAME OUT to support the Glenn family. Lee's friends and neighbors filled every pew at Smith Funeral Home, and there wasn't a dry eye in the house. The celebration of Lee's life had an open invitation to anyone who wanted to tell a story of Lee. Many of the stories Sandy had heard before and a few she hadn't. Lee's death brought Lizzie back to Tennessee and George. They were officially back together. Sandy grinned during part of the ceremony, imagining Lee's spirit among her family and friends. Why not? Sandy liked the notion of Lee's spirit floating among them.

Sandy listened to most of the stories, but her mind began to wander. She looked around the sanctuary and could feel the angels' presence in the room. Sandy closed her eyes and silently prayed to The Creator not to be hard on Baldric and to consider them as a couple. Sandy reminded Him how much she and Baldric loved each other. Sandy prayed He would give a message to Baldric and let him know she would wait for him, and she missed him very much. Sandy had an emptiness only Baldric could fill.

She glanced over at Harry in the front row, and her heart ached for him. Harry and Lee's love wouldn't dissipate, but Sandy would bet her life Harry experienced a similar kind of emptiness after the loss of his most beloved wife.

After the burial service, Sandy, Anna, and Ruby sat in the chairs under the funeral tent, staring as the cemetery maintenance crew shoveled fresh dirt into Lee's grave. At the edge of the artificial grass carpet rug, Reed stood with a cane talking to George while Lizzie held little Joe in her arms. Harry spoke with Hugh, Sally, David, and Christine at the back of the tent.

Ruby smoothed out her dress. "I had a dream last night. I met Mama in the In-Between." Ruby began to tell them about her dream.

Ruby woke to the pleasant aroma of peach preserves and music from the 1940s playing on the radio. Ruby was back in the old cabin lying on the couch in the breezeway with the old rotator fan blowing from her granddaddy's old desk.

Ruby sat up on the sofa and looked around for her grandmother. A warm breeze flowed through the cabin, and suddenly she was caught up in an embrace. Ruby blinked back her tears as Lee held her in her arms. Granddaddy and Grandmama Campbell stood behind them, smiling.

Lee said, "I'm so proud of you, Ruby. Taking over when I know you wanted to stop. I came to tell you a secret you can share with Reed and your dad. Tell them you're going to have another baby. A little girl named Alisa after Harry's mother. And tell Harry that I will see him in his dreams."

Ruby wiped the tears away with her hands and asked, "I'm pregnant?"

Her mama smiled and said, "Not yet, but soon. Joe's going to have a baby sister."

Ruby's eyes widened, and she hugged herself. "Will she have power?"

Granddaddy Campbell said, "Not this little 'un. She's a regular human. But she'll break hearts just like her mama."

Ruby went over and hugged her grandparents. "I miss you. I'm glad Mama is with y'all."

Lee said, "Ruby, we'll always be here. We never left. Love never dies but lives forever."

Sandy said, "Have you told Reed and Harry yet?"

Ruby turned to Sandy and then looked over at Reed and smiled. "Not yet. I have life and death dreams. I want to wait until I know for sure. I'll tell Dad about the dream and how I spoke with Mom. I'll let him know she'll visit him in his dreams. That's the best part about my power. To see my loved ones and know they still exist."

Anna reached over and squeezed. "Maybe you should stop by the office next week, and we'll draw blood."

Ruby raised a brow and said, "I didn't think I could get pregnant while I was breastfeeding."

Anna hesitated and said, "Well, if you're breastfeeding full-time, you shouldn't have a period or ovulate, but the last week or so hasn't been typical. I promise to give you a sticker and a lollipop." Ruby elbowed her, and Anna elbowed her back.

Sandy grinned and stood up. "Let's go to the house. People will get there before we do."

Sandy went over and kissed Harry on the cheek. "Love you, Harry."

"Love you, too, pumpkin."

Chapter 18

Take My Breath Away

THE NEXT DAY, THE GUARDIANS called a meeting in the red barn. They requested that the wards bring Harry and George. A shiver ran up Sandy's spine as she stepped across the threshold into another realm. A choir of angels raised their voices in the sweetest song she'd ever heard. Sandy couldn't understand their words, but it was beautiful nonetheless. The light of love wrapped her in a cocoon of warmth.

The alternate realm seemed like earth, but the grass was too green and the sky too blue. The lush forest had hills and valleys, and in the distance, there was a mountain with a cascading waterfall. A brilliant light Sandy thought was the sun rising over the hill began to move toward them. As the light came closer, Sandy watched as one by one the angels fell on their knees and bowed their heads while stretching their hands toward the light in song.

Sandy turned to her left and right. Following the angel's lead, everyone in her group dropped to their knees and fell face first to the ground without looking up at the light. Without being told, she knew they were in the presence of The Creator.

The Creator's light moved over them, and at once Sandy knew, no matter how bad things got on earth, in the end, everything was going to be all right because they were going to return to the light which created them.

Then He spoke. "I come today to pay honor to Lee who served

humanity well. Please rise, my wards. You may look upon me in my human form. Walk with me."

On the ground, Sandy cut her eyes toward Ruby, who nodded and raised her head. Sandy did the same. Sandy's breath escaped as she looked into the sparkling sapphire eyes that glowed with the same intensity as the first time she had held the totem in the Campbell Ridge cave. The Creator smiled at her, and she wept with joy.

Anna and Jerry, George and Harry, and Ruby and Reed walked with the light, and Sandy brought up the rear. The Creator walked to the most incredible tree. Its outstretched branches resembled arms, and the bright leaves began to sway in the wind as if the tree greeted The Creator. The tree had a chair elaborately carved into the massive trunk out of a material that resembled ivory.

The Creator wore no shoes, only a long sleeved white linen tunic hitting at His ankles with a golden belt gathered at His waist. His silver-white hair shimmered like tiny diamonds in the light of love. He turned and sat down in the tree's carved chair. The Creator motioned with His hands for them to sit on the plush grass. Sandy glanced over her left shoulder, and as far as the eye could see there were rows and rows of angels—all except her angel, Baldric. She didn't see Baldric with any of the other guardians. Sandy's chest tightened, and tears rolled down her cheeks as she grieved for her love.

The Creator opened His hands and said, "Lee is a remarkable creature, and she is alive and well with her family in heaven." He waved His hand in front of them. "We sit at the gateway to the Garden of Eden. You're the chosen few to gain access to this sacred place. I see the questions in your eyes. Why? I've watched the love you have for each other and the sacrifices you all have made on my behalf. Lee's sacrifice received a standing ovation when she entered the courtyard in heaven, which is a place where angels gather. She earned their respect, as have each of you."

The Creator motioned to the guardians. "Erinelle, bring your team to me."

Erinelle along with Raphael, Luwenia, Seneca, and Simon approached The Creator and went down on one knee. She said, "Your Grace, we are here to serve."

The Creator grinned and said, "Good, I'm glad to hear it. Erinelle, you've earned a rest after serving consecutive terms on Campbell

Ridge for the AAF with exceptional valor, and your impeccable reputation will make your shoes hard to fill." He turned to Seneca and said, "Seneca, you'll take over the command of the Campbell Ridge. I have every confidence you're up to the task. But we're missing someone."

The Creator turned to Sandy, and she held her breath. "Sandra Daireann, I have heard your prayers. I believe you're missing your guardian." He turned and shouted over His right shoulder, "Hey, Michael, bring Baldric to me."

Michael and Baldric materialized in front of The Creator and bowed before Him. "Baldric, you and I were having a conversation that was cut short. I believe you had just pleaded your case for pairing with Sandra. I've given your predicament much thought. While I'm not prepared to relinquish the law forbidding angel and human pairings, I have seen the genuine love you share with Sandra. I'm willing to sanction your union to watch and observe your lives. Baldric, you must, however, give up your guardianship, and you will remain on earth aging as a mortal. I will allow you to retain your powers and stay a part of the Campbell Ridge team. How well you live with Sandra will determine if the law should change. What say you?"

Baldric wiped the tears from his eyes with his fingers and bowed before The Creator and kissed His hand. "Thank you, Father. I agree to your terms."

The Creator pointed to Sandy and said, "You may approach, Sandra Daireann."

Sandy couldn't contain her excitement as she approached The Creator and Baldric. She noticed Baldric's rapid pulse beating along the cord of his neck and the tears glistening in his eyes. Baldric tried to hold himself in check, but as she grabbed his hand, he released thousands of shimmering, glittering golden sparkles into the air and onto her skin.

The Creator burst out laughing as He rose. The tension in the air released, and everyone laughed, with a few whistles and catcalls from George, Jerry, and Reed. The Prince and the Spirit of Man materialized and stood on either side of The Creator as He lifted His hands. "May love light your way. May the love of light guide and direct each of you." The Creator smiled and nodded to Baldric. Happy crinkles surrounded His eyes, and with a raised brow, He said, "You may kiss the bride."

Baldric bent Sandy backward as he sealed the sanction with a pretty spectacular kiss to the roar of the crowd. More golden sparkles released into the air like confetti from a parade.

The Creator turned to Harry and the other wards. "Love and laugh often throughout your life." He bowed before them and pressed His hands into prayer mode. "Blessings and Thanksgiving."

They replied, "Blessings and Thanksgiving."

In the blink of an eye, Sandy and Baldric, along with her friends, returned to the center alley of the red barn, each looking around in what Sandy could only describe as wonder.

Baldric picked up Sandy and wrapped his arms around her waist. "Hi, there, baby girl."

Sandy circled her arms around his neck. "Hey, Big B."

Jerry coughed and kicked up dust from the floor. "Um, I think maybe we should retire to the house and help Harry finish off that apple crumb cake."

Harry draped an arm around Jerry's shoulder and said, "I'm with you, brother."

Sandy tossed a glance over her shoulder and said, "I think Baldric and I will pass. We have some catching up to do."

Anna and Ruby started singing, "Baldric and Sandy sitting in a tree..."

To which Sandy rolled her eyes. "Yeah, yeah, and then some."

Reed took his cane and ran it up Ruby's dress. Ruby turned around and said, "Looking for something?"

Reed raised his brow and with a sideways grin, he said, "Oh yeah, baby. I'm looking for something."

Anna grabbed one of Jerry's hands and one of Harry's. "Let's go. The crap in here is getting knee deep."

Sandy yelled out, "Love you, too!"

Sandy and Baldric walked hand in hand out of the barn and to her car. Before opening the door, he kissed her hand. She melted and sighed. "Let's go home. I'll even stop by the store for some bubbles."

"Aw, you remembered."

On the drive into Nashville, Sandy and Baldric talked about Lee and the beautiful example she made out of her life. How one person's life could touch so many other lives. Sandy relayed the events of Reed's injuries and recovery. The supernatural wound would take time to heal, but he would eventually experience a full recovery.

Baldric alternated holding her hand or touching her thigh. "I had to meet in front of the council of nine. They battered me with questions about why I would want to pair with a human."

She cut her eyes to him before going back to the road. "What did you say?"

Baldric smiled. "Your beauty is more precious than the rarest of gemstones. But your spirit, compassion, and sick sense of humor are why I fell in love with you in the first place. The night in the elevator last December, I knew, and when your sassy ass stripped in front of me? Oh man, I shook so bad I thought the building would collapse. You said—"

"I couldn't see you, and I said, 'You might as well show yourself because you smell like hot chocolate, and I could smell you even if I were standing on Capitol Hill.'" She laughed.

Baldric chuckled and said, "I released my paring scent, and the golden sparkles floated in the hallway. I couldn't materialize until I gathered my thoughts. I love you so much that I can barely breathe, and my heart is beating so hard I may not be able to contain it." She sighed.

Sandy stopped quickly at the corner store to pick up champagne and orange juice. She ran out to the car and then drove to the parking garage across from her building and parked in her spot. Turning off the ignition, she turned in the seat and cradled Baldric's face in her hands, rubbing her thumbs along his square jawline. "My sweet and beautiful warrior. Your words seep into the marrow of my bones and heal the wounds from the last week. I was afraid, but I held onto our love and replayed our wedding night over and over with the cords of light that gave me hope and strength."

Baldric leaned in and kissed her gently and slowly, kindling a fire deep inside her. Breathlessly, Sandy released him and said, "I want to make love to you, husband."

Baldric swiftly made it to her door and opened it. His armor materialized into street clothes: jeans, a white T-shirt, and a black leather jacket paired with black boots. Her eyes widened, and she wet her lips. "Baby, I've never seen you in jeans, and me likey a lot."

He reached down and drew her into his arms. "Ruby said you'd like it."

"Oh, honey, I love it." She reached up and kissed him again. Several people passed by, staring at them. She asked, "Can they see you?"

"Uh huh. I'm mortal. Well, sort of." He kissed her again.

Sandy broke from his kiss and grabbed his hand. They ran across the street and into her building.

On the elevator, Baldric backed her against the wall, running his hands along her torso and around her curves, kissing her neck, and he traveled down in between her breasts. Muttering against her skin, he said, "Why are you quivering?"

Her head fell forward onto his left shoulder. "I want you to make love to you."

Baldric scooped her up in his arms and strode to her door. He opened the door with his mind, no keys needed. He took her into the bedroom and carefully laid Sandy on the bed. Kneeling on the floor, Baldric slowly opened Sandy's blouse, one button at a time. With each button he opened, Baldric pressed a kiss. It was agonizingly fantastic. He made love to her with a kiss, and his kiss was better than any sex she'd ever had in her life.

Removing her blouse, he leaned down and clipped the material of her bra with his teeth, freeing her breasts. The golden sparkles released and he moaned as he placed his hands over each, kneading and squeezing, making sure neither went without attention. Sandy arched her back and rolled onto her side. "Unzip my skirt?" she asked.

Baldric unzipped her skirt and lifted her with one arm. With his other hand, he rolled the skirt over her hips, down her legs, and off the bed. She wore no panty hose. He trailed his fingers around each breast, down the line of her flat abdomen, and slipped his fingers inside her panties. He repeated the snip of fabric with his teeth until she lay before him nude.

"Oh, sweet Daireann. You're a goddess." He ran his hand over her bent knee, down her calf. He rolled her onto her stomach and began to kiss the soft skin behind her knee, trailing his tongue up her thigh as he stretched his hands upward along the curve of her spine. "You're perfect to me."

Baldric rolled her again onto her back and spread her legs, dipping down to kiss and tug on the inner softness of her thighs, and moved his way upward. She screamed once he hit the right spot that made her quiver and nearly jerk off the bed. Sandy grabbed fistfuls of his hair as he worked her up into a frenzy.

Baldric rose over her, his smoldering green eyes locked with hers, and he entered her with languorous strokes while whispering over and over in her ear, "I love you."

Sandy dragged in a ragged breath as Baldric buried his face in the soft skin of her neck, kissing and sucking her skin and alternating with her mouth. She ran her hands along his muscular arms and then down the inside of his abdomen. He chuckled and said, "Bet you didn't know I was ticklish."

"Good to know." Sandy tickled him again, and he jerked and laughed. Inhaling deeply, she loved Baldric's incredible pairing scent and arched her back, while she slid hands over his nice tight ass and squeezed. It seemed like a dream—this warrior angel was her husband, for all time.

Baldric slid his warm tongue over her lips and into her mouth with slow strokes, circling her tongue with his. Her heartbeat hammered until release came and she relaxed in his arms. Baldric's thigh muscle tensed against hers until he trembled with release. His powerful chest glistened with sweat, and he nuzzled his cheek against hers. "Hey, FYI, I'm just getting started."

Sandy sighed and nipped his lip. "I'm game, Big B," she agreed, brushing the hair away from his eyes.

Hours later, Sandy lay weightless in Baldric's arms. She was spent and ravenous for food, but she didn't have the strength to get up. Sandy reached over, picked up her phone on the nightstand and dialed The Bistro down the street. She placed a huge order for Chicken Francese with roast potatoes and two loaves of bread.

Baldric stroked her back and placed a kiss on her shoulder. She flipped around into his arms. "I'm not a great cook, but I order great takeout. Mimosas? That is if I can still walk." She giggled.

Baldric jumped out of bed and pointed. "I'll get the mimosas. You need your rest for what is it now? Round three or four? I can't keep up."

Sandy laughed as Baldric walked into the kitchen. *Holy moly.*

Chapter 19

Higher Love

One year later

SANDY SAT IN THE CONTROL room at Channel 3 News working on her latest story. She'd been called early in the morning by Art, her boss. Cole Steele hung himself in his jail cell. Somehow he'd managed to get a work detail in the prison's laundry room. Based on the warden's testimony, Cole had smuggled extra sheets into his room and hung himself during the night.

Baldric went with Sandy to the prison to interview the warden and the guards on duty. She had procured a job for Baldric as a cameraperson at the station along with press credentials. Sandy expressed to her boss that she and Baldric would work as a team, or she'd walk. After much discussion, Art relented and hired her husband. Once Art got the chance to know Baldric, he and Baldric became fast friends. Baldric had many gifts, including the art of persuasion.

The AAF had assigned Caiojezeal as her official guardian once he completed his reconditioning period. The three of them had entered the prison and noticed straightaway the place crawled with demon angels from various divisions.

After interviewing the warden, he allowed Sandy access to Cole's prison cell to shoot cutaways and clips from the guards. Editing her piece in the control room, Sandy scanned through the video and froze the clip from a group of guards hanging around watching her and Baldric work. She zoomed in on the video and looked at Baldric. "Look at the guard, second to the left on the back row. Who do you see?"

Baldric leaned into the screen and shouted, "That son of a bitch. He never learns. I'll call a meeting for tonight and make sure Seneca contacts the AAF."

Sandy took a deep breath and said, "Betcha a hundred dollars Luc killed Cole. The D.A. was looking into tax evasion with Steele Enterprises." She picked up the phone and dialed her legal eagle in the D.A.'s office. "Cheri, hey, it's Sandy. I'm working on a piece for tonight's news on Cole Steele's death. Any chance you guys were talking to Cole?"

Cheri had a catch in her breath and said, "Hold on a second. I need to shut my door." Sandy heard heels clicking on the floor and a door closing. A couple of seconds later, Cheri said, "This conversation is off the record. How did you know? It was classified information. Cole decided to turn state's evidence for a reduced sentence."

Sandy sighed and said, "Just a hunch. I won't mention it in the story. Hey, thanks and let's do lunch soon."

"You got it." Cheri hung up.

Baldric placed his hand over hers. "Luc was probably covering his investments. We scared him, Daireann. Together, we could've killed him, and he knows it. Caiojezeal? You here, bud?"

Caiojezeal materialized and said, "Yeah. I reached out to my contacts on the other side. Luc killed Cole, but he's gone, disappeared somewhere in central Africa deep inside the rainforest. I'm fairly sure Luc was tying up loose ends. He needs money to fund his human operations. He couldn't allow Steele Enterprise to collapse after placing Jackie at the helm. But you just never know with him."

Sandy shook her head and began to splice the tape to delete Luc's image. She turned back to Baldric and said, "Jackie. Can you believe Luc promoted a female? Fencing tonight?"

Baldric rubbed his hands together. "You bet! I have a need to clash steel, for real."

Sandy chuckled. Baldric had acclimated into the human world with ease. The worst part of having him visible was the chicks. Grocery stores, concerts, and even in the station, women wanted to touch him. He attracted them like bees to honey. Sandy didn't sweat it because she was honey to his buttered biscuit.

SANDY AND BALDRIC EVENTUALLY LET the lease go on the downtown condo and bought a house in Brentwood with a huge backyard. It was late spring, and the temperature neared eighty degrees as Sandy and Baldric squared off in a fencing bout. Sandy's skills had vastly improved along with her new skills of porting, which upped the ante for Baldric. She made him promise not to cut her any slack if she was going to get better. Plus, the winner got a *do*, as in do anything.

After an hour, Baldric called time. "It's getting dark, and I don't want to risk accidentally hurting you."

"Hurt me. Are you kidding? So, if you're throwing in the towel, I get the do." She threw her head back and laughed. Dropping her sword, she ported into his arms and wrapped her arms around his neck and her legs around his waist.

Baldric walked with her hanging onto to him to the patio and sat down in one of the wooden chairs carved out of oak they'd bought from a local vendor. "I sense a change in you, Daireann. Are you keeping something from me?"

Sandy cocked her head to the side and smiled. "I hate it when you do that. There's just no fooling you, Daddy."

Baldric's eyebrows rose, and his eyes widened in surprise. "What?"

Sandy nodded and kissed him soundly on the lips. She pulled slightly away and said, "Yup, you're going to be a daddy."

Baldric hugged her and tears ran down his face. "Ah, uh, I never dreamed. I hoped, but I never dreamed The Creator would bless us with offspring. You'll need to see Anna right away. Half angel and half human could prove to be an interesting nine months and an unpredictable delivery." He pressed kisses all over her face. "I'm going to be a daddy," he crooned, hugging her to the rock wall of his chest.

"You know I love things interesting."

Epilogue

Who Loves You

Present day

SANDY SAT AT THE KITCHEN table placing her hand on the Ditch Lane Diaries. Baldric had gone to bed hours ago. She couldn't sleep and went to the bottom bookshelf to retrieve the large book. At first, she read through the pages of her life. She was reminiscing the good and bad times along with the downright scary times.

The diary held all of the pertinent information on the wards of Campbell Ridge. Ruby and Anna had stopped journaling around ten years ago when the new wards took over the primary roles of the wards of Campbell Ridge in the war. Sandy stopped on the page where she described her time as a captive with Luc and included notes from both Ruby and Anna explaining the battle Sandy hadn't seen.

Could it be she was older now than when Lee died?

Sandy turned the pages and read over the notations of her pregnancy. The first half-angel, half-human pregnancy since the great flood. Sandy found out during her first ultrasound that she carried twins. Anna couldn't tell the sex because their little arms had been wrapped around each other.

Sandy glanced up over the mantel to the family photo with her grown kids. She smiled at her beautiful boy and girl. My, how time flew when you were having fun. Sandy flipped to the next page. The birth of the twins had been a little precarious in the delivery room. It wasn't typical for a primary care doctor to deliver twins. But Sandy and Baldric had insisted, and the hospital eventually granted Anna privileges. The babies had required a Cesarean section. Both babies came into the world beautiful, Elena with her blonde hair and Eric with his dark chestnut hair. The twins were completely healthy and had the appearance of being entirely human.

Sandy flipped through a few more pages and remembered the first time Elena and Eric revealed their powers. Sandy stood at the kitchen window watching Baldric as he taught the two teenagers how to fence. The twins were very competitive, and suddenly, Elena disappeared and reappeared behind Eric, knocking him to the ground with her foot and placing the blunted sword at his throat.

Eric became enraged, and before Sandy could reach them, his wings appeared, and he flew up in the air. The look on Elena's face had been priceless. Baldric roared and ordered them to sit at the patio table. Sandy ran to each of her children to make sure neither was hurt.

In the blink of an eye, Baldric appeared before them not as a dad but as a warrior angel in full AAF gear with his wings extended. Both teenagers' mouths dropped open. Baldric proceeded to explain to the kids their life story and how the two of them were unique beings in The Creator's eyes.

Sandy closed her mind as she traveled along the cords of light until she could see Baldric and her kids, as they were then, in the backyard.

Baldric said, "Everyone in the heavens watches our family. If we fail, then the law will remain unchanged. You both will have to receive special sanction should either of you desire to marry."

Eric rolled his eyes at his sister and said, "Ew, too bad for you and Joe."

Baldric straightened his shoulders and said, "What did you just say?"

Elena flipped her brother off, but Sandy caught on quick.

Sandy said, "Stop arguing. I take it, Elena, that you're dating Joe. Do Ruby and Reed know about it?"

Elena crossed her arms over her chest and bulled up.

Eric said, "Are both of you blind? She and Joe have been together since birth."

Elena yelled at her brother, "Shut up, ass wipe. You're just mad because Amy doesn't look at you twice."

Sandy said, "Watch your language, young lady."

Baldric huffed and puffed, and Sandy felt certain he could blow the house down. He blew out a breath and locked eyes with Sandy. He calmly said, "Amy, as in Jerry and Anna's Amy?"

Sandy grinned and opened her eyes, the memory as fresh as if it happened yesterday. Elena and Eric had both fallen in love with her best friends' children.

Sandy scribbled a few notes before closing the Ditch Lane Diaries. The wards of Campbell Ridge had faced battles throughout life, but none of the battles had been as brutal as the Battle of Arrington Estates. Thankfully, Sandy never had another face-to-face encounter with Luc.

There are hard moments in life, moments that are almost unbearable at times. Sandy made a habit to enjoy those rare moments of laughing so hard that tears ran down her cheeks and loved every precious second with the people who made her heart sing with joy and happiness.

Sandy and Baldric held up their promise to The Creator. Their love story had been one that broke the mold of marriage. She closed the diary and walked into the den and placed the journal back on the bottom shelf of the bookcase. Then she walked down the long hall to her bedroom. She slipped out of her day clothes and into her gown before climbing into bed with Baldric. She draped her arm over his back, and he turned around.

Baldric released his chocolatey scent, and the room engulfed in golden glitter. Sandy grinned and cupped his face in her hands. "I guess fairy tales do come true after all." She kissed him and muttered against his lips, "And they lived happily ever after."

Books by D.F. Jones

RUBY'S CHOICE
Ditch Lane Diaries, vol. 1

ANNA'S WAY
Ditch Lane Diaries, vol. 2

SANDY'S STORY
Ditch Lane Diaries, vol. 3

ANTIQUE MIRROR
a short story

Projects on the horizon:

JOHNATHAN'S CURSE
the prequel novel to Antique Mirror

SPINNING TIME
a time travel romance

THE WARDS OF CAMPBELL RIDGE
the spin off series to the Ditch Lane Diaries

Register for my updates on new releases and for buy links go to
http://dfjonesauthor.com

Follow me on my Amazon Author Page
https://www.amazon.com/D.F.-Jones/e/B011YUN8HG

Follow me on social media
https://Facebook.com/DFJones.author
https://twitter.com/Author_DFJones
https://instagram.com/D.F.Jones_author
https://www.goodreads.com/GoodreadscomdfjonesAuthor

About the Author

After years of developing creative advertising for my clients, I had the compelling desire to write something for myself. If you love to read and get immersed in the characters of a book, then you'll catch a glimpse of how incredible it is to write characters and breathe them into life. I fell in love with writing and trust you'll enjoy my books.

I'm happily married to the love of my life and my best friend, KJ. We have two gorgeous sons whom I love and adore more than life itself. I love to laugh, and my husband keeps me in stitches.

D. F. Jones